CHEREE ALSOP

Werewolf Academy Book 7

Chosen

By Cheree L. Alsop

ISBN
Cover Design by Robert Emerson and Andy Hair
www.ChereeAlsop.com

CHOSEN

To my family—
the love within my books
Comes from the love outside of them.
Thank you for real adventures,
Movie nights, and walks to the park.

A special thanks to my beta readers- Cathy Pontious and Marie Efromson.

Thank you for helping these books become the very best they can be.

BOOKS BY CHEREE ALSOP

The Silver Series-
Silver
Black
Crimson
Violet
Azure
Hunter
Silver Moon

The Werewolf Academy Series-
Book One: Strays
Book Two: Hunted
Book Three: Instinct
Book Four: Taken
Book Five: Lost
Book Six: Vengeance
Book Seven: Chosen

The Seven Series
Book 1-

The Haunted High Series-
The Wolf Within Me
The Ghost Files
City of Demons
Cage the Beast
Ashes of Night

Heart of the Wolf Part One
Heart of the Wolf Part Two

The Galdoni Series-
Galdoni
Galdoni 2: Into the Storm
Galdoni 3: Out of Darkness

The Small Town Superheroes Series-
Small Town Superhero
Small Town Superhero II
Small Town Superhero III

Keeper of the Wolves
Stolen
The Million Dollar Gift
Thief Prince
When Death Loved an Angel

The Shadows Series
Shadows- Book One in the World of Shadows
Mist- Book Two in the World of Shadows

The Monster Asylum Series
Book One- The Fangs of Bloodhaven

Girl from the Stars
Book 1- Daybreak
Book 2- Daylight
Book 3- Day's End
Book 4- Day's Journey
Book 5- Day's Hunt

The Pirate from the Stars

The Dr. Wolf Series

CHOSEN

Book 1- Shockwave
Book 2- Demon Spiral
Book 3- The Four Horsemen
Book 4- Dragon's Bayne

The Wolfborne Saga
Book 1- Defiance
Book 2- Ricochet
Book 3- Dark Coven
Book 4- Ghost Moon
Book 5- Demon Crew
Book 6- Hunter's War

The Prince of Ash and Blood

Game Breaker

Orion's Fall

Sira and Solace

The Trouble with Timekeepers

Demon Guard
Book 1- Prophecy
Book 2- Underground
Book 3- Catalyst

The Rise of the Gladiator Series
Book 1- Forgotten Planet
Book 2- Dark Universe
Book 3- The Godking Conspiracy

Chapter One

Alex felt every eye in the Great Hall on him. The sounds of breakfast had vanished. If he was a lone wolf before, he was truly by himself now.

"What are you saying?" Jaze asked. There was a hint of steel in the dean's voice as if he had already guessed the direction of Alex's thoughts.

Alex took a steeling breath and let it out. "We don't need to hide anymore. The best thing we can do is to let the nation know we exist just like they do, students and professors who are trying to make the world a better place in which to live. Tolerance is there, but it has to start with us."

"It's not safe," Dean Jaze said. "We can't protect our students beyond these walls, and if the Academy is known for what it is, they'll tear it down around us."

Alex watched Jaze closely. Something flickered in the dean's eyes. Alex's chest tightened when he realized the emotion Jaze tried to suppress was fear. Jaze had seen so much death and destruction when he revealed werewolves to the world the first time, the dean was afraid for his students. That was why he had worked to hide them for so long. He didn't dare risk the werewolves who looked to him for protection.

"They won't," Alex replied. "They can't. They've seen what we can do." He hesitated, then said, "They've seen what I can do. They know we exist. We can pretend to be ghosts, telling ourselves that wolves can live happily behind walls, or we can embrace our heritage and be strong enough to live outside of them."

Jaze shook his head. "We're not ready."

Alex met his gaze. "You might not be ready, but we are."

The students and professors around the cafeteria were completely silent. Not even so much as a fork scraped against a tray. They had the Academy's complete attention.

Jaze rose to his feet. "Alex, you're in over your head. We can't protect our students if we make them a target."

"We've been targets our whole lives," Alex replied without stepping back. "The only way to take the gun away is to force the world to accept that we deserve to exist."

"I've tried," Jaze replied, his tone heartbroken. "It doesn't work like that."

"It does," Alex told him firmly.

"Alex." Siale said her fiancé's name quietly and touched his arm.

Alex kept his gaze on the dean. "It's time, Jaze. We need to reveal the Academy to the world. They might not have accepted werewolves years ago, but we've shown them that we'll put our lives on the line to defend humans. We sacrificed to save Greyton and the hospital. We made ourselves targets for the curs to help end their threat. We gave the humans their lives back. Now is the time to ask the nation to return the favor."

"I won't let you risk this Academy," Jaze said, his voice laced with steel.

"Then I'll fight you for it."

Gasps spread across the Great Hall at Alex's challenge. A shiver ran down his spine at the enormity of his actions.

"What?" the dean asked.

Alex's heart thundered in his chest. He kept his focus on Jaze. "I challenge you for the right to reveal the Academy to the world."

"It doesn't work like that," Jaze began.

Alex cut him off with a motion toward the student body. "You taught us that rank duels separate those who lead from werewolves too weak to be the leader. I am ready to lead, Dean. I challenge you for that right."

Jaze's gaze traveled around the room, then back to Alex.

"Fine. I accept your challenge," he said shortly.

The dean's jaw clenched and his right knee bent slightly. With an outlet of breath, Jaze threw the first punch.

Alex ducked and answered with a jab. Jaze dodged the attempted hit to his ribs and threw a fast uppercut that connected with Alex's jaw. Alex staggered back a few steps. The pain cleared everything else away. Alex was no longer fighting the werewolf who had been a father figure for most of his life. He wasn't attacking the dean under the gaze of every student and professor at the Academy. He wasn't the lone wolf student fighting to find his place in a life that kept shaking him from his feet.

With the blow to his jaw, Alex's instincts took over. His wolven need to defend himself fused with the human side that had practiced for hours upon hours until blocks and punches came from muscle memory and Jaze was just another attacker intent on keeping him from his goal. To Alex, instead of the crazy world of tangled grays he tried to wade through, the fight was tangible, black and white. He would win or die, because that was the way he had always fought.

Alex threw punches and blocked, kicking and spinning out of the way of the dean's answering blows. Jaze was unlike any fighter he had ever come across. Instead of defending and attacking as though he had been trained to do so, the dean's movements appeared so natural it was as if he had been born to fight.

When Jaze crouched, Alex saw his brother Jet in the way the dean's feet moved into the perfect defensive stance. When Jaze lashed out with a fist and brushed away Alex's answering chop with a two-handed block that sent Alex into one of the nearby tables, he could almost see Jet within the lines of Jaze's movements. He felt as though he wasn't fighting Jaze, he was fighting his older brother.

Alex spun to the left and threw a punch that glanced off Jaze's shoulder. The dean turned with the hit and slammed a fist into Alex's chest so hard the ribs gave. Alex staggered back a few feet. He should have seen the blow coming.

The Demon surged at the pain, but Alex forced it down. The fight was between him and Jaze. Freeing the Demon was against the way of the wolf. If he couldn't beat Jaze himself, he didn't deserve to win.

Yet his memories of Jet merged with those of Jaze. Instead of the dean, his older brother stood in front of him. The dean's brown eyes changed to dark blue, and his blonde hair to black. When Jaze threw a punch, Jet's fist connected with Alex's chest and then stomach. Alex staggered back, his head spinning.

Two punches to the face made Alex see spots. He tasted blood. The dean was faster than any werewolf he had ever fought. Jaze didn't become the recognized Alpha leader of werewolves for nothing; he had earned it with every blow and scar. Despite the years Alex had trained, he couldn't match the dean. Jaze had him beat.

Jaze tackled Alex around the waist and drove him to the ground. He spun so that he had an arm locked around Alex's neck. Jaze turned, blocking the cafeteria from view.

"Don't stop fighting," the dean said in his ear.

Jet's voice echoed in Alex's head. They were the same words his brother had told him before he was killed by Extremists. Alex had lived with those words as his mantra since the day he and Cassie became orphans. For better or worse, fighting was what he had and what he knew. He wouldn't give up no matter who he fought.

Alex grabbed the dean's arm and tucked his chin, slipping out of Jaze's hold. He rolled back to his feet and bent his knees, his hands open and jaw clenched with determination. Jaze dove at him and slammed him into the closest table with the strength of a bear. Someone in the crowd screamed. Alex's head rebounded off the wood as it splintered to pieces beneath them. He rolled to the right and stood in time to block a kick and answer with one of his own. It connected with Jaze's jaw.

The dean fell back two steps and lifted a hand to his mouth. Blood trickled from the corner of his lip when he took the hand away.

"Good kick," Jaze said, his stance at ready.

Jaze attacked with a left and then a right. The left hit home and Alex breathed out to ease the force from the blow, but fire burned angrily through his already bruised ribs.

When the right connected, Alex grabbed Jaze's fist and spun inwards, using Jaze's momentum to draw him off balance. Alex kicked low and threw his weight to the right, driving them both to the ground. Alex turned on one knee and wrapped his elbow around Jaze's neck. In the next moment, his had his other knee in the dean's back and his spine extended to the point that if Alex jerked back at all, it would cause fractures.

Alex's heart thundered and his breath was ragged and loud. The taste of blood coated his mouth. He could hear the dean's heartbeat and felt him take a tight breath.

At that moment, the Demon surged. Instinct bade Alex to finish the dean, to end his reign and take over, to lead the werewolves to a new life of freedom. The Demon fought against the thought of anyone having control. When Alex struggled to keep it at bay, it lashed out, sending physical pain surging through Alex's body. He gritted his teeth and forced his mind to stay clear despite the Demon's wishes.

It promised that ending Jaze's life would give him the freedom he yearned for. The thought was tantalizing within the heat of the fight.

Alex held onto the thought that werewolves were meant to live in packs, to protect each other, to learn together. The Demon flooded his mind with images of the Academy walls, of cage bars, of being tortured. Alex felt his arm tighten around Jaze's neck. He shook his head, trying to regain control.

The Demon battered him with the images he had seen while on missions with Jaze's team, werewolves tortured, mutilated, left to die, finding Siale in the body pit, setting free so many others who would never live a normal life after all they had been through. The Demon argued with needle-like teeth and razor-sharp claws that cut him from the inside. Alex's knee pressed harder into the dean's spine. The Demon refused to sit back. It wanted to gain peace by force.

The Demon's thoughts mirrored Drogan's; the thought washed over Alex like a rush of cold water. He let out a breath through his clenched teeth. He wouldn't take things by force. He wouldn't hurt others to gain his own advantage. That wasn't the werewolf way.

The dean grabbed Alex's arm and rolled, using strength Alex didn't know the Alpha possessed. Alex was thrown into the closest wall. The cement cracked. Before Alex could rise, Jaze picked him up and threw him again. Alex slammed through two pillars that reached to the ceiling of the Great Hall and landed against the back wall in a daze. Jaze was behind him with an arm around his neck and a knee against his spine.

Alex struggled, but he couldn't break the dean's hold. The silence in the Great Hall was palpable as if every student and professor was holding his or her breath.

Alex felt Jaze shift slightly as if he looked around the room. Alex wished he could see the expressions on the faces of the students and professors, but he could only see the wall in front of him.

Jaze released him and stepped free. Alex gasped and drew in a breath. Jaze held out a hand and he rose shakily to his feet.

"Jaze?" Alex asked softly, worried he had damaged his relationship with the dean by instigating the fight.

"We'll bring the Academy into the open," Jaze said.

"Are you sure?" Alex asked in surprise. "I lost."

The dean nodded. "We'll do it together."

Alex smiled and a cheer surged through the Great Hall. Trays struck the tables and students clapped. A glance at the professors showed apprehensive but hopeful expressions.

"It could work," Alex heard Professor Mouse say quietly to Lyra.

"It really could," she replied.

Jaze barely appeared winded after the fight. Alex was still trying to catch his breath. He was amazed at how strong the dean had shown himself to be. Alex thought he had been

17

winning; to be beaten by Jaze so easily unsettled him. He realized he still had a great deal to learn.

Expectant silence filled the room. Alex didn't know what to say. Luckily, Jaze did. With a hand on Alex's shoulder, he turned to face the Great Hall.

"I knew this term would be different." He squeezed Alex's shoulder. "And I should have guessed Alex would be the one to spur that on." A few chuckles sounded. The dean took a calming breath and smiled. "Change is inevitable for progress. Werewolves can't hide forever. I know I've been guilty of hoping we could live behind our walls and the world would leave us in peace." He looked over at Nikki. His wife rested her hand on her burgeoning stomach and smiled back at him. "But werewolves weren't meant to be caged. Our students, children, and faculty deserve to live in peace, and though the first steps may be shaky, we'll learn to walk together with the humans."

Another cheer sounded, louder this time. Students looked excited at the prospect of living a normal life. The professors gave answering smiles, though Alex could read the worry behind their gazes. He hoped he wasn't making a mistake, but he had gone too far to turn back.

"Let's eat before Jerald's amazing cooking gets cold," Jaze concluded.

"It's already cold," Brock pointed out from the table behind them. He glanced at the doorway to the kitchen and Cook Jerald gave him a disgruntled look. Brock picked up a forkful of eggs and waved them. "But you know me. I'll eat anything!" The human swallowed it down with a huge grin that showed bits of waffle in his teeth.

Alex took a seat back at Pack Jericho's table. Siale slipped her hand into his. He didn't realize until he picked up his fork with his free hand that he was shaking.

"Seriously, Alex?" Trent said from across the table. "I

questioned if you had a death wish before. Now I know it! Going against Jaze? You must be insane!"

"He could have beaten me easily any time during that fight," Alex said quietly.

His friends stared at him.

"What?" Jericho asked. The Alpha watched him closely, his usually calm gaze troubled.

Alex glanced over his shoulder at the dean. Jaze was talking with Mouse and Nyra while little William attempted to share a bite of syrupy waffle that ended up in the dean's lap. Jaze didn't appear to notice. Nikki's expression showed her worry as she cleaned up the mess.

Siale squeezed Alex's hand. "Are you sure?" she asked.

The dean's voice sounded again in his head. "Don't stop fighting." Jaze and Jet's voices melded into one, echoing back and forth in his thoughts.

As much as Alex may have wanted to tell himself that he beat Jaze fair and square, the truth was obvious. "He wanted to show me that I'm not the strongest werewolf here. He's still the top dog, but he still agreed to reveal the Academy to the world." Alex shook his head, confused.

Trent nodded with a dawning smile of awe. "Of course he did. The first time he revealed werewolves to the world, it was a bloodbath. He can't lead it again. You've become the face of the younger werewolf generations. The world knows you as the Demon of Greyton. You've proven that you believe in the cause enough to fight for it. You're something he can stand behind."

"He's right," Cassie said, leaning across the table from where she sat next to Tennison. "You've given the world something to believe in."

Her fiancé nodded. "Maybe it'll be enough."

"It has to be," Jericho said. The Alpha smiled at Alex. "If werewolves stand a chance, now is the time. That was a bold move."

"Let's just hope I don't regret it," Alex replied.

"It's not like you make irrational, spur-of-the-moment decisions," Trent said.

After a pause of silence, Pack Jericho broke into laughter.

Alex grinned. He had definitely had more than his share of controversial actions; becoming the Academy's first lone wolf and challenging the dean to change the course of the school were only the most recent.

He looked around the room and his grin faded. Students talked excitedly and the snippets of conversation that came to him said everyone spoke about werewolves being accepted into society. Alex's decision would change the lives of every student and professor at the Academy. He could only hope the change would be for the better.

Chapter Two

Familiar footsteps paused outside the door a moment before it creaked open.

"Alex, are you busy?"

Alex shook his head. "Come on in."

Trent glanced around at the dusty quarters Alex had picked for himself.

"Nice," he said, his tone doubtful. "Are you sure you don't need a tetanus shot to sleep here? And wouldn't you rather take a room instead of the couch?" He looked meaningfully at Alex's duffle bag that lay open and sifted through next to the clean, if somewhat dust-layered, couch.

Alex shrugged. "It works. Did you need me?"

Trent's eyes widened as if he just remembered why he was there. "Yes, Jaze needs you. He said to bring you to the

Wolf Den right away."

The thought of the new classes they should be going to fled Alex's mind. He hurried to the fireplace and slid the hidden panel aside. Trent followed down the dark stairs toward the basement lair. Alex knew better than to ask what Jaze needed. The dean liked to have the entire team together before he told them the details of a mission. The thought of heading back out sent a thrill of excitement through Alex.

He pushed open the door and stepped into the Wolf Den. His heart slowed at the images on many of the screens above Brock's elevated platform in the middle of the vast cavern.

It was the fight, filmed from across the Great Hall. Alex and Jaze circled each other. As Alex walked to the platform and climbed slowly up the steps, he heard his argument for bringing the Werewolf Academy public.

Jaze, Nikki, Brock, and Mouse watched the video in silence. On the biggest screen, Jaze threw the first punch. Alex blocked it and countered.

"I didn't know how much Jet had trained you," Alex told the dean quietly.

Jaze nodded. He turned away from the video and motioned for Alex to walk back down the steps. When they were away from the others, he said, "Jet said he wouldn't always be there for me."

The dean took a seat on the steps that led down to the helicopter.

Alex leaned against the railing.

"Your brother became my protector ever since the day I saved his life." Jaze glanced up at Alex. "When I saw him in the ring, I knew I had to get him out of there."

Alex knew some of the history between Jet and Jaze. Jet hadn't been one to talk about his past, but Jaze knew how much Alex's brother meant to him. Just hearing his name was enough to make Alex's heart tighten from the pain of losing someone he looked up to so much, yet he yearned for it. He had gone so long without hearing others talk about his brother; hearing about him now felt like a breath of fresh air after being under water.

As if Jaze understood that, he said, "Jet was raised as one of the only Alpha werewolves in a werewolf fighting ring. He was pitted against dreadful odds, and he won because fighting was the only thing he knew." Jaze stared out across the cave beneath the Academy. "Winning meant killing his opponents. The werewolves had a pact that they wouldn't leave the losing members of a fight to be ended by the silver bullet from a guard. It was the only form of honor they could give each other in such a situation."

Jaze was quiet for a few moments before he continued, "When I found out about the fighting rings, Mouse, Chet and I went to scope it out. I got there just as Jet entered a fight. He must have smelled me in the audience, because he stopped and looked straight at me through the fence. Even though he was bleeding and trapped in a horrible situation, there wasn't anger or frustration in his eyes. Instead, I saw only determination to see it through. He was a fighter, a survivor, and he did the best he could with what he had."

Jaze let out a slow breath. "But the last fight Jet was pitted in wasn't fair. We had plans to break him out before the fight, but there was just no possible way to do it. They sent Jet into the fight outnumbered in every way possible, and his *owner*," he said the word with a grimace as though it tasted bad, "Bet on him to lose."

The cold of the metal bars beneath Alex's hands seeped up his arms. He stared out at the helicopter in front of them without seeing it.

"Jet won," Jaze continued softly. "Against all odds and after taking what were potentially life-threatening wounds, Jet defeated his attackers. In return, his owner sent him out in a cage and instructed her men to shoot him with silver bullets." His voice lowered. "They were told to make him suffer before he died."

"So much for honor," Alex said quietly.

Jaze nodded. "I tried to get to him, but we were delayed by security. By the time I reached him, he had already been shot. But even though most werewolves would have died from the wounds, Jet was stronger. He survived to bring down the rest of the fighting rings at my side."

Jaze turned so that he leaned against the railing and looked up at Alex. "That's when he began to train me. Jet said he wouldn't always be there, and teaching me how to fight was the best way he knew how to protect me even when he was gone." Jaze's forehead furrowed. "I think Jet always knew he wouldn't make it to this stage in life, married, having kids. He once told me that fighting was all he knew how to do. When the fighting stopped, there wouldn't be a place for him."

Alex sunk down on the other side of the steps and leaned his back against the railing. "There would have been," he said quietly.

Jaze nodded. "Yes, there would have." He glanced at Alex. "Imagine if every student at the Academy could fight like Jet."

Alex smiled. "We'd be a force to reckon with."

Jaze chuckled. "Yes, we would." He motioned toward the screen where the images showed Alex's argument and the fight over and over again. "That's out in the world now."

Alex stared at him. "What?"

"Someone had a cell phone despite our policies. They recorded the fight and released it on the Internet. Brock says he's never seen a video go viral so quickly."

Alex was amazed at how calm the dean was being. "Get it

taken off," he said, rising to his feet. "They'll know about the Academy, about you, about everything here! We need to erase it or—"

Jaze shook his head with a small smile. "You fought for the right to reveal the Academy to the world. Now it's done."

"But not like this," Alex said. He motioned toward the screens. "Not with arguing and fighting. We're supposed to be civilized and…and…."

"And human," Jaze said, rising to stand next to him.

Alex hesitated. The word was exactly what he meant, but agreeing felt wrong. They weren't human, they were werewolves. He wanted the world to accept them for who they were, not pretend to be something different.

"You said what we would have wanted to say in a public statement," Jaze told him quietly.

At that moment, Alex on the main screen said, "You might not be ready, but we are."

"I wasn't rational," Alex told the dean quietly. He glanced away from his image on the monitor.

"You were acting in the heat of the moment. To the public, the dean of the Academy is brawling with a student. It's not my best moment."

Alex shook his head. "You're an Alpha. That's what Alphas are supposed to do."

"Then don't feel like we have to hide it from the world," Jaze countered. "You want the world to accept us, they need to know the real werewolves."

"You really think that's the best way?" Alex asked, watching him and Jaze smash through a table.

Jaze smiled. "It's our way."

"We'll up the detectors for the luggage," Brock called down from the platform. "I don't know how a phone got inside, but we'll be more careful next time. All of the news stations have picked it up. I swear it's running in a loop all

25

over the nation."

Trent followed Alex back up the tunnel to Alex's lone wolf quarters. Alex sat on the couch with a shake of his head.

"I didn't expect that to happen."

"Guess I should hide this," Trent said. He pulled something from his pocket.

Alex stared at the cell phone. "You took the video?" he asked in shock.

Trent nodded. "You wanted to bring the Academy to the world." He slipped the phone behind a picture of a mountain at sunset on the mantel piece.

"But bringing a phone to the Academy is against the rules," Alex replied. He was unable to get his mind around the fact that Trent was the one who had taken the video and posted it to social media.

"Being a werewolf used to be against the law. Things are changing," Trent replied.

"Trent, you directly disobeyed Jaze's rules. He's the dean," Alex pointed out.

Trent shrugged his small shoulders. "But you're my Alpha."

Alex's heart slowed. He stared at his friend. "Trent, I'm nobody's Alpha. I'm not even really an Alpha, and with the whole Demon thing, I may not fully even be a werewolf. I don't know what I am, and that makes me entirely unfit to be in charge of anything, let alone anyone."

Trent ran a hand across his buzz-cut hair. "I know what you are, Alex."

"Then you should know that I'm the last person here you should be calling your Alpha," Alex replied, staring incredulously at his friend.

Trent gave Alex a straight look, the first one he had since hiding the phone. "Alex, you have to understand something. You may not have a completely black coat, but the last time we phased, you were almost there. You may not have it all together as a leader, but I would argue that neither do Boris or Torin. You may morph into a rage mode Demon, but that's not entirely a point against you."

"What are you saying?" Alex asked when the little werewolf paused.

Trent crossed his arms and leaned against the wall. "What I'm saying is that you already beat the two strongest Alphas at the Academy. You have pretty-much single-handedly wiped out the biggest threat to werewolves and this nation to date, you take out danger heedless to the harm it might cause yourself, and you always take the time to care about the opinions of small, pretty much invisible werewolves to the rest of the school. You sound like a good Alpha to me."

Alex rested his head in his hands. He stared at the floor through his fingers. "It's not that simple."

Trent sat down on the couch next to him. "It never is."

Alex glanced at him. "What about Jordan?"

"She'll be moving her stuff in here tonight."

Alex stared at him. "What about Jericho? He chose you both. You're part of his pack."

"Like I said. Things are changing." The bell rang. Trent smiled. "Let's go. Dean Jaze asked all the seniors to meet him in his office before class. We can worry about semantics later."

"Semantics?" Alex sputtered. "You say I'm your Alpha and call it semantics?"

Trent pulled the door open and said over his shoulder, "Demon, Alpha...who says they're not the same thing." He disappeared down the hallway.

"I do!" Alex called after him.

His friend's footsteps didn't slow.

Alex shook his head. "Great," he muttered. "Now I've really done it."

27

He grabbed a notebook from beside his duffle bag and followed Trent's path down the stairs.

Students hurried to the classrooms on the ground floor. New first term students followed their Alphas with wide eyes and nervous expressions. Alex couldn't help smiling. The Academy was a great place to grow up.

He crossed the hall to the wing with the professors' offices and paused at Jaze's door. Professor Colleen was addressing the other seniors with the dean looking on.

"Torin and Boris, you'll be with Professor Vance."

Both Alphas looked unhappy about their assignment to the gruff football coach.

"Cassie and Siale, I'd like you to be my assistants."

"Yay!" Cassie said. A blush of red ran across her cheeks as though she hadn't meant to say it out loud.

Siale gave her a warm smile.

"I appreciate the enthusiasm," Colleen said with a pleased expression.

"Trent, you're with Professor Mouse, and Tennison, Professor Dray would appreciate your assistance in the green houses."

"You get to smell like fertilizer," Torin said with a laugh.

"At least he'll have a reason to stink," Boris replied.

Torin glared at him.

Professor Colleen ignored them. "Jordan and Terith, I'd like you to be with Professor Gem. She'll be teaching Art History this term."

"I love art," Jordan said.

"Me, too!" Terith seconded. "We'll be the best assistants ever!"

Professor Colleen assigned the rest of the seniors to their professors. At the end, Alex was the only one who hadn't been given an assignment.

"Head to your teachers for the first class. They'll let you

know what they expect from you and how you can help out in their classes," Colleen told them. "For you Alphas, there will be some juggling with getting your new first termers settled in, so lean on your Seconds to split tasks." She smiled at them. "You can go."

Siale hung back with Alex. "Professor, who is Alex with?" she asked.

Colleen looked at Jaze. Her violet gaze showed a hint of concern.

The dean merely smiled. "I have a special assignment for you. Come with me."

"Why do I have a feeling this isn't going to be easy?" Alex asked.

Siale slipped her hand into his and walked beside him down the hall. She gave him a warm smile. "Nothing you do is easy."

"She's right," Jaze said over his shoulder. "If I gave you an easy assignment, you'd find a way to make it difficult."

"I'm going to take that as a compliment," Alex muttered.

Siale laughed and squeezed his hand. "I'm sure it is."

Jaze led them down the second wing of classrooms. With the increase of students at the Academy, the professors had opened the second wing to create enough space for teaching. The dean opened the door to the office at the end.

"Alex Davies, I'd like you to meet Mr. O'Hare. Mr. O'Hare, this is Alex."

Alex stepped into the office with a smile, but it faded quickly. The look of disdain on the face of the man behind the desk was unmistakable. The man had graying black hair, a goatee, and glasses that he glared through directly at Alex.

Despite the look, Jaze's smile was warm. "Mr. O'Hare, I feel that having Alex as your assistant would be the best way to give you a true impression of what goes on at our Academy." The dean turned to Alex. "Alex, Mr. O'Hare was sent by the Board of Education after our announcement of our academy in order to review our practices and procedures here. You are to be his assistant, guide, and informant on anything he needs to know."

"Uh, okay," Alex said uncertainly. He was surprised the man had reached the Academy so quickly after the video. He must have been sent out the instant it aired. Concern filled Alex. He glanced back at Siale. His fiancé peered through the door with a matching uncertain expression. Alex steeled himself and crossed to the desk with his hand out. "It's good to meet you, Mr. O'Hare."

The man rose from the desk with a huff as though it was a burden to stand for such an event. His scent reached Alex; the werewolf couldn't help but staring. Mr. O'Hare was human.

He gave Alex's hand one quick shake before returning to his seat.

"Is there anyone else?" he asked, finally turning his loathing gaze from Alex to the dean.

Jaze shook his head and appeared completely composed as though he had anticipated such a question. "The rest of our seniors have already been assigned to professors. I reassure you that Alex will be a willing and helpful assistant and will do his best to meet your needs."

"I'm sure he will," Mr. O'Hare replied dryly.

Chapter Three

"Why did you assign me to him?" Alex asked with confusion as he and Siale followed Jaze back to the dean's office.

Siale's expression said she was wondering the same thing. Though she hadn't spoken a word during Alex's introduction to Mr. O'Hare, he could tell she was bothered by the situation. It wasn't every day Alex met someone who flat-out hated him.

He changed his mind at that thought. Boris and Torin had both gone through months of extreme hatred. He should be used to it; yet, he wasn't accustomed to meeting a human who completely loathed him before he had even spoken a word.

31

Jaze didn't speak until they were back in his office with the door shut. He sat behind his desk and let out a sigh that said as much as the weary acceptance in his gaze.

"I've been bombarded with phone calls from various government agencies since the video of our fight aired," Jaze said quietly. He looked up and when he saw that they were still standing, he motioned for Alex and Siale to take the seats facing his desk.

"Are they going to bomb the Academy?" Siale asked.

Jaze gave her a half smile. "No; at least, not yet. There are agencies fighting for our rights and motions being put into place to counterbalance the fight. I think Mr. O'Hare is the weapon of choice in this type of dispute."

The thought filled Alex with discomfort. "What do you mean?"

Jaze motioned to the door. "You saw how much he hates werewolves. If those humans who want werewolves wiped from the earth can't banish us through war, they'll do so with a means even more devastating."

"With politics," Siale answered.

The dean nodded. "The Board of Education has very strict regulations on primary and secondary academic facilities. Mr. O'Hare has been placed here to find any holes in our system that will enable him to shut us down."

"Will he?" Alex asked. The thought of losing the Academy through politics was entirely unfamiliar to him. How could he fight something based on the interpretation of laws and rules? The school was his home. He was responsible for bringing its existence into the open. After everything the school and students had survived, he couldn't bear the thought of losing it.

"I don't think so," Jaze replied. "At least, I hope not. When we established Vicky Carso's Preparatory Academy, Mouse and Lyra took charge of ensuring that we adhered very closely to the Board's guidelines in case something like this happened. While a few of our particularly specialized classes may not be in the standard curriculum, we have maintained a disciplined schedule and our students are on the same track as the humans." His mouth twisted into a wry grin. "Although, thanks to our werewolf students' quick learning capabilities, they are far ahead of students their age. I don't think that'll be a problem, though."

"So why Alex?" Siale asked. "Mr. O'Hare obviously hates him."

"Hate's a strong word," Jaze began.

"Oh, he hates me. The room stunk with it," Alex replied.

Jaze let out a little snort that was part laughter, part acceptance. "Okay, so he hates you. That's why I assigned you to him."

"That doesn't make any sense," Alex told the dean.

"It does."

Alex stared at Siale. She was watching Jaze with a small smile of her own.

"If he hates you, you'll be the one he would want to scrutinize the most." She looked at Alex. "Dean Jaze just gave you to him."

"Seems like a bad idea to me," Alex said.

She shook her head. "It's the opposite. Would you agree that you are the student most prone to creating trouble?"

Alex rolled his eyes. "I'd rather call it disturbances, but yes, you're right."

Siale grinned. "So if you're right in front of Mr. O'Hare all the time, he'll be busy watching everyone else because you'll be right there. It's like hiding in plain sight."

The thought both appealed to Alex and troubled him. "What if I mess up?"

Jaze lifted his shoulders in a shrug. "We'll deal with it if it comes to that. The curriculum from the Board of Education doesn't give leeway for students caught up in midnight escapades freeing werewolves from the hands of malicious terrorists."

A pit formed in Alex's stomach. "I have to give up the team?"

When the dean shook his head, relief rushed through Alex.

"Not at all," Jaze said. "We couldn't do it without you."

Alex decided it wasn't time to point out that they had managed through the summer just fine without him. The voice in the back of his head argued right back that the key to defeating Drogan's mutant army had been his idea.

"We'll just have to be more careful when we leave and make sure you get all of your schoolwork done in a timely manner." The dean paused, then said, "Without your professors looking the other way."

"What?" Alex protested in a tone of false surprise. During the time when Siale was injured and several other occasions related to injuries or his determination to defeat his half-brother or the General, which turned out to be quite a few times, Alex knew his studies had slipped. Luckily, with Trent, Siale, and Cassie, along with a few professors like Professor Mouse and Professor Kaynan, he had still managed to squeak by to his senior year. That was apparently the last time it was going to happen.

"Okay, fine," he said. "I'll get my studies done without help."

Siale took his hand next to her chair. "You'll still have help if you need it," she promised.

The phone on Jaze's desk rang.

"I need to answer that," the dean told them. He gave Alex a frank look. "I would appreciate it if you escorted Mr. O'Hare around the school and grounds, then brought him to lunch in the Great Hall. He can dine with the professors."

"I'll do that," Alex said. He rose to his feet and held out a hand to Siale. She walked with him toward the door.

"Alex?"

He turned at Jaze's voice. "Yes?"

"Mr. O'Hare is under your protection while he's here at the Academy," the dean said.

Alex's chest tightened. While the dean's assignment of him to the government official may have been for the reasons he said, Mr. O'Hare's obvious hatred for werewolves had the potential to make him a target for the other students. Werewolves were nothing if not territorial.

"I'll make sure he's safe," Alex promised.

Jaze nodded and answered the phone.

Alex pulled the door shut behind him just as the bell rang.

"I've got to go assist Professor Colleen," Siale said with an apologetic tone.

"Go ahead," Alex said. "I'll be fine."

"Are you sure?" she asked, throwing a skeptical look down the hallway to where Mr. O'Hare's makeshift office resided.

"I'm sure," Alex told her. He knew he shouldn't, but he couldn't help the impulse to pull her close and kiss her on the nose. She was just so cute when she worried, and kissing her like that made her giggle.

She stepped back with a smile and a blush that ran across her cheeks. "You be careful, Alex Davies. Don't start any of your disturbances."

Alex grinned at her. "I'd rather start some trouble."

She rolled her eyes with a laugh. "See you at lunch."

"Bye, love," he replied.

She paused on her way down the rapidly filling hallway and blew him a kiss. He smiled at the warmth that flooded his chest and watched her dark brown hair sway across her back as she walked toward Colleen's classroom. He missed her already. Lunch seemed way too far away. He shook his head, amazed that at a second away from her, he was already thinking about when they would be back together.

A chill ran down his spine. He glanced to his left and met Mr. O'Hare's gaze. The man was watching him over the flood of students rushing to their next class. The disapproval on his face was stark before he turned away and disappeared back into his room. Alex took a steeling breath and followed.

He found the man marking something down in a small notebook.

"What are you writing?" Alex asked.

The human paused and glanced at him. "I don't have to explain anything to you," he said cuttingly. "You will do what I ask, and only that. I won't answer any questions you might have, so you should probably just save your breath. You're going to need it when I get this place shut down."

The barb hit Alex like a knife in the ribs. He gritted his teeth. As much as he wanted to shout or tear the man's tiny notebook apart, he reminded himself with considerable effort that he was the school's first line of defense against the government that wanted to shut it down. He would try to maintain at least some semblance of control, and it was only the first day.

"Are you ready for a tour of the Academy?"

A hint of surprise showed in the man's gaze before it was smothered in his disdain. "What? No growling or chewing up my homework like a bad little werewolf? I'm a bit disappointed, Alex. Perhaps all the rumors have been misplaced."

"Perhaps," Alex replied with a forced smile that felt like plastic on his lips. "Give me time," he muttered quietly so the man wouldn't hear him.

"Even though I feel it's pointless to get familiar with this doomed establishment, it would be a relief to stretch my legs and get some fresh air. It does smell a bit like dog in here," Mr. O'Hare noted. He brushed past Alex.

When their shoulders touched, Alex felt the man shy away from him. A slight whiff of fear flooded in his wake.

Alex stared after the man. Was it possible that his loathing was a front to hide fear at being in an Academy filled to the brim with students whose race he hated? Alex shook his head. If that was the case, Mr. O'Hare had gotten himself into a nightmare.

"Coming, Fido?" Mr. O'Hare asked.

Alex was grateful all of the students had made it to their classrooms. He didn't know if he would have been able to control himself otherwise. If a student attacked the representative from the Board of Education, Alex knew that would be it for the school. The human had no idea how dangerous Alex was. Or perhaps he did. The thought was unsettling. Would the man put himself in serious danger just to prove a point?

Alex stifled a growl and followed Mr. O'Hare down the hallway.

"Here is where Professor Mouse teaches biology, anatomy, and chemistry," Alex explained a few classrooms later. A glance inside showed the desks full and students watching the small professor sketch a cell on the whiteboard.

"A werewolf named after a mouse. A bit emasculating, don't you think?"

Mr. O'Hare walked off down the hallway without waiting for Alex's reply.

After a moment, the human said, "A bit like using the name Davies. Aren't you really a Carso, like the General and his son who's at the top of the nation's most wanted list?" Mr. O'Hare glanced back over his shoulder to give Alex a dry look. "I suppose hiding out under the name Davies is wise considering your unsavory relations."

Alex bristled. "My sister and I were adopted. Our parents were Davies, so we kept the name. Carso is a good name, especially when you consider that Dean Jaze carries it."

Mr. O'Hare appeared unruffled at his outburst. "Claiming to be related to Jaze Carso isn't exactly the best idea considering his own follies in werewolf and human relations. He was wanted for most of his life before opening this school."

Alex's hands tightened into fists. "Jaze's only *folly* was putting his life on the line a million times to save werewolves from the hands of humans who only wanted to hurt or kill them. Families were destroyed and even his own mother was killed. He lost friends in the battle, good friends." Alex's throat tightened and his voice cracked with his outrage. "Jaze is a hero."

Alex paused. His heart thundered in his chest and his hands opened and closed. He wanted to make the man pay for his attack against Jaze. The dean had been like a father to him. He wouldn't stand by while someone slandered Jaze's name.

Alex realized with a start that that was exactly what Mr. O'Hare wanted. Alex already knew the man's goal was to provoke him into fighting. Mr. O'Hare's stay would be cut short and his job done. Students fighting administration would without a doubt be entirely against the Board of Education's policy. Why else would they only send one man to survey the school? Perhaps Mr. O'Hare was the only one who dared.

Alex looked closer at the human. Mr. O'Hare's lips were pressed into a tight line and he waited with anticipation on his face as though he knew what his words would mean. There was fear hiding in the depths of his cold green eyes. His glasses were held in one hand. Alex couldn't remember when the man had taken them off. Perhaps he didn't relish the

38

thought of having them slammed into the bridge of his nose.

Alex let out a slow breath. He willed his hands to relax and lifted his shoulders in a small shrug that felt like it weighed a thousand pounds.

"If there wasn't anyone holding true to the name, maybe I'd consider taking up the name Carso, but Jaze is doing a great job." Alex forced a smile. "Someone needs to do the same for Davies. I guess they'll have to settle for me."

He turned away before he could see the human's expression. Turning his back on Mr. O'Hare meant going entirely against his instincts. Of any enemy he had, the human armed only with his tiny notebook was the most dangerous. Alex had no problem retaliating with only himself on the line, but if he lost control at all, the Academy would pay. Alex walked down the hallway with chills running along his spine.

"I hope you know what you're doing, Jaze," he whispered quietly.

Chapter Four

"Your cafeteria smells better than most of the schools I've been to," Mr. O'Hare noted when they reached the Great Hall for lunch.

Alex looked at him in surprise. "You do this at other schools?"

Mr. O'Hare gave him a look that said he clearly thought Alex was stupid. Alex was getting used to the expression.

"Of course I've been to other schools. Checking for violations is my job." His eyebrows pulled together in a disapproving expression. "Don't assume your school is the only one on the verge of being shut down. There are plenty of violations out there. I just happen to be very good at what I do, and," he hesitated, then said, "And the only one brave enough to come to an Academy of mutts who might want to eat me."

When they stepped into the Great Hall, every eye locked on them. Gazes shifted from Alex to Mr. O'Hare. The sounds of forks on trays and talking ceased. Torin rose halfway from his seat at his usual table; Shannon set a hand on his arm and he slowly settled back down with a glare at the human.

Alex glanced at Pack Jericho. Trent met his gaze with a worried look. Jericho gave Alex a half-smile, though it didn't touch the question in his eyes when he looked from Alex to the human.

"What are you doing?" Cassie mouthed.

Alex gave her what he hoped was a reassuring smile and motioned for Mr. O'Hare to follow him to the kitchen.

"I've never felt more on the verge of death in my life," the human muttered when the sounds of talking and eating picked up again. "They really do hate humans."

"They don't hate humans," Alex told him. "Professor Thorson is human, and Nikki, Dean Jaze's wife. Humans aren't the issue."

"Then what is?" Mr. O'Hare asked when they entered the kitchen. A breath of relief escaped him at being shielded from the accusing glares of the students.

"Your obvious disdain for werewolves," Alex told him. "They can smell it. It wafts from you like sour eggs."

The human stared at him. "You can smell how much I don't like you?"

Alex nodded. A brief rise of humor filled him at the dismay in the man's voice. "It's pretty obvious."

"Great," Mr. O'Hare turned away and grabbed a tray from the table. "That's got to be an infringement of privacy if I've ever seen one."

"We can't help what we can smell," Alex told him. "It'd be like telling a cow not to moo or a bird not to fly."

"You realized you just used all animal references in your

example," Mr. O'Hare replied drolly.

Alex was aware of Cook Jerald watching them. She didn't appear at all pleased to have Mr. O'Hare in her kitchen.

"Werewolves are part animal, Mr. O'Hare," Alex replied. "We're not ashamed of our lineage, so the sooner you accept it, the better."

He expected a displeased reply from the human, but the man kept silent as Cook Jerald ladled pasta and her amazing made-from-scratch Alfredo sauce onto his tray. Alex followed behind.

The human was about to enter the Great Hall again, but Alex grabbed his arm.

Mr. O'Hare looked completely outraged that Alex would dare to touch him. Alex dropped his hand.

"Look," Alex said. "You may hate my guts and all of my race, but one thing is certain. You are a human in a school of werewolves, and your hatred follows you around so thick I can't even smell the Alfredo right now."

Mr. O'Hare glanced at his tray and back at Alex.

"You might find it annoying that Jaze assigned me to be your assistant, but after everything I've done here, I get a bit of respect from the students. Consider me your protection. I don't want this Academy to fail." His eyes narrowed and he gave the man a straight look. "No matter how much you might. So listen to me when I say that you need to either hide your hatred of werewolves better or carry silver in your pocket. Werewolves are loyal, and I don't want you to get hurt because you can't hide your disgust for children."

Mr. O'Hare was quiet for a moment before he said, "I have silver in my pocket."

"I know," Alex replied. "I can smell it."

The man stared at him.

Alex turned away and walked out the door. It wasn't until the human wandered over to join the professors at their table that he felt like he could breathe again. He knew as a lone wolf that he should have sat alone, but spending so much time surrounded by such great quantities of hatred had exhausted him. He walked to Pack Jericho's table and smiled at the empty seat Siale patted next to her.

"Hey guys," Alex said with an outlet of breath. He set the tray on the table harder then he intended.

Siale leaned her head on his shoulder when he sat down. "Rough day?" she asked.

"Yeah," he admitted with a dry chuckle. "Class is easier than being an assistant to Mr. I-Hate-Werewolves."

"What's the deal with that guy?" Trent asked. "Why is he here?"

Alex glanced over his shoulder at the human. While the professors made small talk with Mr. O'Hare, it was obvious they were uncomfortable with his presence. Alex shook his head and turned back to his friends.

"The esteemed Mr. O'Hare is here to shut down our school."

"What?" Terith exclaimed.

"They can't," Cassie protested.

Alex nodded. "My job is to prove that we have nothing to hide."

"But we have plenty to hide," Jericho replied. "I'm sure students in other schools don't run around at night rescuing their comrades."

"Yeah," Alex said. "That's why we're going to have to be more careful. He can't know when we get called out, and we can't let missions with the team affect our schooling or assisting the professors. Got it?"

Everyone nodded.

"What if he looks for you and you're gone?" Von asked. Terith's boyfriend wasn't on their team for missions with Jaze, but they had never hidden the missions from him. With his closeness to Terith, keeping secrets would have been impossible.

If she trusted him so much, Alex decided he could as well. "Then you'll have to cover for me. Think you can do that?"

Von's eyebrows rose at the enormity of such a task, but he nodded quickly. "Yes, definitely. I can tell him you're sick or something and," he adjusted his glasses, "I can be his assistant until you are available again."

"I appreciate it," Alex replied with a warm smile. "I need someone I can count on, and I know you'll do a good job." He hesitated, then told the werewolf, "Just be careful. He tries hard to rile students up. If we let down our guard at all and lash out, the Academy's done for."

"What has he done?" Siale asked, her expression worried.

Alex gave her a reassuring smile. "Nothing I couldn't handle. We'll be fine."

She smiled back at him. "I knew Dean Jaze picked the right werewolf for the job." She paused, then leaned over and kissed him on the cheek as though she couldn't help herself.

"Careful, you two," Jericho warned. "Public displays of affection are against school policy."

Everyone looked at the professors table. None of the teachers were talking and everyone ate their lunch in silence. Apparently Mr. O'Hare's warm personality had gotten to them. Luckily, he didn't seem to have noticed Siale's kiss.

"We'll be more careful," she said with a hint of reluctance in her voice.

"I can't blame you," Jericho told her. "Maybe with the opening of the Academy to the public, we can allow human students in. I would love it if Cherish could be here. It's hard to be so far away from her."

"That's not a bad idea," Terith said. "A lot of the students here haven't had much exposure to humans besides the few we have at the Academy. It would be good for them to see that not all humans are out to kill them. We have as much prejudice to work through as the humans do. Welcoming human students to the Academy might be just the way to do that."

"As long as they don't come in with as much hatred as your guy," Cassie said. "I don't know how you can stand to be around him with that stench."

"I don't exactly have a choice," Alex told his sister. "Believe me, both of us would rather be elsewhere. I'll just have to do what I can to break him."

"You mean work with him," Jericho corrected.

Alex grinned. "Of course. What did I say?"

The Alpha rolled his eyes with an answering smile.

"Guess what," Trent said as if he couldn't hold it in any longer. "Brock says werewolves are coming out of hiding left and right."

"What?" Cassie replied, her eyes wide. "You mean because of the video?"

Trent nodded. "Apparently revealing the school gave others the courage to come out of hiding. They say if the Demon doesn't cower behind walls, they won't, either."

"How is the nation taking it?" Alex asked worriedly. He had heard enough of the repercussions from when Jaze revealed werewolves to the world to know they could be met with extreme hatred.

"Surprisingly well," Trent told them. He took a bite of his food. "Apparently, everyone's tiptoeing around trying not to make waves until the government decides how to approach the issue. Hopefully Mr. O'Hare won't do a belly flop in the middle of it all."

"Are you comparing werewolf politics to a swimming pool?" Terith asked her brother. "You can do better than that."

Trent grinned. "I was going to say wolves in a hen house, but I thought that was in bad taste."

Terith rolled her eyes.

"This is good," Alex said. The promise of what Trent was telling them caught up to him. It was hard to keep his voice quiet. "If werewolves keep coming out of hiding, the government will realize that there are families, students like us, just trying to survive. They'll see that we're normal citizens and that we're not dangerous."

"Not all of us," Jericho reminded him. "Drogan's another issue."

Siale nodded from Alex's side. "But at least he was an enemy before all of this. The nation's united against him, which puts the humans and werewolves on the same side."

"'The enemy of my enemy is my friend,'" Terith quoted.

"Exactly," Siale replied. "Now all we have to do is find Drogan."

Everyone looked at Alex. "We'll get him," he promised. "Our team and the Black Team have been searching everywhere. We'll find where he's been hiding."

"And when we do, problem solved," Trent replied.

He and Alex exchanged a look. They both knew it wouldn't be that easy, but their words appeared to satisfy the others who returned to eating and their own conversations.

"Problem solved," Siale repeated softly from beside Alex. She leaned against him.

Alex spread butter on her nose with his spoon.

"Ew!" Siale exclaimed.

Alex grinned. "Just lightening the mood."

Siale rolled her eyes, but couldn't stop smiling.

***

"Where do we go next?" Mr. O'Hare asked when they left the Great Hall.

Alex knew it wasn't his imagination that made the talking louder behind them as soon as the human exited the cafeteria. He was just glad Mr. O'Hare couldn't hear the expletives that followed their swift retreat.

"Take it easy," Vance ordered.

The talking quieted at the coach's brusque command.

"You've seen all the classrooms," Alex replied. "Where else would you like to go?"

"I'd like to view the students' quarters," Mr. O'Hare replied.

That was the one place Alex hadn't wanted to take him. Werewolves were very territorial. They wouldn't take kindly to the intolerable human in their living spaces. Alex hoped that during the lunch hour they would find the quarters empty.

"Up this way," Alex said, motioning to the stairs.

He led the way along the hallway toward Pack Jericho's quarters. If any Alpha would give him leeway for bringing the Board Representative in their rooms, it was Jericho, though Alex could still pay for the infringement.

Alex pushed the door open. He tested the air for signs that anyone was there, but none of the smells were fresh. Relief filled his chest.

"Each group of students, what we call a pack, gets their own separate quarters. The Alpha is in charge of making sure the others in his pack get their homework done and have all of their other needs taken care of." Alex pointed down the left hallway. "The girls sleep down there and the boys have the other hall. The Alpha takes the first room."

"The quarters are co-ed?" Mr. O'Hare asked in surprise.

47

"Yes," Alex replied with a hint of uncertainty as the man jotted something down in his small notebook. "Is that a problem?"

"It's highly unusual," Mr. O'Hare replied, apparently forgetting his earlier proclamation that he would never answer any of Alex's questions. He finished making notes and peered around the room. "You've never had any problems from cohabitation?"

Alex shook his head. "Never. The Alpha protects all members of his or her pack. No one would be unsafe in their own quarters, or anywhere in the school, for that matter. If anyone messed with a werewolf in a pack, they would have to answer to the pack's Alpha."

"So the Alpha is the first line of accountability before the professors or dean?" Mr. O'Hare asked with interest.

Alex swallowed when the man jotted something else in his infernal notebook. "Yes. That way there is security for the students at all times. It really is a good system."

Mr. O'Hare looked at Alex over the top of his glasses and asked dryly, "Because you know differently?"

Alex fought back a surge of defensiveness. "Yes, I do. I was here when the Academy was created and I've worked with Jaze on many, uh, trips to different areas on, uh, school-related outings." He met the man's doubtful gaze. "I've seen enough to know that humans could do better in pack situations where they have someone to protect their backs at all times. It's better than being out there alone and defenseless."

The man studied him for a moment before he asked, "And how did your schooling fare during these so-called school-related outings?"

"I have excellent marks that I've worked hard to earn," Alex replied; his tone was steady and left no room for argument.

Mr. O'Hare watched him for another minute in silence. He finally motioned to the door. "Fine. Let's move on."

Alex stepped into the hallway and his stomach clenched.

"We followed the stench," Boris said. He waited at the end of the hallway with his entire pack behind him. "What are you doing with that human up here?"

"He's surveying our school for the Board of Education," Alex said, hoping the answer would appease the Alpha. He and Boris had come to friendly terms, but an Alpha's instinct to protect his pack was nothing to be trifled with.

"Could they have sent someone less rotten-egg like?" Boris demanded. "The entire lunchroom stinks."

"If you have a problem, you will address it to me," Mr. O'Hare told the Alpha.

The man attempted to push past Alex, but Alex didn't budge. The human's second, harder attempt didn't even move the student.

"Boris, we don't have a problem here. Mr. O'Hare and I were just leaving. We won't come back up this way."

"No, you won't."

Boris' pack stepped to the side at the sound of Torin's voice. The other Alpha made his way through them as if he didn't see any of Boris' werewolves. Torin's gaze burned with anger.

"Did you come here to threaten our students?" he demanded.

Mr. O'Hare seemed to realize why Alex was standing between him and the Alphas. He stopped pushing and even had the presence of mind to take a step back into Pack Jericho's quarters.

"I came here to ensure that the quality of education provided by Vicky Carso's Preparatory Academy meets the standards set by the Board of Education," Mr. O'Hare replied, though his tone was a bit less haughty than Alex was used to.

"So why are you investigating our living quarters?" Torin demanded.

It seemed Boris was content to let the other Alpha do the questioning. He folded his arms and leaned against the wall as if enjoying the show.

"Because where a student eats and sleeps is also essential to success. If you were living in shambles, it goes to follow that your grades would be diminished as a result of poor living conditions."

"And what did you surmise?" Torin asked, his tone matching the human's.

Alex saw Mr. O'Hare's reluctant acceptance out of the corner of his eye.

"Your quarters are acceptable," he said. "We have concluded our business here. Alex?"

Alex stepped out of the man's way. When Mr. O'Hare brushed past him, the human's hate-filled scent was intermittent with the sour lemon smell of fear. A slight, begrudging amount of respect surfaced in Alex's chest when the man walked past both packs and down the stairs without showing any of the fear Alex knew he carried.

Thankfully, both Alphas let him go, though the occasional growl or disgruntled mutter from the packs voiced how the other students felt about that.

As soon as the man was down the stairs and out of earshot, both Alphas grinned.

"Did you see the look on his face?" Boris asked.

"I thought he was going to pee his pants!" Torin exclaimed.

Alex stared at them. "You were joking?"

Boris chuckled. "Of course. Do you think we're stupid? We're not about to attack a human on school grounds. Let him wander the forest, though…"

Alex rolled his eyes at what the Alpha left unsaid. "You guys are ridiculous," he admonished. "My job is to help him approve our Academy, not let him be scared half-to-death by the students."

Torin's smile faded. "He already hates us, Alex. He's not going to pass the Academy; you know that."

"He'll pass it out of the sheer fact that he'll have no reason to fail us if I can keep the students," he speared them both with a glare, "from messing things up."

Both Alphas had the presence of mind to look somewhat apologetic.

"Sorry, Alex," Boris apologized. "We don't like the way he treats you like a lapdog. We've all seen you showing him around. He's an entitled tool."

"A tool with the power to shut down our home so we have nowhere else to go," Alex reminded him.

Torin nodded. "Just the same, nobody has a right to treat anybody else like that, regardless of their race. How do you think it looks to the other students that he can push you around?"

Alex lifted his shoulders in a shrug to hide how much it bothered him. "I can handle it. Just trust me and try not to scare him so much that he leaves the Academy. As it is, he's the only Board member who dared to come out. We have to give him credit for that."

"Do we?" Sid, Torin's Second, muttered from behind the Alpha.

"Yes." Torin's response was firm. "We'll trust Alex." He gave Alex a steely look. "But if that fails, we will rely on our own means to protect our Academy."

"I understand," Alex said.

He walked down the stairs after the human.

Chapter Five

Alex found Mr. O'Hare sitting in his office with his forehead on his desk.

"Mr. O'Hare?" Alex asked.

"Get out," the man growled in a voice that would have done a werewolf proud. He raised his head and glared at Alex. "Didn't your *dean*," he said the word with heavy sarcasm, "teach you manners? You don't walk into an office without knocking and waiting for a response. Get out. Now."

Alex didn't move. He knew it was fear that made the man so gruff. He hoped that perhaps he could get through to Mr. O'Hare with sympathy.

"I know it's a strange school and—"

"GET OUT!" Mr. O'Hare shouted so loudly Alex knew half the school heard it.

"Fine," Alex snapped. He spun on his heels and retreated through the door, pausing only long enough to slam it behind him.

Alex leaned against the wall with his heart thundering in his chest. He felt like he had run a hundred miles. His muscles tightened and released, and it was all he could do to keep the Demon from forcing its way forward. Nothing in all of his experiences had taught him how to deal with someone like Mr. O'Hare.

"I need a run," he muttered.

He crossed to the back doors and shoved them open. The warm sunlight fell on his face and shoulders. Alex took a deep breath of the fresh air. The scents of the forest filled his nose. Pine and aspen heated by the August sunshine mixed with the loam and mushroom smell of the shadows. A tickling hint of clover and clay told him that a rabbit was eating beneath the bushes inside the wall. Alex made a mental note to mention it to Dray. It wouldn't do for the rabbit to get into the professor's greenhouse, and the other werewolves weren't especially kind to animals they found within the grounds.

Alex pulled the gate open and stepped outside the wall. He phased in the shelter of the trees and left his clothes next to another bush. He shook himself, grateful to be in wolf form once more. The colors became more segregated with heavier shades of gray, and the scents separated into the stories of the individual plants and animals that gave them. He could tell in his wolf form that the rabbit had been grazing beneath the bushes all morning. The scent of dew from the early hours still lingered on its soft, downy fur.

Alex glanced down at his forearms, then stared. He looked over his shoulder and his chest tightened. Alex gritted his teeth and took off running.

His paws knew the forest. Each fallen trunk and windfall

was a part of his home. The scent of the sunflowers that grew thickest in the meadow just south of the river flooded his senses, but he barely thought about it. The rush of deer hiding in the next thicket failed to pike his interest.

Alex didn't slow until he reached the lake. The cliff that towered above it gave shade to half of the water. Alex stopped just outside the shadows and looked down at his reflection. The wolf that stared back at him with his same dark blue eyes had a coat of solid black. His scars showed through his fur as patches of gray, the only reminder of the wolf he had been. Looking down at his reflection, it was unmistakable. Somehow, and for reasons he couldn't explain, Alex had truly become an Alpha.

His best friend Trent knew it, and the way the other students, especially the Alphas, treated him said they guessed as much. The fact that Torin and Boris had acted with such amiable deference when he asked for them to lighten up on Mr. O'Hare said they regarded him as an equal. His coat announced that he was an Alpha; whether he felt like he deserved it or not didn't matter.

"Help!"

Alex's head lifted. He stared back in the direction he had come. A growl sounded. Alex's eyes widened. It hadn't been the growl of a wolf, but of a bear.

"Help me!"

Mr. O'Hare was the one in trouble.

Alex spun and ran back toward the Academy with a speed only a few of the students could even match. Thanks to the challenge presented by Tennison's skills, Alex had constantly pushed himself to work harder. Since his heart no longer gave him problems, he usually stopped when he was on the verge of collapse. Luckily, Mr. O'Hare was much closer than that.

Alex slid to a halt just inside the sunflower-filled clearing. He stared at the sight of Mr. O'Hare cowering at the base of a windswept pine. A grizzly stood on its hind feet and towered over him. A snarl of rage rumbled from the animal's deep chest.

Alex searched the area quickly. The only things he knew made a bear upset was when someone got between the animal and its chosen food or the animal and its cubs. Alex's heart slowed. A glance in the pine tree the human huddled beneath showed two cubs up in the branches. One gave a plaintiff cry. The grizzly bellowed at Mr. O'Hare again.

Alex knew he had to get the human away from the tree before the animal attacked. Whether Mr. O'Hare was aware of the cubs didn't show. He merely cowered lower at the bear's angry advance. If Alex could get to him before the animal dropped to all fours, he might have a chance.

The bear lowered back to the ground with a thud Alex felt through his paws. Before he could so much as bark a warning, the animal charged.

Alex darted through meadow and hit the bear's side just before her huge, swiping claws could reach Mr. O'Hare. The force of the blow rolled the grizzly along the ground and threw Alex over her shoulder. He leaped back to his feet and placed himself between the bear and human. The animal rose to her feet and shook her head from side to side, her small eyes narrowed in anger at this new threat to her cubs.

Alex had to get Mr. O'Hare away from the tree. The bear wouldn't stop until her little ones were safe. As long as the human cowered beneath the pine, Mr. O'Hare's life was in danger.

Alex backed up next to the man without letting his gaze drop from the bear. He pushed Mr. O'Hare with his shoulder.

"Get away from me!" the man shouted. He hit Alex on the head.

Caught off-guard by the surprise attack, Alex growled at

him. The bear, taking the growl as a danger to her cubs, attacked. Alex jumped to the left to avoid a swipe of the bear's huge claws and latched onto her shoulder, stopping a second swipe at the human.

The bear tried to shake him off. When she couldn't, the animal dropped onto her right side in an effort to dislodge him. Alex leaped free before he was crushed and placed himself between Mr. O'Hare and the danger once more.

He didn't know how to convey to Mr. O'Hare that he needed to get away from the tree. If he didn't, they might both get killed.

Alex barked as the bear lumbered back to her feet. Mr. O'Hare merely stared at him with wide eyes like a startled deer. Alex barked again and motioned with his head.

"W-what?" the human asked.

The bear charged. Her angle of attack meant that she realized Mr. O'Hare was the weaker of the two. If she could take one of them down, perhaps she could then focus on the other and eliminate the threat to her cubs.

Alex saw Mr. O'Hare tense out of the corner of his eye. There was only one thing he could think of to do to get the human out of danger. As the bear rushed past him with the speed of a raging bull, Alex surged around the animal at full speed and charged headlong into the human. Mr. O'Hare went sprawling to the ground the same time that the bear's thick claws sank into Alex's back. He let out a yelp of pain and spun around to protect himself.

Using the strength of the Demon, Alex dove at the grizzly's throat. The force of his attack propelled the animal up and over onto her back. Alex held tight. The bear swiped at him, but he closed his jaws tighter and gave the grizzly a warning growl. The animal did something that seemed completely opposite of her instincts. Instead of fighting him, she held still like a wolf in the same submissive situation.

Alex saw her small eyes flicker to the cubs in the tree. They were about the size of a small wolf, probably born that winter. Both cubs had thick brown hair and gave plaintiff calls. A small moan of worry came from their mother.

Alex glanced below the tree. Relief filled him that Mr. O'Hare had found the presence of mind to leave the area. The bear struggled for breath beneath his grasp.

Alex knew letting go might be the last thing he did, but he wasn't about to kill a bear, especially one with cubs. He slowly released his grip and took a few careful steps away from both the grizzly and the tree.

The blue faded from the edges of his vision as the Demon vanished. Every muscle tensed when the bear rolled to her side, then back to her feet. The animal was breathing heavily. She looked from Alex to the tree. He could smell her relief that the human was gone.

The grizzly rose on her hind legs and bellowed at him. The animal's breath smelled of dirt and grubs from the rotten log next to the tree where the bears had probably been foraging before Mr. O'Hare surprised them. When the animal hit the ground again, he could also smell the fear she had for her cubs.

Alex took a step backwards, then another, hoping space would give the animal peace of mind. For a moment, she glared at him, swinging her head from side to side in a warning. Then, to his relief, the bear turned away and ambled back to the tree. She gave a grunt and the little bears answered with happy cries. They more tumbled than climbed down the tree and wrestled happily with their mother. Alex left the clearing to the sounds of the mother bear's reassuring grunts.

He could smell Mr. O'Hare's progress through the trees. The journey pulled at the healing wounds along Alex's back. He wished it was night so the moonlight could help while he padded back toward the Academy, but evening would be soon enough as long as Mr. O'Hare avoided angering any other animals.

Alex reached his clothes and phased. He stifled an exclamation at the pain when he lifted his arms to pull his shirt on. The stickiness of the blood made the material cling to his back. Alex wished he could skip the shirt altogether, but he didn't want to alarm anyone. He had visited the Academy's medical ward far too many times, and his mother, as the main nurse, wouldn't be thrilled to see that he had managed to get injured once again. The wound would heal quickly enough on its own.

"I thought students weren't allowed outside of the grounds during school hours."

Alex's head jerked up at the sound of Mr. O'Hare's voice.

"Technically, the forest is part of the school grounds. It was given to Rafe as a grant from the government in gratitude for—"

"Save it for someone who cares," the man said, cutting him off with his curt tone.

Alex stared at him. "I just saved your life."

The human glared at him. "Am I supposed to thank you? It's probably your fault the beast went after me in the first place. You probably sent it."

Alex sputtered. "I can't send a bear after you even if I wanted to!"

"So you admit that you want to," Mr. O'Hare replied with heavy venom in his voice.

Alex shook his head, then changed his mind and nodded. "Yes, maybe. Not to kill you, but perhaps to show you how much this school means to me. This is my home, Mr. O'Hare, and you are intent on destroying it."

"From what I've seen, you're doing a pretty good job of that on your own."

Alex glared at the human. "What does that mean?"

Mr. O'Hare met his glare. "If a werewolf student has the ability to send a bear against an academic professional, who's to say that the world would be safe coexisting with such a creature?"

"I didn't send the bear to attack you!" Alex protested. "You were between the grizzly and its two cubs in the tree. It would have killed you to get to them!"

"So you admit that it wanted to kill me."

Alex clenched his hands into fists in an effort to stay calm. "Mr. O'Hare, I didn't send the bear to attack you. You had the stupidity to stand between a mother grizzly and her two young cubs. Any person, or werewolf, for that matter, would get mauled to death in that situation. As it was, we got off with our lives, so we should consider ourselves lucky."

Alex spun on his heel and stormed toward the Academy. He didn't care if the man followed; he would almost rather Mr. O'Hare go visit the grizzly again.

"Hey, Alex!" Trent said as soon as he stepped through the doors.

Alex turned so his friend wouldn't see the blood through his shirt. "Hey, Trent. How are things going?"

"Great!" Trent exclaimed. "Professor Mouse let me demonstrate electrolysis using a battery and pencils. It was awesome!"

"I'm glad," Alex told him. Trent had always been the science expert of Pack Jericho. It was good to see him in his element. "You didn't blow anything up?"

His friend grinned. "Nope. That's your job, remember?"

Alex chuckled. "I guess that's why they assigned me to Mr. O'Hare instead."

"So you can blow him up?" Trent asked.

Alex lifted his shoulders and was reminded about the lacerations down his back when his shirt stuck to the skin. "I might, if things keep going the way they are."

"Not so good, huh?"

Alex shook his head. "He hates me, and before you say I shouldn't be surprised, he hated me before he got here. I could save him from a bear and I don't think it would matter." Alex grimaced at the poorly veiled truth.

"I'd stick with something smaller than a bear," Trent said, missing Alex's expression entirely. "How about a raccoon? Of course, those things are mean, and a lot of them carry rabies. Plus, they're born with masks. How good can you be if you're born wearing a mask?"

"Trent?"

"No, seriously, Alex. Perhaps we should look into that. Raccoons are always breaking into Professor Dray's greenhouse and stealing stuff. Maybe there's something to that. It could be ingrained into their genetic makeup, and nature's given us a warning, like how poisonous frogs have bright skin or—"

The bell rang, cutting him off.

"I guess I should get to class," Trent said.

"Back to Mouse's?"

Trent shook his head. "All the senior boys are supposed to be with Vance to help train the football team. You might have to fight for quarterback against Torin and Boris."

The thought of throwing a football with his back all scratched up wasn't a pleasant one.

"Don't worry, you'll win," Trent reassured him, misreading his expression. "You're a great quarterback, and you had all that practice on the beach during the summer. You've got it; no problem."

"I've just gotta grab something in my room," Alex told him. "Let Coach Vance know I'll be there in a sec."

"Okay," Trent called over his shoulder. "But you know how much he hates it when we're tardy."

"I'll be there," Alex promised.

Chapter Six

Alex sat on the couch in his quarters and gingerly pulled off his shirt. The wound was healing, but it would do better if he washed it. Luckily for him, Trent didn't pay as much attention to scents as some wolves. Cassie or Siale would have been all over the smell of blood.

He dabbed at the lacerations along his back the best that he could. From what he could tell by feel, there were four gouges that ran from the base of his neck to about midway down his spine. It wasn't exactly the easiest place to clean.

Footsteps sounded in the hallway. Alex grabbed a shirt, but the door opened before he could get it on. He glanced back and saw Mr. O'Hare in the doorway. The man's expression was unreadable.

"You're missing class?" the man asked, his gaze on Alex's back.

Alex drew on the shirt, grateful he had chosen a black one that would hide any blood that leaked through during practice.

"I'm leaving right now," Alex replied. He grabbed the torn shirt and tossed it in the corner he had turned into his laundry pile.

"Nice," the human said dryly. "Bachelor quarters, huh?"

"Lone wolf quarters, really," Alex said. He glanced around the room. "It's a bit messy," he admitted. "But it's home."

"Until I get it shut down."

Alex stared at Mr. O'Hare. There wasn't any budging in the man's expression. "I saved your life today," Alex reminded him quietly.

"That's a matter of opinion," the Board Member replied. "But what's not an opinion is that a student from Vicky Carso's Preparatory Academy violated the school grounds policy and trespassed during school hours."

Alex tried to remain calm. "Wouldn't that be on the student's head instead of the school?"

Mr. O'Hare met his steely gaze. "That depends on how your school board decides to handle it."

"My school board?"

The man nodded. "Whenever there is a violation of school policy, a board meeting should be called to address the punishment for the action."

"Punishment?" Alex repeated. He hated miming the man's words like a parrot, but he couldn't believe his ears. "For fighting a grizzly to save your life?"

"For leaving the school property during the hours in which you should have been assisting your administrator, namely, me."

"You trespassed, too," Alex said, his tone barely above a whisper in his struggle to remain calm.

"I wouldn't have if you hadn't forced me to go looking for my assistant," Mr. O'Hare replied curtly.

Alex's hands balled into fists. "You're putting this on me." The lacerations down his back stung. He had to fight down the Demon that rose in the face of his outrage.

Mr. O'Hare turned away. "See that you report it to the dean so that the appropriate actions can take place."

Alex stared after him. It wasn't until he heard the man's footsteps hit the bottom stair that he could will his muscles to relax again.

The bell rang.

Alex slammed his door shut and ran down the hallway. He jumped down the stairs and hit the bottom floor running. By the time he slid into Coach Vance's classroom that was situated closest to the football field, he was a minute late.

The huge coach's unforgiving gaze locked on him from where the werewolf was taking role at the front of the class. "Thirty laps and two hundred pushups, Alex. It won't do for a senior to show a bad example to our first year students, would it?"

Alex knew better than to argue. He shook his head. "No, Coach." He headed to the outside door.

"Sorry, Alex," Trent whispered when he went by.

Alex looked back at his friend. "You told me so."

Trent's response followed him outside. "Sometimes I wish I wasn't right all the time."

Alex jogged around the field. By the fifteenth lap in the warm afternoon, sweat dripped down his back and stung the scratches. All he could think about was Mr. O'Hare's demand that he ask Dean Jaze for a punishment for leaving the school grounds during class hours. He had saved the man's life. Mr.

O'Hare had no way of knowing Alex had been outside of the school until the incident with the bear. He couldn't get his mind wrapped around what was happening.

"Done with your pushups yet?"

Alex looked up at Coach Vance. The rest of the seniors were on the field warming up.

A wry smile crossed Alex's face. "I lost count somewhere around eighty."

"I counted three-hundred and seven, so if you're done showing off, you're welcome to join us." The coach held out a hand.

Coach Vance wasn't one to give any show of kindness toward the students. He had lost his wife during the same werewolf annihilation that Jet died in. Even though Vance's wife had been human, her relationship with a werewolf had made her a target. Nikki had told Alex that Vance never forgave himself for losing Nora. Because of that, he seldom let anyone else in.

Alex took the coach's hand and rose to his feet.

"Your mind somewhere else?" Vance asked.

As badly as Alex wanted to tell the coach about Mr. O'Hare, he was determined to handle things on his own. Jaze had asked him to be a good representative of the school. He needed to do just that.

"I've got to talk to Dean Jaze," Alex said. "Can I be excused?"

"You'll miss tryouts for starting quarterback," Coach Vance replied.

Alex nodded. "It's probably for the best. I've got a lot going on and I wouldn't want to let the team down."

Vance looked at him carefully. Finally, he nodded. "You're excused."

"Thank you," Alex said with relief. He turned toward the school.

"Alex?"

Alex glanced over his shoulder.

"Get your back looked at," the coach said. "It's bleeding."

Alex's stomach tightened into a knot at the searching look the huge werewolf gave him. He nodded, grateful that the coach didn't ask any questions. "Will do." He jogged toward the school feeling as though Mr. O'Hare had just managed to avoid an encounter with another bear.

Jaze stared at him from behind his desk a few minutes later.

"Let me get this straight," the dean said. "You want me to punish you for going into the forest?"

Alex shook his head. "I want the school board to decide an appropriate punishment for violating school rules."

"But we don't have a rule about leaving the school grounds," Jaze protested.

Alex sat back in the chair, then winced when his back touched the wood. He scooted forward again. "Yeah, I didn't think so, but there is one; at least, there should be one." He realized he was rambling and said, "Mr. O'Hare saw me leave the school and go into the forest. He suggested that I talk to you so that the school board can make a decision as to the best way to handle the situation."

Jaze watched him closely. "By suggest, you mean that Mr. O'Hare said he could use your violation of the rules to shut the school down."

"He more or less implied it."

Jaze shook his head. "I don't like him holding something like that over you. It's not your individual duty to keep this school from getting shut down."

"It is." At Jaze's surprised look, Alex said, "I'm pretty sure Mr. O'Hare has taken a personal vendetta against me and if the school shuts down, it'll probably be my fault. Let

66

me do this and clear my name. It could go far toward improving our relationship with the man."

Jaze sighed. "I don't like this."

"Trust me," Alex told him. "I don't like it either, but I don't see another way. I can take it."

Jaze nodded. "I know you can, but you shouldn't have to. We've had classes held out in the forest before. Technically, that makes it part of the school grounds."

"Only if you want to tell Mr. O'Hare the nature of the classes," Alex shot back. "I'd rather take this one then open that can of worms."

A slight, begrudging smile spread across Jaze's face. "You're starting to think like a dean."

"What?" Alex replied in surprise.

Jaze nodded. "Listen to you. You're more worried about the school than the punishment you're going to receive for a violation you didn't even know about. You're willing to put your pride aside to keep this investigator in check, and I haven't once heard you talk about your own problems since the moment you got in here."

"What problems?" Alex asked uneasily.

Jaze speared him with a look. "Alex, you smell like blood and bears. What's that about?"

Alex studied the dark wood of the desk in front of him. It was familiar, like the slight curve of the railing on the stairs or the board near the backdoor that creaked whenever he walked on it. He could have just not stepped on the board, but that wasn't the point. The board was a part of him as much as the school.

The wood of the desk was covered in the tiny scratches and marks of years as a part of the dean's furniture. 'Torin' had been scratched along the edge where Jaze wouldn't see it from his seat. The letters were crude and oiled, as much a part of the desk as the wood itself.

"I went for a run in the forest," Alex finally said. "I heard a scream and found Mr. O'Hare cornered by a bear. Somehow he had gotten between the grizzly and her cubs. I fought the bear so he could get away."

The dean's gaze was sharp. Alex could feel it even though he kept his gaze on the desk. He had never known Jaze to miss anything.

The dean's voice was quiet when he said, "So you saved his life and he wants you to turn yourself in?"

Alex gave a reluctant nod.

Jaze sat back in his chair. "It's not worth it."

The words were so quiet Alex barely caught them with his sensitive werewolf hearing. He looked up at the dean.

Jaze was watching him with a concerned look. "It's not worth it," he repeated, louder.

Worry filled Alex. "Worth what?"

"This," Jaze said, motioning to Alex. "I'm not going to stand by while one of my students goes above and beyond to protect a human only to be punished for it. I'd rather lose the Academy than stand by while injustices like that happen."

Alex shook his head quickly, shocked by the dean's direction of thought. "No, Jaze, you can't do that!"

"Werewolves take care of their own, Alex. You may have chosen to be a lone wolf, but you'll always be like a son to me. My pack is your pack, and I won't stand by while some anti-werewolf activist tears down someone I care about."

Alex stared at him. Jaze had truly been his father figure for most of his life. To hear the dean say as much in his own way gripped Alex's heart in a tight fist.

"We're not going to lose this place," Alex said with determination. "It's worth fighting for."

Jaze watched him, his gaze distant as though he saw something other than Alex standing in his place.

"Don't stop fighting," Jaze said quietly.

Alex nodded at Jet's words. "Never stop fighting."

Jaze let out a slow breath and nodded. "Alright, then what do we do. Should I remove you from being his assistant?"

"And give someone else the torture?" Alex replied with a half-smile. "As much as I'd like to give the honor to Torin or Boris, I think they would have killed Mr. O'Hare by now. I've already conquered one bear. How much harder can it be?" He gave a smile he hoped didn't look as forced as it felt. When dealing with Mr. O'Hare, he knew better than to hope it would get easier.

"Alright," Jaze gave in. "I'll talk to the school board and figure out what the appropriate punishment should be. In my opinion, maybe you should have let the grizzly eat him."

Alex chuckled. "Good thing you're not his assistant."

Jaze nodded. "I agree with that completely."

Alex rose and made his way to the door.

"Hey, Alex," Jaze said.

When Alex turned back, the dean's smile had faded, replaced by a look of respect. "I'm proud of the way you've handled this."

His words took some of the weight from Alex's shoulders. The younger werewolf nodded. "Thank you."

He walked back up the hall with the knowledge that not only had he lost his position as starting quarterback, he had solidified his position as assistant to the most unforgiving, cruel, and spiteful man he had ever met. Yet Alex couldn't help the smile that spread across his face. Through it all, Jaze was proud of him. He would do anything to stay worthy of the look of respect in the dean's eyes. As long as Jaze thought he deserved even a tenth of the dean's high opinion of him, Alex could survive anything. He hoped.

Chapter Seven

"Time to go."

Alex opened his eyes. He had almost forgotten that Trent had kept true to his word and slept in his quarters. Alex had pulled the couch beneath the window where he could get the strongest moonlight for his healing back and had almost fallen asleep when the door had opened. Trent entered, tossed his pillow on the ground in front of the unlit fireplace, wrapped himself in the blanket he had brought, and fallen asleep without a word. Alex had decided not to question his friend. He was tired enough for the both of them.

Now, the croak of Trent's tired voice brought him to full alert.

"Jaze?" Alex asked.

Trent peered at the small screen of the watch he wore. "Yeah, he's calling the team. I'll go get the others and meet you down there."

"It'd be easier if you were already in their quarters," Alex said meaningfully.

Trent nodded. "It would, but I'd rather stay in *our* quarters," he answered, stressing the word. He pushed open the panel on the wall and stepped inside without waiting for Alex to respond.

Alex made his way down the dark tunnels and pushed open the door to the Wolf Den. The screens were lit and Brock sat on his throne in the center surveying the information that came across. The human's throne was a swivel chair with various Kick-Me signs stuck to the back and surrounded by wrappers from many different types of snacks. Jaze's best friend held a candy bar in one hand and a corndog in the other. Alex knew it was time to start worrying. Brock was usually a one-food-at-a-time person unless the situation was particularly intense.

Alex walked up the stairs. "That bad, huh?" he asked quietly.

Brock nodded without looking at him. The human's gaze was glued to a screen with words running across it.

"I got it," he said into his earpiece. "They're on their way."

He looked at Alex. "You might want to go armed to this one."

Caden, Brock's cousin, stood behind a long table already covered in a vast array of weaponry.

"Want the usual?" he asked.

At Alex's nod, the human handed him the Glock the werewolf carried on their risky missions. He double-checked the slide and magazine before buckling on the shoulder

71

holster Caden held out.

"Food in both hands?" Alex heard Cassie say to Siale. "We're in trouble."

"Gear up accordingly," Dean Jaze said, entering closely behind them.

Jericho, Terith, and Tennison followed. The werewolves went straight to the table.

"Good to see you're still at the Academy," Jericho said with a nod at Alex. "We missed you at dinner."

Alex stifled a grimace. "I was busy cleaning the bathrooms."

"Seriously?" the Alpha asked. "I thought you'd had enough of toilet duty after your stint with Pack Torin."

The thought of his time as Torin's Second sent a shudder down Alex's spine. He had thought he was done with cleaning toilets after that term. Unfortunately, Jaze's board members didn't feel the same way. He knew the smirk he had seen on Mr. O'Hare's face when the man 'accidentally' walked in on him scrubbing the tiles would linger in his mind for days. He wondered if he had unintentionally become the human's pawn, and the thought rankled his pride more than he liked to admit.

"What can I say?" Alex asked lightly. "Don't leave the school grounds during school hours. If there isn't a class being held in the forest, it's outside the boundaries."

He felt everyone's stares. Alex didn't want to explain further. He shoved his Glock into his holster and focused on Jaze. "What's the situation?"

The dean's gaze said he understood exactly how Alex felt. He saved Alex from further scrutiny by answering, "We've found Drogan's trail."

Alex's heartbeat sped up at the proclamation. After they had defeated the mutants Drogan created in his attempt to make a Demon like the one Alex could turn into, Drogan had vanished. Though the summer went by much more peacefully, the thought of Alex's half-brother lingered in his mind. Drogan had vowed to kill Alex for leaving him in Dr. Kamala's clutches. Despite Alex's pleading on national television for Drogan to leave the werewolves in peace, he knew his brother wouldn't give up. The Extremist's silence had only increased his certainty.

Alex was already heading for the helicopter.

"Fill us in on the way," he called over his shoulder. "Let's move!"

Everyone hurried to join him. Jaze climbed into the back of the helicopter and let Trent sit next to Mouse at the pilot's seat.

"I could use the practice," Trent urged.

"Not on a mission," Mouse replied. "We'll see about the trip home if everything goes well."

The small professor guided the helicopter up through the floor and past the greenhouses designed to slide to each side of the hidden cavern passageway. They rose above the dark Academy and turned to the horizon.

"Drogan's not there," Jaze said in answer to Alex's questioning gaze. "But we know he was there less than a week ago. He set up shop in an old water treatment facility and turned it into his own private laboratory."

"A lab for what?" Cassie asked.

"For his own twisted experiments," Jaze replied, his tone showing his distaste. "He's trying to make something, but we don't know what, yet."

Alex was grateful Siale had been assigned a permanent position with Brock. After all she had gone through as a victim in one of Drogan's labs, he was glad she would be spared finding another of his half-brother's lairs. Mercy wasn't one of Drogan's virtues. He had promised to shield his fiancé from such things; he hoped Brock would use discretion if what they found proved too difficult for her to see.

"The Black Team's arrived," Mouse called over their headsets. "They say it's dark. Do you want them to move in?"

"How far away are we?" Jaze asked. The white of his knuckles from where he gripped the side of Mouse's chair was the only sign of his anxiety.

Alex realized his own fists were clenched and forced them to relax. He wasn't going to find another body pit. Memories of mutilated bodies and a single hand reaching toward the sound of his voice swarmed him. He had held Siale close against his body, willing her heart to keep beating despite the potentially fatal wounds that lined her body. He couldn't think of the corpses beneath them, nor the fact that after the explosion, their only hope of escape had been cut off. He concentrated on the sound of Siale's heartbeat and attempted to keep her from slipping away by telling her about his life.

"Alex, you ready?"

Alex realized they were no longer moving. The helicopter had landed in an empty parking lot with unlit streetlights. The buildings around them were dark at the late hour. Alex looked up to see everyone watching him. Jericho and Terith were already outside. Cassie and Tennison exchanged a worried look from the other side of the helicopter.

"Ready for this?" Trent repeated. He tried to hide the worry he felt, but it rounded his tone.

Alex pushed up to his feet. "I'm ready," he said.

Trent ducked outside with a hand on Alex's arm. Mouse and Jaze were busy conferring with Darian, the head of the Black Team. Alex was grateful Jaze hadn't seen his lapse in attention.

Mouse jogged back over to them. "Darian will take the Black Team through the back. He's already got snipers on the roof. Heat signatures show a dozen guards, but there's no sign of Drogan. We're going in on three."

"You got this?" Trent asked quietly when the others fell into their usual pairs.

Cassie and Tennison ghosted around the front of the building. Terith and Jericho followed close behind.

"I've got this," Alex replied. He jogged after his sister, careful to keep to the shadows in case there was anyone watching from the buildings around them. The fact that Mouse had landed them in the middle of the building's parking lot said that they weren't as concerned about the element of surprise as they were about rescuing whoever might be inside.

In one of Professor Chet's rants during combat training, the werewolf had explained how letting an enemy know an attacker was coming could put them into their standard defensive procedures; while the element of surprise was valuable, knowing how defenders reacted to an attack told valuable information about whoever was in charge.

"Are we concerned about hostages?" Darian asked over their earpieces.

"From what Mouse's surveillance has shown, all warm bodies appear to be performing tasks. Be alert for armed guards." Jaze paused, then said, "Mouse, the lights."

"Got it," the small professor replied.

A moment later, the lights went out in the building. Alex could hear the commotion inside. His muscles tensed and his senses strained, following the movements of the people they were about to confront.

"Slow and steady," Jaze said quietly over their earpieces. "Ready, go."

Jericho kicked the door open, then spun to the right in case anyone charged out.

"Clear," Alex said after a moment. He ducked inside.

His wolven eyesight made out the empty first floor. By the sound of things, the men and women in the building were on the second and third floors. Alex led the way to the stairs.

"Cassie, Tennison, sweep this floor in case we missed anyone," Alex ordered.

"Got it," Tennison replied. His sister nodded, her gaze searching the darkness.

"Be careful," she said.

"Will do," Alex promised. He walked silently up the steps. Trent followed close behind, their footsteps soundless the way Professor Colleen and Professor Rafe had trained them to walk during their outdoor classes in the forest.

"We're taking the back stairs," Jaze said into their earpieces. "Wait for my command."

"Four bodies on the second floor," Brock told them from the surveillance equipment. "They've been walking set routes. Prepare for armed guards."

Alex slipped his gun from the holster. They avoided using firearms whenever possible, but if Jaze felt it was necessary, things could get out of hand.

Jericho reached for the handle to the door at the top of the stairs. Alex waited on pins and needles.

"Go," Jaze said.

Alex nodded and Jericho opened the door. Alex dove through. Two guards spun and shot from the end of the hallway. Bullets tore into the wall next to Alex's head. Alex shot the one on the right and Trent took the left. Both guards fell with small paralyzing darts sticking from their necks.

"Machine guns?" Terith noted quietly. "That's a bit much."

Her brother gestured to the liquid silver that dripped from one of the bullet holes marring the beige wall. "They're armed for werewolf."

"Is that silver?" Brock asked over their earpieces. "Terith, get a closer look."

She complied, angling her head so the camera attached to her earpiece could capture the view.

"Get a sample," Mouse said. "I'd like to know what concentration they're using."

Terith dipped a swab in the liquid and put it in a bag in her pouch.

"They definitely knew we were coming," Jericho said quietly.

"Be careful," Alex told them. "Jaze?"

"Clear," the werewolf said. "Let's move on. Brock?"

"The other six are on the next floor," the human told them.

"There are some strange readings at the end of your floor, though," Siale said. "Someone should check it out."

"Will do," Alex replied. "Jericho, Terith, cover us."

He and Trent made their way down the wall to where the guards had fallen. Alex kicked the machine gun free from the closest guard's hand even though the dose from the dart would keep him out for hours. It paid to be careful. He fought back a smile at the thought. Siale would be proud of him.

"What is that smell?" Trent asked quietly.

The door they stood in front of was made of thick metal and sealed all the way around. Alex stepped closer and took a sniff of the scent that shouldn't have been able to make its way through, yet a faint smell touched the air. Alex's stomach twisted.

"This isn't going to be good," he said, his voice tight.

"What did you find?" Siale asked.

Alex touched the doorknob. Trent set a hand on his arm. "Maybe we should let someone else go first."

Alex shook his head. "Let's do this."

Chapter Eight

Alex tried the doorknob, but it was locked. He used his werewolf strength to force it to turn completely. A metallic pop sounded and the door swung inward.

The smells rushed out, surrounding them in death and decay. Alex fought back the urge to stumble outside and never look back. Instead, he forced one foot in front of the other. Memories attempted to swarm him, but he pushed them down. Alex blinked in the dim lighting. His eyes focused and the knot in his stomach turned into a burning pain of dismay.

Bodies strapped upright to tables lined the walls. I.V.s

with empty bags protruded from withered limbs. The bodies looked mummified as if they had been drained completely of blood.

"What is this?" Trent asked.

"Alex, what did you find?" Siale demanded. Concern for her fiancé filled her voice.

"Uh, I'm not sure yet," Alex answered honestly, his voice rough.

He steeled his nerves and made his way to the first body. Alex avoided looking at the hollow-cheeked face. Plugs had been removed from the human's arms and legs where the major arteries ran. He could smell Drogan's scent in the room. His half-brother had definitely drained their blood, but Alex couldn't fathom why.

Alex's hands started to shake. He reached for a chart on a nearby table, but hit the side of it, sending both the chart and a tray of operating tools crashing to the floor.

Trent was immediately at his side.

"Steady," his friend said quietly.

"Are you guys okay?" Terith asked. "Oh my goodness!"

Alex rushed to the doorway the same second that Siale's gasp of dismay sounded through his earpiece. He covered the camera at the side of Terith's head and turned her back to the hallway.

"Wait outside," he demanded, his voice words gruffer than he meant them to be.

"O-okay," Terith replied quickly. Jericho took her arm and steered her down the hall.

"We've reached the third floor," Jaze said over their earpieces. "Hold up. We'll take care of things and call you if we need you."

"Ten-four," Alex replied.

Spots showed in his vision. He barely heard Trent retreat from the room. Alex pulled the door shut and leaned against the heavy metal. His legs gave out and he slid to a sitting position.

"Guards are down," Jaze said.

Alex barely heard him. He buried his face in his hands. "Siale," he said, his words quiet. "Siale, are you okay?"

It was a moment before she answered, "I-I don't know. Are you?"

Alex shook his head, but couldn't make himself respond. A hand touched his shoulder. Alex jumped at the contact. The world around him spun. He felt as though he was back in the room and one of the corpses was after him. He knocked the hand away and drew his gun within the space of a heartbeat.

His eyes focused and he found himself staring down the Glock's barrel at Trent.

His best friend's hands were raised and eyes wide. "Alex, it's okay. Lower your gun. It's just me!"

Alex's vision warred between memories, nightmares, and reality. The scent of the room clung to his clothes and his nose, refusing to leave him in peace. He kept seeing withered hands reaching for him. He told himself it had been Trent's hand on his shoulder, but he wasn't sure if he believed his own words.

"Alex, give me the gun." Trent's voice was calm. He crouched slowly so that he was eye-level with Alex. If he felt any anxiety at the gun that followed him down, he didn't show it. "Come on, man. We need to get out of here. Let's go get some fresh air. Hand me your gun, okay?"

Trent was a pack mate. He had told Alex he would follow him no matter what he did. The voice in the back of Alex's mind noted that aiming a gun at his best friend's face might change that. His hand shook. He lowered his arm.

"That's it," Trent said.

Alex's training took over. Instead of handing his friend

80

the gun, he slid it back into his holster and attempted to stand. Trent grabbed his arm and helped him to his feet.

"Third floor's clear," Jaze said. "Alex, get your team outside. We'll sweep for leads and meet you there."

Jericho led the way down the stairs. Alex barely saw the stars shining down from outside. His back stung slightly beneath the blanket of moonlight.

"Alex, you're bleeding," Trent said.

Alex nodded. "Bear," he said numbly.

Trent gave him a strange look, but didn't ask questions as he led Alex to the helicopter.

Alex vaguely remembered giving his gun back to Caden when they returned to the Wolf Den. Siale held him as if she knew just how much he needed to know she was alright. He kept looking down at her to reassure himself that she hadn't been left strapped to a table in the room of corpses. Siale and Trent walked with him back to his quarters and he fell into a dazed sleep on the couch with Siale under his arm.

***

When Alex awoke, the faintest gray of dawn showed through the window. He wanted to go back to sleep, but the things that had happened flooded his mind so stark and real that rest evaded him. He slipped his arm from beneath Siale's head at the same time that scents touched his nose. He looked down at Trent's familiar form on the floor.

His friend was awake. When Trent met Alex's eyes, he tipped his head to the left. Alex followed his gaze. His heart slowed at the sight of Jordan, Terith, Von, Cassie, and Tennison sleeping on the floor wrapped in their own blankets.

Baffled, Alex whispered, "What's going on?"

Trent put a finger to his lips and motioned toward the hallway. Alex nodded. Both werewolves made their silent way outside Alex's lone wolf quarters.

"Why is everyone in there?" Alex asked quietly as soon as Trent shut the door.

"They've chosen you, Alex," his friend replied.

Alex shook his head. "It doesn't work that way."

"It does in real life," Trent replied. At Alex's questioning look, the werewolf made a sweep with his hand. "Out there, in the real world, wolves choose their Alpha just as much as their Alpha chooses them. Your pack has chosen you."

"That's ridiculous," Alex replied. "I'm not an Alpha."

"You know you are," Trent shot back.

Alex shook his head. He leaned against the wall and crossed his arms, unable to meet Trent's gaze. "You know very well I'm not fit to lead anyone, let alone my own pack."

Trent was quiet for a moment before he asked, "You mean what happened on the mission?"

Alex nodded. He glanced at his friend. "I could have shot you."

"But I'm still here," Trent replied with forced humor. His

smile fell when Alex refused to smile back. "Okay, so you flipped out. It happens."

"Not like that," Alex argued. "I was supposed to lead my team, and what did I do? I freaked out at the sight of a few bodies and almost shot my best friend. What kind of a leader is that?"

Trent sat on the carpeted floor and motioned for Alex to join him. When Alex kept standing, Trent patted the carpet. "Come on. You might be tough, but I'm tired. Humor me."

Alex gave in and sat. The pressure of his back against the wall hurt far less than he thought it should have. Despite the whirlwind of his mind, his body was healing the way it was supposed to.

"Okay, what?" he asked into the silence.

"Alex, you have PTSD."

"What?" Alex asked to confirm Trent's proclamation.

Trent gave him a steady look. "PTSD. It's short for Post-Traumatic—"

"I know what it is," Alex replied. "We've talked about this before. But I think you're wrong."

"Really?" Trent asked. "Did the sight of dead bodies take you back to the night you rescued Siale? It sure seemed like you were looking at something other than me when you were pointing the gun at my head." He paused, then said, "Please tell me I'm right so I don't think my best friend really was trying to kill me."

The hint of worry in his voice made Alex give in. "Fine. You're right." He shook his head without looking at Trent. "I couldn't control it. The memories took over and I felt like I was trapped. I was on the verge of a meltdown."

"I think you had a meltdown," Trent replied, his voice gentle. "You couldn't control what was happening. Shutting down and running on instinct alone is a meltdown. You were in survival mode."

"Yeah, but survival mode shouldn't account for aiming a gun at you."

Trent gave a small shrug. "So. It's different for everyone, I hear."

Alex looked at him. "You hear? From who?"

"From whom," Trent corrected. At Alex's exasperated look, he explained with a hint of trepidation, "From Meredith."

"You told my mom?" Alex asked with dismay.

Trent stiffened slightly at the sound of frustration in Alex's voice. "Yes, I did. I know you think I have all the answers, but sometimes I don't. It helps to have someone else to talk to." He paused, then said, "It's the same thing I keep encouraging you to do."

Alex wasn't thrilled with the fact that his mom knew what was going on. She had been through enough without having to worry about him. The voice in the back of his mind answered that mothers were supposed to worry. It came with the title.

Alex let out a slow breath. He could feel Trent's worried gaze on him. His best friend was obviously afraid that he had crossed an unspoken line. By his expression, the small werewolf wondered if he had damaged their friendship. Alex felt bad for the fact that apparently everyone around him was worried and it was his fault.

Alex forced a small smile. "I think you have all the answers?"

The relieved answering smile that crossed Trent's face eased Alex's stress.

"Yes, you do, and no, I don't. Sorry to take that away from you," Trent replied.

A chuckle escaped Alex. "I guess I'll recover. It'll be hard, though."

Trent nodded with mock solemnity. "Just understand that

once in a while, once in a very rare while, I might have to go to someone else for an answer. In this case, it was your mother. She said she's noticed the same symptoms, but thought you would come talk to her if it got too bad." He watched Alex closely. "She asked if I would send you to her."

As tempted as Alex was to let himself vent everything to his mother, he shook his head. "I can't." At Trent's fallen look, he rushed on to explain, "Not yet. There's so much counting on me. I have control of it, if only a little bit. If I open that box, I may not be able to close it again."

"But Alex…" Trent began.

Alex shook his head, cutting his friend off. "I need you to trust me, Trent. We're on Drogan's trail. I can't let go now. What if they need the Demon and I'm too far into this breakdown to help out. I won't let the other werewolves suffer because of me."

Trent's gaze was sharp. He ran a hand over his buzzed hair before he finally said, "Okay, if you're sure."

"I'm sure," Alex told him. He hesitated, then said, "As long as I have someone who can help keep me in check; someone who knows what's going on."

A smile crossed the smaller werewolf's face when he realized what Alex was asking of him. "I'm there for you; I promise."

Alex grinned at Trent's sincerity. "It's getting a bit mushy out here. Jordan's going to start getting jealous."

Trent laughed. "Don't worry. She's the one who thought we should stay in your quarters tonight. She says sometimes wolves need to look after their Alpha."

Alex snorted. "I don't think I've heard that one."

Trent gave him a serious look. "You should listen to her. She knows what she's talking about. She's even smarter than I am."

The awe in the small werewolf's voice made Alex happy.

"I'm glad to see you're engaged to someone who will challenge you."

"Trust me," Trent replied. "I feel like I'll be catching up to her my whole life, and it'll be time well spent."

Alex grinned. "Me, too. Siale keeps saying she's happy, but being engaged to her makes me the luckiest werewolf in the world."

"Second luckiest," Trent shot back.

"I'm still going with luckiest," Alex said.

"Second."

"You're right; you're second. I'm the luckiest," Alex told him.

Trent shook his head with a sigh and a pleased expression. "We're both pretty darn lucky."

"It's true," Alex gave in. "So you just have to help me get through this so I can be the husband Siale needs."

"Will do," Trent said. "Just make sure I don't get shot."

"Deal," Alex agreed. "We both have our work cut out for us."

Trent laughed. "You're right about that. If I'm in charge of your sanity, we might be in trouble."

Alex stood and held out a hand to Trent. His best friend rose to his feet.

"A bear?" Trent said.

Alex shook his head. "Don't ask."

Trent grinned and opened the door to Alex's lone wolf quarters that was quickly becoming much more crowded than he had anticipated.

Chapter Nine

"Let's go."

Alex stared at Mr. O'Hare. "Go where?"

"I need to run to my office," the man explained with obvious annoyance as though he shouldn't have to explain himself to his assistant.

"And you need me to go with you?" Alex replied.

Mr. O'Hare gave him a straight look. "You are my assistant, are you not? So, hurry up. The helicopter's landing at the airport in ten."

"Minutes?" Alex didn't know what was going on. After a too-short night's sleep, his brain was having a hard time following what the human wanted from him.

"Yes," Mr. O'Hare replied with a grimace. "I thought werewolves were smart."

"We are," Alex snapped back. At the human's raised

eyebrows, he took a calming breath. "Let me go tell Jaze where we're going."

"Seriously?" Mr. O'Hare replied. "Do you run to your dean for everything? Is there some sort of Alpha protocol for kissing Jaze Carso's shoes whenever he calls?" He grabbed his briefcase and waved for Alex to go out the door. "I've already cleared it with him. There's no time for you to double-check me on everything I tell you. You're my assistant, so assist me by carrying this."

He shoved the briefcase at Alex and stormed through the door, leaving Alex with no choice but to follow. The students and professors had already gone to their first classes. Alex glanced down the halls they passed in the hopes that he would see Jaze. He wasn't worried about leaving the school; he had done that enough times not to have any concerns about going outside the walls. But something about the man's request bothered him.

Alex had no doubt that he could handle himself. Though the situation was beyond what he had thought was within the scope of his duties as an assistant, perhaps Jaze wanted him to tag along with Mr. O'Hare to make sure the man didn't report anything about the Academy that would place the school in a bad light.

A blue car picked them up at the Academy gates.

"Couldn't spring for the ominous black one?" Alex asked.

"What?" Mr. O'Hare replied as he climbed inside.

Alex shook his head and followed. He didn't ask questions at the tiny airport in Haroldsburg and climbed silently into the helicopter behind Mr. O'Hare and the short, bearded man who had been waiting for them.

"First time in a helicopter?" the man asked over the headset.

When Alex realized the man was talking to him, he shook his head. "I've been in one before."

When he didn't expound, the man smiled. "It's a bit intimidating. You'll get the hang of it."

Alex nodded. He glanced at Mr. O'Hare, but the man was busy studying the documents from his briefcase.

They landed a few hours later in the helipad of a short, unmarked building surrounded by many others.

"Assistants are supposed to be silent. Observe everything, but keep to yourself," Mr. O'Hare instructed on their way inside. He paused, then said, "Especially you."

Alex chose not to be ruffled by Mr. O'Hare's comment. He nodded at the uniformed man who opened the door and studied the security guard who scanned the card Mr. O'Hare pulled from his pocket.

"Is he with you?" the guard asked, eyeing Alex with uncertainty. Alex had the distinct feeling the guard knew exactly who he was.

Mr. O'Hare sighed. "Unfortunately, but at least we'll be brief."

The guard waved a hand.

Mr. O'Hare nodded and accepted the card back. As Alex made his way up the hall, he felt the guard's eyes on his back. He was grateful when they turned the corner and left the guard's line of sight.

"Stand here."

Alex glanced at the door. The nameplate beside it said 'Jamison P. O'Hare- National Education Analyst.'

"You want me to stand out here?"

"Do you really have to repeat everything I say?" Mr. O'Hare replied dryly.

Alex crossed his arms and leaned against the wall near the door without a word.

Mr. O'Hare gave a satisfied nod and went inside.

Alex couldn't believe that he had followed Mr. O'Hare in an uncomfortable helicopter for hours only to be told to stand outside the door like some creature unworthy of stepping past the threshold. He made a mental note to tell Trent that he was much better at landing a helicopter than the pilot who had flown them.

Guilt touched Alex's thoughts. He knew he should have told Trent where he was going. Whether or not Jaze actually knew where they were, and Alex highly doubted Mr. O'Hare had actually run Alex's absence by him, Trent was the one who was usually concerned whenever Alex disappeared off the map. Although the small werewolf was sneaky with his tracking chips, Alex doubted even Trent had been given the opportunity to know they were leaving.

The building was quiet, even to what Alex felt were standard office terms. He told himself he was just being paranoid. Perhaps everyone was busy working in offices whose doors were soundproof enough to keep in the keyboard clicks and paper shuffling he assumed should inhabit the numerous rooms.

After an hour of leaning against the wall, footsteps sounded down the hallway. Alex listened to them through sheer boredom, sure whoever was walking in a group had somewhere more important to go than Mr. O'Hare's office.

As if to prove him wrong, the footsteps turned down their hallway. The five men in suits didn't look at all surprised to find Alex there. In fact, they walked straight to him. He pushed casually away from the wall and stood.

"Is Jamison O'Hare in?" a bald, burly man asked.

"Yes," Alex replied.

The man glanced at the door and then back at Alex.

"Would you like to talk to him?" Alex asked.

"No, I wouldn't," the bald man replied. He glanced at his companions.

Alex could smell the man's anxiety; he kept an outward appearance of calm, but his muscles tensed.

"We're here to talk to you," a tall man with a goatee said.

Alex wondered if he and Mr. O'Hare went to the same barber. He had the distinct feeling the men weren't exactly friends by the hostility he felt from them. Keeping the sarcastic thought to himself, Alex queried, "What would you like to talk about?"

"This," the man said.

His gaze shifted and his shoulders tensed, foretelling of the punch before he threw it.

Alex ducked under the man's arm and spun. "What's going on?" he demanded.

None of the men replied. Instead, they attacked in force.

Alex realized the answer to his question in that moment. Mr. O'Hare had mentioned that there were others who weren't thrilled about his involvement with the werewolves. Alex ducked under another fist, threw one man into another, dodged a kick, and blocked a hammer fist with crossed forearms.

Alex wasn't there for Mr. O'Hare to throw around his authority and tell him what to do. Alex had been positioned at the door as a bodyguard.

He spun, using an attacker's momentum to propel the man into one of his companions. Alex blocked another kick with his forearms and was about to follow-up with a punch to the man's groin when he realized the truth.

None of the men were seasoned fighters. Their skills were methodical and rusty at best, yet they were persistent as if they were under someone else's orders instead of their own. If they hated werewolves so much and would go so far as to attack one within their own building, desperation fueled them. Perhaps Mr. O'Hare truly hadn't found enough to shut down the Academy. If five men could report that Alex had attacked and hurt them as innocent bystanders in their own building, it might be the step they would need to shut down the school entirely.

Alex spun inward, falling into Chet's defensive training. He couldn't hurt any of the men. That much was obvious. They threw themselves at him over and over without appearing to fear what would happen as a result. Alex blocked, ducked, jumped back, and spun, only to block again. The hallway felt much smaller with the five men throwing themselves at him.

Luckily, as long as Alex remembered not to throw the punches and kicks that came with the muscle memory of hundreds upon hundreds of hours of training with Chet and the other professors and students, Alex could block attacks for hours. Even when the men intensified their assault, he was able to keep them at bay with hand flips and blocks that sent them harmlessly down the hallway; yet his attackers refused to give up.

The men gasped and stumbled over each other. The bald man threw a slow fist at Alex's head. The werewolf stepped to the side in time for the man to fall into his friend with the goatee. Both men fell heavily against the door to Mr. O'Hare's office.

Alex was in the middle of blocking punches and a kick from the three other men when the office door opened.

"What's going on out here?" Mr. O'Hare demanded.

Alex looked from the men frozen in their various attacks back to Mr. O'Hare. He had thought Mr. O'Hare had set him up in an effort to launch his political attack against the school; however, it was clear by the expressions on the faces of the exhausted men around him that Alex's theory was wrong.

The bald man lowered his attempt to drive a fist through Alex's jaw. "I, uh, didn't know you were back," he said.

"It appears that way," Mr. O'Hare answered flatly.

"We were just introducing ourselves to Mr. Davies, here,"

a man with short gray hair said, straightening his tie.

Mr. O'Hare gave him the same flat look he often used with Alex. "Are you working on making a good impression for the Board, Welks?"

To the gray-haired man's credit, he looked somewhat uncomfortable when he answered, "Of course."

Silence settled over the hallway. The sound of the men's heavy breathing as they fought to catch their breaths was harsh and loud. Satisfaction rose in Alex at the thought that he, on the other hand, wasn't breathing hard at all. He folded his arms and leaned nonchalantly against the wall; a smile touched his lips at the discomfort of the exhausted grown men.

"I think we're done here," Mr. O'Hare finally said.

The bald man nodded. "Yes, we are." He walked back up the hall. Three of the men followed.

Welks hung back. He glanced at Alex but refused to meet his steady gaze. Welks cleared his throat and gave Mr. O'Hare a straight look. "James, because we're friends, I just want to warn you that the conversations around here haven't been pleasant since you took your position."

Instead of softening at the man's apologetic tone, Mr. O'Hare appeared to stiffen even further. "Don't make assumptions about where we stand, Welks. You know that friendship died long ago."

The man's statement deflated Welks further. "You're not going to let that go, are you?"

Mr. O'Hare's jaw tightened a moment before he said, "There's nothing to let go. This conversation is over."

Welks watched Mr. O'Hare for a brief minute, but the man stared past him at the empty hall. Welks let out a sigh and turned away. His footsteps echoed long after he had taken the turn at the end of the hall.

Mr. O'Hare's answering sigh was so quiet Alex's werewolf

hearing barely caught it. His shoulders relaxed and he turned to Alex with the first sign of concern Alex had ever seen from the man.

"Are you alright?"

Alex nodded. "I'm fine. What was that?" He had his guess, but he wanted to know what the human's thoughts were.

To his surprise, Mr. O'Hare answered his question as though speaking to a peer instead of talking down to him. "That, Alex, is the last-ditch effort of my superiors to bring the question of werewolves as individuals with rights to an end. If you had bloodied and broken them, you would be dragged out of here and probably been given the death sentence in front of the nation to end this fight once and for all. Instead, you managed to save face and merely humiliate them." Mr. O'Hare watched him closely. "Are you sure they didn't hurt you? Remember, I've seen you fight a bear and walk away."

Alex fought back a slight smile. "They didn't touch me, though I'll admit it took nearly every bit of self-control I have to defend instead of attack." He paused, then said, "Until I realized how poorly trained they are."

Mr. O'Hare actually let out a short laugh. His eyebrows rose as if the sound surprised him. "Sergeant Ryker would have something to say about that, I'm sure. Our saving grace will be that each of those men has too much pride to admit that an eighteen-year-old werewolf beat them without gaining so much as a scratch, and they have nothing to show for it. You may have single-handedly saved your precious Academy."

"Really?" Alex kept his tone guarded, unwilling to give the man too much.

Mr. O'Hare raised one shoulder slightly. "That's left to be seen, but you didn't doom it."

94

He turned away. Alex caught the briefest hint of fear in the air.

"Mr. O'Hare?"

The man paused with his hand on the open door to his office.

"Is that why you brought me here?" Alex asked. "Did you know they'd attack?"

Mr. O'Hare hesitated as though he debated what to say. He finally gave a slight nod, more to himself than to Alex as if he had made up his mind. "To be honest, I had no idea what to expect. The correspondence I have received since taking up my position at the Werewolf Academy—" He paused, then corrected himself, "At Vicky Carso's Preparatory Academy, have been hostile to say the least. Many feel that if we approve the education at your school, it'll close the gap between werewolf citizenship approvals."

Alex couldn't contain the enthusiasm he felt at the man's words. "That's great!" he exclaimed.

The candidness Mr. O'Hare had shown vanished behind his expressionless wall once more. His look was flat when he replied, "As far as I'm concerned, I'm doing my job here and it's a job that needs to be done. Prejudice aside, children need an education and it's my duty to see that they are educated to the same degree as the rest of the nation. Until things are decided otherwise, Vicky Carso's Preparatory Academy is still under intense scrutiny for educational measures and extremes of student activity beyond the guidelines approved by the Board. I'll be done shortly. Stay here."

Mr. O'Hare pulled the door shut with a sharp bang. Alex leaned back against the wall, baffled by what he had heard and seen. His trip to Mr. O'Hare's office hadn't cleared anything up. Instead, many more layers of politics had been revealed than he had imagined existed.

Chapter Ten

Alex's eyes snapped open. Something was wrong. He could feel it in his bones. A shiver ran through his skin. He looked around the room.

Despite his insistence that the werewolves rejoin Jericho in his quarters, the pack that had chosen him had refused to listen. He thought back to the argument earlier that evening. It replayed in his mind as it had happened.

"You're our Alpha," Terith said and Von nodded at her side with a stubbornness the scrawny werewolf seldom showed.

"But what about the Choosing Ceremony?" Alex pointed out.

"You didn't choose anyone."

Alex stared at his sister. "Of course I didn't! I'm not an

Alpha."

"You are," Trent replied with the quiet persistence that showed up whenever Alex tried to debate the point.

Jordan nodded at her fiancé's side.

Alex shook his head. "I'm not, and I'm not a good leader."

"We're still alive because of you."

Silence filled the room after Tennison's response. Alex let out a slow breath.

"I could argue that," he finally said.

"But you'd be wrong," Trent replied. "As your Second—"

Alex stared at him. "You're my Second now?"

"Of course," Trent told him. "I handle the details you don't have time for; I make sure someone covers for you when you're gone." He gave Alex a straight look. "Like when you took off gallivanting with Mr. O'Hare without letting anyone know where you'd gone."

"I wasn't gallivanting," Alex sputtered. "What does that even mean? I was forced to go with him and…" Alex shook his head with a huff. "That's beside the point! I shouldn't have a Second because I'm not an Alpha!"

"You are," Trent replied.

Alex didn't know whether to punch something or jump through a window. He felt as though the werewolves looking to him to be their leader had no idea how unworthy he was to lead them. He could barely keep his own thoughts under control, much less meet the needs of seven other students who watched him with matching smiles as though they had already known the outburst he would make at their decision.

"Alex."

He turned at the gentle touch to his arm. Siale's gaze was soft and understanding. It took some of the frustration from him just to see it.

"Yes?" he asked quietly.

The little furrow formed between her eyebrows. "You need us, Alex."

Her words were completely different than what he had expected.

"I need you," he repeated with a hint of confusion.

Siale nodded and a slight smile turned the corners of her lips. "Werewolves need Alphas, and Alphas need their pack. You chose to be a lone wolf, but no werewolf is meant to be alone. A pack brings support, love, and stability."

She held his gaze. He felt in that moment like they were completely alone. The instinctual part of him still tracked the werewolf students who watched them, but for the human side of him, everything else fell away. He held onto Siale's words because he felt how much he needed them.

"Alex, you've done so much for all of us and for this school, and we know that the things you've had to do have scarred you."

Alex felt laid bare as if her words took away his clothes, his skin, and exposed the marks on his soul that he carried from his encounters with the General, with Drogan, and in his rescues. He dropped his gaze, ashamed of how weak the scars made him.

"Alex," Siale said softly. When he didn't look up, she continued, "Someone once told me that my scars were beautiful because it meant I survived."

Alex's eyes burned when he looked back at her. "Yes," he said, his voice rough through his tight throat. "But I think I'm past the point of beautiful. Sanity doesn't feel like my strength anymore."

Siale set a hand on his cheek. He closed his eyes, concentrating on her touch.

"That's why we're here," she said just above a whisper.

The silence that settled around them was filled with the

breaths of the pack that had chosen him. Alex felt unworthy to be their leader, but they wouldn't leave. He didn't know what to do or how to face them.

"In the wild, wolves don't choose the flashy new young wolf to lead them," Cassie said from somewhere behind her brother.

Tennison spoke up when she stopped. "They choose the grizzled, scarred veteran wolf who knows how to protect them."

"Nobody wants a leader that hasn't been proven," Von said.

"Yeah," Terith echoed. "The point of leading is using what you've learned in your experiences to protect those who look to you for guidance."

Alex turned around to face them. He asked the question that bothered him the most. "But what if I can't lead?"

"You already have," Trent said.

Tennison nodded. "You've led this entire school, Alex. We fought against Drogan's men together, survived the mutants, and you've led our pack numerous times on Jaze's missions. You lead all the time."

Alex fought back a smile at the werewolf's encouraging tone. "It's a lot easier when there's a mission to follow." He waved a hand to indicate the room. "It's this that I'm not good at, the everyday, making sure everyone's needs are met stuff."

"That's why you have such a good Second," Trent pointed out.

Jordan smiled from his side. "Yeah, and why you have a pack that can take care of itself. We picked an independent Alpha because we're self-sufficient. You don't need to walk us through our homework or anything."

Everyone laughed at the thought. Alex had barely squeaked by the last several terms by studying Trent's notes well past midnight for weeks and weeks. The little werewolf was the sole reason Alex had made it to his senior year. His best friend had been looking out for him ever since their very first term at the Academy.

He looked at Trent. "You've been my Second since we started here, haven't you?"

A light of pride appeared in the smaller werewolf's gaze. He lifted his shoulders in his usual shrug, but the same pride could be heard in his voice when he replied, "Someone had to help you survive the boring stuff."

Alex made up his mind. He held out a hand. "Welcome to Pack Alex. Will you be my official Second?"

Trent stared at Alex. He shook his friend's hand with a look of awe as though he hadn't actually expected their argument to work. "Yes, I will," he said, his eyes wide.

The other werewolf students laughed at his expression.

Alex grinned. "Thank you." He looked around at the rest of his new pack. "And thank you for giving me a chance. I'll try my best."

"You already do," Siale said.

Now Alex sat up, careful not to disturb his fiancé as she slept beside him on the couch. Despite his insistence that everyone pick a room in his quarters, they had all come back to sleep on the floor of the main room again. He couldn't help the smile that crossed his face at the still forms on the floor. The sound of steady breathing and a few snores from Von's corner filled the air.

Another chill ran across his skin. At that same moment, the watch Trent never took off his wrist buzzed. The small werewolf's eyes flew open and he glanced at the screen.

"Alex?" he whispered.

"I'm up," Alex replied. He climbed off the couch.

"Is everything okay?" Siale asked sleepily.

"I'll find out and let you know," Alex told her.

He followed Trent to the panel and stepped inside.

"What do you know?" he asked when they were far enough away from the others so as not to wake them.

"They found another lab and there's a chance Drogan's there."

Alex paused. "Why aren't we waking the others?"

"I'm not sure," Trent said. His watched buzzed again. He glanced at it and his eyes widened. "Nikki just went into labor."

Both boys took off down the tunnel into the darkness. Instead of turning to the Wolf Den, they took the branch for the medical ward. A few seconds later, the panel for the medical wing opened and they stepped through.

All of the professors already lined the halls. Vance gave Alex a nod while Gem smiled at them, her short blue hair askew at the late hour. Her hand strayed to her own noticeable belly. Colleen and Rafe sat in the chairs at the end of the hallway next to Mouse. It was one of the few times Alex could remember seeing Rafe within the Academy walls. The thought sent a thrum of worry through him.

"Is Nikki alright?" he asked Brock.

The human ran a hand through his messy brown hair in an effort to straighten it. His hair refused to obey. "I'm not sure. They've been rushing in and out. The last thing your mom said is that the umbilical cord is wrapped around the baby's neck."

Ice ran through Alex's veins. He wanted to go inside the operating room, but knew better. He was about to ask Gem what would happen to the baby when Jaze came out.

All eyes looked at him hopefully, but Jaze motioned only to Alex. Alex's heart was tight as he followed the dean down the hallway to the small waiting area set aside for the nurses. Jaze leaned against the nearest couch looking more exhausted than Alex could ever remember seeing him.

"Alex, I need your help."

"Anything," Alex said immediately.

"We need to hit Drogan's lab, but I've got to stay here with Nikki and the baby. You need to lead the team."

Alex stared at the dean. "What about Chet or Vance? Surely there's someone more qualified—"

Jaze shook his head. "You know Drogan, and you know what it takes to get everyone out of there alive. I need someone I can trust to lead my team. Can I count on you?"

Alex wanted to say no. He wanted to tell Jaze that there were so many other werewolves who should be entrusted before him. But Alex took another look at the dean who had been a father figure for most of his life. Instead of the strong, determined leader of the Academy, he saw a father worried for his wife and unborn child; instead of the man who had taught him to fight like Jet, he saw his brother's best friend pleading for a favor from someone he had never let down. Alex drew in a small breath and nodded.

"You can count on me."

Jaze gave him a tired smile. "I knew I could." He stood, his shoulders a bit straighter. "Brock will keep me posted on your progress. Be careful."

"I will," Alex promised.

He followed Jaze back up the hallway. The dean disappeared into the operating room without another word. All eyes shifted to Alex. Trent already stood by the panel waiting for Alex's orders. Alex realized then why all of the professors were there. Many waited to see how Nikki and the baby were, but the others were Jaze's team wondering if Alex would be able to take on the role of his mentor.

"Never stop fighting," Alex whispered. He squared his shoulders and met Trent's gaze. "Wake the others. We have a mission to accomplish."

Trent nodded with a grin and disappeared back inside the

hidden passage.

"What's the plan?" Professor Chet asked.

Alex looked at his combat instructor. "If Drogan's there, he'll be protected. We need to make sure everyone is prepared for a firefight."

"Got it," Chet said. The Alpha motioned to Vance and Dray. The werewolves ducked inside the passage.

"Mouse," Alex began.

The little werewolf cut him off. When Alex looked down at the little professor, he was surprised to see the older werewolf drop his gaze the way he did whenever he addressed an Alpha.

"I would prefer to stay with Jaze in case they need help with the delivery," Mouse asked with his eyes on the floor.

Caught off-guard, Alex didn't know what to say. His gaze flickered to Brock. The human nodded encouragingly.

"Alright," Alex replied. "Trent can fly the chopper. I'd appreciate it if you'd keep Jaze posted of what's happening." He paused, then said, "Unless, of course, things here need his attention more."

Professor Mouse gave a relieved smile. "Thank you."

"Rafe and I will get in contact with the Black Team," Kaynan told Alex.

Alex had forgotten the Black Team entirely. He gave the red-eyed professor a smile of gratitude. "Thank you. Let's be prepared to leave in ten."

"Will do," Brock replied.

All of the adult werewolves from Jaze's team left the medical wing. Alex looked up to find his mother watching him from the doorway of Nikki's operating room.

He gave her a quick hug. "How is she doing?"

"It's going to be rough," Meredith replied. "Dr. Benjamin says we might have to do a cesarean." Worry creased her brow. "But you have a job to do. Stay focused and get back

103

here as fast as you can."

"I will," Alex promised his mother.

He put a hand on the wall panel.

"Alex?"

He turned.

Meredith hugged him again. "I'm so proud of you. Be careful, okay?"

He nodded and stepped into the darkness.

Chapter Eleven

Alex jogged down the sloped tunnel toward the Wolf Den. He could hear the commotion of Caden handing out guns, Brock setting up headsets and earpieces, and Trent starting the helicopter.

Kaynan's voice reached him. "Keep it tight and follow Alex as you would Jaze," the professor said.

"He's younger than all of us," Chet pointed out.

Alex paused in the darkness just inside the door.

"I've seen his leadership skills," Vance replied. "Alex can do it."

"What if he freezes again?" Brock asked.

Alex's heart clenched.

"Again?" he heard Dray ask curiously.

"You shouldn't have said that," Trent said.

Alex was surprised at the anger in his best friend's voice.

"Alex has this." Trent's tone was firm. "If Dean Jaze believes in him, you should, too."

Silence filled the Wolf Den for the space of a heartbeat.

A deep voice broke it. "Of course, Trent. We'll follow Alex. Jaze would never turn his team over to someone who wasn't worthy." Vance's voice was light, but carried truth when he said, "But Alphas question authority because we should. We're born to lead. Alex is young and hasn't taken up the reins as a true Alpha yet. We follow our instincts as much as our heart. If there is reason to question, we should."

"There's no reason to question."

The surety of Siale's words calmed the doubt that had filled Alex at the professors' questioning.

"Alex has this," Trent echoed.

Alex stepped into the room. "Let's go." He grabbed the gun Caden held out and checked it on his way to the helicopter.

"Did he hear them?" Terith whispered.

"I'm not sure," Cassie replied.

Alex climbed into the helicopter and was grateful when Kaynan and Vance did the same. His team and the rest of Jaze's followed without question. Kaynan took the seat next to Trent and put on his headset. Trent's hands shook slightly as he checked the helicopter equipment. Alex squeezed his shoulder.

"Trent, you've got this," he said into his headset.

Trent threw him a worried look. "I've never flown by myself before."

"You built me a motorcycle."

A slight smile touched the small werewolf's eyes. "What does that have to do with flying a helicopter?"

Alex gave his friend a confident look. "Anyone who could build a motorcycle from scratch can handle this. Trust me."

Trent let out a breath. "You're right. I've got this."

Alex sat back. He watched the chopper rise through the split greenhouses and into the night.

"These missions always happen at night," Tennison said. "Why do you suppose that is?"

"Our sources sweep at night," Vance replied. "They're sneaky like that."

Alex stared at the huge professor. He had never known Vance to joke about anything. When the Alpha looked at him, he realized the coach was trying to lighten the mood. It worked to ease the tension a bit in the helicopter.

"Brock, what do we know?" Alex asked.

"A few things," Brock replied. "We know that Drogan's given up his apparent penchant for warehouses. They've taken up residence in a mansion purchased under an alias, and by the looks of things, this operation has been going on for quite a while. We also know that there are thirty-five guards, give or take."

"Where does Drogan find these guys?" Jericho asked with a shake of his head.

"Good question," Chet answered. "I don't suppose there's a network for muscle looking to be hired by homicidal werewolves in the middle of an identity crisis."

"We should search for that," Kaynan said.

Dray shook his head. "I think you'd have to throw in torture-inclined and willing to die for someone else's losing battle."

"Term too broad?"

"Exactly," Dray told the red-eyed werewolf. Both of them grinned.

"Also," Brock cut in as if slightly annoyed at the professors' banter, "We're not positive that Drogan's there, but I'd be willing to bet he is." The sound of a wrapper crinkling ended his statement.

"What are you eating?" Dray asked.

"A cupcake," Brock replied. He paused, then said, "I have a stress-eating disorder."

"It's okay," Kaynan said. "The first step is admitting it."

"The second is not eating the box of donuts under your desk," Chet said.

"It's impossible to hide anything from werewolves," Brock muttered.

At Alex's orders, the helicopter landed within the hills at the edge of the city's limits. They jogged silently through the trees until they could overlook the location Siale guided them to.

Alex stared down at the mansion that made the one Kalia had lived in look tiny.

"What's the power situation?" Alex asked in a whisper.

"I'm going to cut the grid," Brock answered. "Less chance of questioning that way. I'll give them a wild goose chase for a bit on locating the source to buy you guys some time."

"Thanks," Alex answered.

Without Jaze to guide him, the task looked intimidating. Guards patrolled the walled lawn and rooftops. Three separate buildings made up the main living structure along with a pool house and series of sheds and garages.

"How do you suppose our pal got the financing for this place?" Kaynan whispered.

"Politics," Chet replied. "Someone on each side of a war makes the money. Drogan apparently has the ear of some very influential individuals."

"Let's hope we catch him in the act," Vance said, his low voice a quiet grumble.

Alex nodded in agreement. "Kaynan, Rafe, sweep the left lawn. Chet, Vance, take the right. Dray, you, Jericho, and

Terith clear the front and set up a post to monitor traffic. We don't want anyone coming in or out while we search the place. Trent, Cassie, and Tennison, you're with me. We'll hit up the back. As soon as we get the signal, move in. Take the lights as go."

Everyone stared at him. Alex fought back an embarrassed smile at their shocked expressions.

"Huh," Chet said. "I guess he won't do too badly."

Trent gave Alex a thumb's up when the others left, but didn't say anything they would overhear on the ear monitors. The pride that shone on his friend's face warmed Alex.

"Ready?" Brock asked into his ear.

"Ready," Alex answered.

A moment later, the lights shut down.

"Low and fast," Alex said quietly. "Take out all guards. We don't want to alert Drogan if he's in there. He'll have at least three escape routes if I know him at all."

The near silent buzz of darts from their guns answered. A shadow fell near the porch. Dray caught him before he hit the ground and pulled the man out of sight. Two others disappeared.

After a second, Kaynan said quietly through their earpieces, "All clear. There's lots of movement inside, but no one seems concerned. We need to hurry before they call for their guards to check in."

"Got it. Move in," Alex commanded.

He ran down the hill with Trent on his right and Cassie and Tennison on his left. They reached the back door just as Kaynan and Rafe crept through. At Alex's motion, the professors angled left. Alex's gun felt warm in his hand as he led the others to the right.

Two shadows appeared in the darkness. Alex shot each square in the chest. He dove forward to catch the first before the guard knocked a chair to the floor. Trent grabbed the second, but the man fell against a marble bust. It teetered, then tumbled backwards. Alex cringed, but only a muted thud followed.

"That's why you need girls," Cassie whispered. A quick glance showed that the bust had fallen on a pillow.

"How did you do that?" Tennison asked.

She lifted her shoulders with a grin.

"Thanks," Alex whispered. "Stay alert."

The smell of blood touched Alex's nose. He reached the landing. Stairs led to the basement while another set went to the second floor.

"Any sign of movement in the basement?" Alex asked in a whisper. His senses strained. While he heard confusion in the darkness upstairs, below was quiet. Kaynan and Rafe met them in the hall. Chet and Vance paused close behind.

"Heat signatures aren't reading belowground," Siale replied. "But the equipment might not be able to pick up through the building material. The mansion has a strange layout."

Alex motioned to Vance. "Take a quick look below. If things are sketchy, don't take any risks. Call us and we'll bring the team."

"The Black Team is here," Dray said over their ear monitors.

"I've got them on the frequency," Brock said.

"Good," Alex replied. "Darian, take the second floor from the outside. By the sound of things, the more, the merrier. We'll go as soon as you give the word."

"Ten-four," Darian's gruff voice replied.

A few seconds later, he said, "Go."

Alex led his team upstairs while Chet and Vance went down. Alex's footsteps were silent on the stairs. He could hear the confusion as the Black Team broke through the windows. Alex reached the top step and dove to the left.

Trent did the same to the right, leaving Cassie and Tennison to clear out the center.

Two shots took down two guards. Alex rolled and shot two more entering the room. The smell of blood was thicker and human, tangling in the air with a scent of iron so heavy Alex could taste it. He searched the darkness for the source.

It was strongest near the door to the south. Alex put a hand on the doorknob.

"Ready?" he whispered to Trent.

"Maybe we should send Kaynan and Rafe," Trent replied with a hint of worry in his voice.

Alex knew his friend was concerned about a repeat performance of last time, but Alex refused to back down. Both teams counted on him. He would be the leader they needed.

Alex shoved the door inward with his shoulder. The blood scent rushed out so strongly it clouded his senses. He blinked, focusing on the objects in the darkness.

Humans were strapped to the vertical tables like last time. Tubes filled with blood ran from the plugs in their arms and legs. The only thing missing was the scent of death.

One of the humans moaned.

Alex let out a sigh of relief. "We have live ones," he said. "Get them down."

Trent, Kaynan, and Rafe quickly responded. Kaynan cut the first set of straps with his wristband blade. The man would have hit the floor if Trent didn't catch him.

"Darian, we're going to need a medevac," Alex said, glancing quickly at the other humans. They were all pale and lethargic, but strength appeared to be returning to them at the prospect of escaping from Drogan's clutches.

"Our chopper's ready," Darian replied. He entered the room with three of his werewolves at his back.

"You've got the humans while we continue our sweep,"

Alex said.

"Got it," Darian answered.

Alex left the room with Trent close behind.

"What was that?" Siale asked into their headsets.

"It looked like the other place. Drogan's collecting their blood," Trent answered.

"For what?" Brock asked.

"I'm not sure," Alex answered. "Run it by Mouse. See if he has any ideas."

"Will do," the human replied.

"Alex, we found a trapdoor in the basement," Chet called into his earpiece. "It's got some sort of contraption keeping it shut. We need Trent down here. Drogan's scent is all over this place."

Alex's steps slowed. "You can smell him down there?" he asked.

"Yes," Vance replied. "This is definitely where he went."

Though the Extremist leader's scent had lingered in the blood room, the faintness of it had given Alex doubt that there was even a chance of finding his half-brother in the mansion. A thrill of excitement ran up his spine at the werewolf's words.

"The third floor is clear," Cassie called. "We took down four guards, but no humans or psychotic lab experiments."

"Way to keep your opinion out of it," Jericho said from the porch.

"She has a point," Tennison replied. "Drogan's pretty psychotic."

"Point taken," Alex said, "But let's stay focused. Kaynan and Rafe, do a final sweep of the second and third floors. Trent and I are heading to the basement."

Terith's voice came over the earpiece. "Alex, there's a truck pulling up to the gates."

Alex's heart slowed. "If they're coming to the mansion at

this hour, it's not by accident. Dray, question the occupants and Jericho do a sweep of the vehicle. Whatever you do, don't let that truck up the drive. If that's Drogan's escape plan, he's not going to make it."

"Will do," Dray answered.

Alex thought quickly through his plan. He wanted to get to the basement to investigate the trap door with Chet and Vance, but the truck was definitely a security hazard. "Cass, you and Tennison monitor the front and back of the house. If Drogan's here and he's called in his escape, it won't be that easy."

"Okay, Alex," Cassie replied.

"We're heading down," he said. "Give us the word when the humans are clear and let us know what you find out about the truck."

Chapter Twelve

Alex jogged back down the stairs with Trent close behind. The scent of blood in the air lessened when they reached the open basement door and continued down. They passed four rooms. Similar tables from the second floor sat in each room. The scents that lingered in the air spoke of werewolf and human along with anger, body odor, stress, and Drogan. The last one made Alex's stomach turn.

"What are we going to find?" Trent asked quietly.

Alex wasn't sure how to respond. He followed Chet and Vance's scents to the last door. Vance pushed it open when they approached. Drogan's scent flooded out along with a strange musk Alex didn't recognize. It smelled of werewolf and human, but something else tainted it that made his muscles tense and his hands close into fists. He approached the strange door in the middle of the floor.

"Leave it to a psychopath to construct some sort of bomb on the door," Chet said with heavy annoyance in his tone. He gestured at the door and crossed his arms as though done with the entire thing.

Trent crouched and studied the apparatus that sat on the door. Two glass vials filled with liquids and another filled with a white, salt-like substance were connected with slender tubes and an array of mechanisms Alex didn't dare to touch.

"What do you think?" he asked Trent quietly.

Alex's instincts screamed for him to smash the entire thing and tear through the door to get at the Extremist hiding beneath, but a lingering need for self-preservation warned him that if it was a bomb, smashing it would be the worst thing he could do. He knew Siale would be glad that his voice of reason still remained. She and Cassie feared he had lost it long ago.

"It's on a trigger system," Trent replied, his voice distant as he worked gingerly through the mess. "One wrong turn and this place will be leveled. Brock, can you put me through to Mouse?"

"Siale already left to get him," Brock replied.

"So he'll blow himself up just to kill us?" Alex asked with a hint of amazement. If anything, his brother had shown more drive to protect himself than Alex had ever had.

Trent shook his head and gestured at the floor. "This cement appears to be coated in a metal alloy that will no doubt protect whoever is underneath from harm. That's why Brock's heat sensors didn't pick anything up." He looked up at Alex. "Drogan could be the only one beneath here, or he could have a hundred guards. There's no way to know for sure."

Alex let out a slow breath. Opening the door could mean death for both teams he had brought to the mansion, but not opening it meant Drogan would escape yet again. They would never know what the Extremist was up to until it was too late. Jaze's orders had been to capture Drogan; they had to go through the door.

"I'm here," Mouse said over their ear monitors. "Describe what you see."

Trent launched in a detailed description of the bomb and mechanisms. Alex paced the room in an effort to contain how badly he wanted to be down that hatch and chasing Drogan. The minute Trent and Mouse took to discuss the bomb felt like hours.

"How long will it take to disarm?" he asked when silence followed.

Trent studied the mechanisms for a moment longer. "Give Mouse and me seven minutes."

Mouse agreed. "If we don't have it by then, we won't have it at all."

Alex spoke into his earpiece, "Darian, how much time do you need to get the humans clear?"

"We're working on the last two," the leader of the Black Team replied. "Give me five minutes. I can send four men down to you."

"Do it," Alex answered.

If the bomb went off, they would all be dead anyway. With the uncertainty of what lay beneath the door, Alex didn't want to risk being caught without the ability to defend his teams.

"Go ahead," Alex told Trent.

"The truck driver is definitely under orders," Jericho said. "He's to drive around back and wait beneath a stand of aspens. The guy's armed for bear." He paused, then said, "Correction. He *was* armed for bear. Dray has relieved him of his weapons and Terith now has the truck's keys. The driver is enjoying a close introduction to the pavement."

"Good," Alex replied. A thought occurred to him. "Jericho, take the driver and Terith with you and drive the truck to the aspens. If something goes wrong here, Drogan might still try to escape. Dray—"

"I'll be in the back," the werewolf replied. "The element of surprise could still be on our side."

"Gently," Mouse said to Trent.

Alex's attention darted back to the small werewolf.

Trent's hands shook as he detached one of the glass vials of liquid from the bomb. He held it up slowly and handed the vial to Alex.

"Don't drop that," the werewolf said.

Alex stared at the container in his hands. He heard the members of the Black Team come into the room, and felt as much as saw Kaynan and Rafe enter as well. All werewolves waited silently for Trent to do his job.

Alex's hands felt sweaty. He wiped one hand and then the other on his pants. Just holding the vial in one hand felt like flirting with certain death. He doubted his promise to his mother that he would be careful covered holding a glass container of explosive liquid. The sarcastic side of him said that he should get someone to take a picture just to show her how very bad he was at keeping his promises.

"Got it," Trent said. The small werewolf held up a vial of colorless liquid.

He noticed Alex's worried expression concerning the vial in his hands.

"It's okay," Trent told him. "You're holding diesel fuel. This is the stuff you have to be careful with. Drogan's concentration of Nitromethane and ammonium nitrate could level this place in a matter of seconds." He set the vial gently to one side. "As long as they don't mix, we're fine."

Alex eyed the container he held. "Are you sure?"

"You can smell it, right?" Trent asked.

Alex focused on the vial. Now that he was concentrating on identifying the liquid instead of being afraid of losing his hand or worse, he recognized the heavy, oily sulfur scent that was much thicker than gasoline. Still careful not to disturb the diesel fuel overly much, he set it gently against the wall.

"So we can open it?" Alex asked.

"You can," Trent replied. At Alex's questioning look, the werewolf explained, "I've got the bomb off, but the bolts are another matter. Unless you know where some bolt cutters are…"

Alex let the Demon through. The beast had been raging beneath his skin with the promise of Drogan feet below them. It took two seconds to channel that strength and tear the trap door from the floor. Chunks of cement and metal ripped free with it.

Alex tossed the door to the side. He willed the Demon to back off, knowing he needed his mind clear to face whatever they met below the basement. The blue faded from his thoughts and he felt like himself again.

A glance to the right showed the Black Team staring at him. Vance and Chet looked at each other. Alex took a calming breath.

"Let's go," he said.

"I don't know if you should—"

Alex jumped into the hole, cutting off any protest Trent had. He hit the ground and drew his gun. The darkness was so complete even his werewolf eyesight had a hard time cutting through.

"Are you still alive?" Trent called down.

Alex glanced up at the gray square above his head. A ladder reached it from the wall.

"I'm alive," Alex answered. "Come on down."

Trent reached for the ladder. Vance and Chet jumped down the way Alex had. Both Alphas straightened and looked around. Three members of the Black Team followed.

"Ever heard of lighting?" Chet grumbled.

"How about cleaning the floor?" Vance replied. "This place stinks and I don't know what I'm stepping in."

A sound cut through the darkness. Everyone froze.

"Well done, Alex."

Alex bared his teeth at his brother's hate-filled voice.

"I wasn't sure if you would be able to open the door," the Extremist continued from the far end of the room.

Alex peered in the direction of his brother's voice, but he couldn't pierce the darkness. The impression he got was that they were in a far bigger room than he had first thought. Drogan's voice echoed slightly.

"In fact, I half-hoped you would blow yourself to pieces and end my headache, but I'm apparently not that lucky."

"Give up, Drogan," Alex growled. He took a step forward to place himself between the Extremist and his team.

"I'm far from giving up."

Alex squinted when Drogan struck a flare. The Extremist held up the red light. It sputtered, and twelve other reflective eyes were revealed.

"What are those?" Chet demanded with true fear in his voice.

Alex took in the creatures' wolfish heads, clawed hands, and bulky muscles. His heart slowed.

"Demons," he and Trent said at the same time.

He looked up at his friend who was halfway down the ladder.

Trent's face was pale and eyes wide. "We're in trouble."

The flare died and the sound of claws on cement filled the air.

"Get out of here!" Alex yelled.

"You can't save them," Drogan called. "You can't save any of them, Alex. You'll watch them bleed and die."

CHEREE ALSOP

"Darian get everyone to the choppers. Leave, now!" Alex shouted.

He shoved the members of the Black Team toward the ladder. Chet jumped and caught the edge of the trapdoor just as Trent disappeared through.

"Come on!" the Alpha yelled.

Vance threw one of the members of the Black Team up and he grabbed Chet's hand. The werewolf pulled him through. The other two scrambled for the ladder.

Alex and Vance turned to face the onslaught. Alex let go of his self-control. The Demon surged through him with fury and blue light. Alex let out a growl of rage and charged the first Demon with the strength of a bull.

Instead of being thrown back the way a werewolf would, the Demon matched him strength for strength. Another barreled up behind the first. Her momentum shoved Alex back. His claws scraped along the concrete as he fought to keep them from Vance and the others.

The Demons were fast. Alex caught claws and returned blows, but every time he shoved one free, another was there to take its place. They shoved him back to the ladder just as the last member of the Black Team was being pulled through the hole.

A female Demon leaped and caught the werewolf by the ankle. Chet's hold slipped and they both plummeted to the floor. The Demons closed in. Vance threw himself on top of the fray. Even the huge werewolf looked small compared to the hulking bodies of the Demons Drogan had created. Claws and fangs pummeled the Alpha as he fought to pull the team member free.

Alex couldn't get past the two Demons he fought in order to help Vance. Instead of taking them down, Alex changed tactics. He charged at both Demons. The attack caught them off-guard, allowing him to shove them back

120

toward their companions. The Demon on his left swiped at his eyes. Alex ducked and grabbed the ankle of the werewolf Vance fought to save. He fell backward and used his momentum to pull the werewolf free. He shoved the team mate toward the ladder. To the werewolf's credit, he began to pull himself up the rungs despite his wounds. Hands reached down to help.

"Vance!" Alex roared.

The werewolf spotted him through the fight. Blood streamed from a huge gash along the Alpha's forehead and he looked as though he was standing by mere will alone. The Demons would tear the coach apart. Alex knew he had one chance to save his professor.

"Drogan."

The rage-filled growl that echoed through the room turned the head of every Demon.

Alex took a step toward the back of the room. He knew that threatening the Demons' Alpha would mean his death, but it was the only way he could think of to draw the attention away from Vance.

"I'll kill you, Drogan," he said, walking further from the trapdoor.

A glance over his shoulder showed the Demons following. Vance stumbled to the ladder. Chet quickly climbed down along with Kaynan and Rafe. They pulled the wounded werewolf up.

Alex continued talking, knowing that the longer he distracted the Demons, the more time he gave the teams to get clear of the mansion. "You've crossed a line, Drogan. You created Demons. What were you thinking?"

Silence met his question. Alex had expected as much. He knew Drogan wouldn't disappear into a hole if there weren't at least a few escape routes on the other end. He could only wonder how long his ruse would keep the Demons following him. The scraping of their claws sent chills of true fear down his spine. They were almost to him. He didn't dare to look over his shoulder.

"Here goes nothing," he whispered.

Alex channeled his Demon strength and ran at the wall. He leaped and hit high on the wall with both clawed feet. Shoving backwards and slightly to the right, Alex tucked and flipped. He hit the ground so hard his claws tore massive cracks into the floor. A quick check showed the Demons behind him and the trapdoor in front with no one in the way.

"I can't believe that worked," Alex exclaimed.

Growls of outrage met his words. Alex scrambled backwards and ran for the trapdoor. The Demons followed hot on his heels. A claw caught his shoulder. Alex threw himself into the air.

He reached, but he had mistimed his leap. The trapdoor was too far away. He could hear the Demons massing beneath him, ready to tear him apart. Alex couldn't beat Demons that matched him strength for strength. There were too many of them. His only hope was that his team would get clear before they made it through the door.

A hand caught his clawed one. Alex stared up into Trent's panicked face.

"I'm not leaving you behind!" Trent said.

The small werewolf pulled. Kaynan and Rafe grabbed Alex's other hand. One quick yank lifted him clear of the hole.

Chapter Thirteen

Alex grabbed the trapdoor from beside the wall and slammed it onto the hole. The raging force of the Demons pounded against it.

"Get everyone to the helicopters," Alex yelled above the chaos.

"The Black Team is clear," Kaynan replied, scrambling to help him hold the door. "Our chopper is in the yard."

The thud of a Demon's body hit the bottom of the door so hard that massive cracks spider-webbed out from the cement around the hole. Alex and Kaynan stared at each other.

"Run," Alex said. He looked at Trent and Rafe. "Get out of here; I'll come after you."

"Are you sure?" Trent asked. The small werewolf looked completely terrified.

123

Another thud hit the door. The ground shuddered.

"I'm sure," Alex replied. "Run. Now!"

At Alex's command, Rafe and Trent took off for the stairs. Kaynan continued to hold on.

"Go," Alex barked. "That's an order!"

Kaynan stayed for one more slam, then ran after the others.

Alex drove his claws into the cement around the trapdoor. With each attack, the flooring crumbled further. Two more blows and he knew there wouldn't be a floor left to hold onto.

Alex prayed that his team mates and pack mates had made it onto the helicopter. His earpiece had fallen out when he morphed into the Demon, otherwise he would tell them to take off. Maybe Trent had seen the futility of remaining. If the Demons got to the helicopter, they would all be killed. Alex could only hope his team was far out of reach.

The floor shook with the next slam. Alex's claws broke free. There were twelve Demons in the room below him and Alex had no way to hold them back. Staying in the basement would be a death sentence. As much as he wanted to fight them all regardless of the losing battle it would be, the wolf drive for self-preservation took over. Alex shoved the door down and scrambled backwards across the crumbling floor. The Demons surged out, werewolf-human-Demon nightmares that could match his strength and were fueled by Drogan's hatred.

Alex took the stairs four at a time. He flew through the mansion's huge entrance hall and out the front doors someone had thoughtfully left open. The sound of the Demons charging after him gave fuel to his flight.

Alex was relieved at the sight of the empty front lawn. The helicopters had taken off. Both teams were gone and the humans with them. He spun, ready to take down however many of the Demons he could.

They spilled out the door. The heavy beating of a chopper sounded in the air. Alex looked up to see the Academy's helicopter lowering above his head. Jericho and Tennison knelt on one of the struts holding a rope ladder. It wavered in the air a few feet above Alex's head.

"Jump!" Tennison yelled.

"Hurry, Alex!" Cassie shouted.

Alex jumped just as the charging Demons swarmed into the yard. He grabbed the last rung of the ladder and was jerked into the air. The Demons scrambled on top of each other. One, a wild-eyed female with patchy red hair and fangs that protruded from her jaws, jumped off the others and latched onto Alex's ankle. He let out a yell as her claws tore into his foot. Alex kicked, attempting to unlatch her as the helicopter rose above the mansion.

She scrabbled to pull herself up and drove her other set of claws deep into Alex's calf. He kicked, but she wouldn't let go. Panic filled Alex. He couldn't let the Demon get to his friends. If she reached the helicopter, there was no doubt of the carnage that would ensue. He had only one choice. Alex grabbed the rope ladder with one hand and raised his other to slice through it with his claws.

The Demon's grip loosened. Alex looked down to see darts protruding from her chest and shoulders. He glanced up and gave a sigh of relief at the sight of a gun in the hand of every werewolf in the helicopter. Four more shots followed. The Demon struggled to hold on. A dart hit her clawed hand. She let go and plummeted to the earth. Alex watched with a faint shred of hope that she would be killed on impact. Drogan's creations had been bred for one thing, to kill every creature in their path. One less Demon could save hundreds, if not thousands, of lives.

To Alex's dismay, at the last moment the Demon spun in

the air and landed on the sidewalk hard enough to split the cement. The other Demons massed on the mansion's front lawn and roared their anger that he had escaped. The battle wasn't over by far.

Alex let his Demon fade as Trent steered the helicopter over the trees. He climbed slowly up the ladder. Hands grabbed his arms and pulled him into the chopper.

Cassie stared at him. "Alex, that was too close," she said with tears in her eyes. She hugged him tight.

"Is Alex okay?" Alex heard Siale ask over and over again in Cassie's headset.

"Yes, he's okay," Trent reassured her. The little werewolf threw Alex a look that said it had been a close one.

"Talk to Siale," Cassie told him. She put a headset on Alex's head.

"Hey, Siale," he managed to get out. Dray pulled him up onto a seat. He glanced over to see Vance bandaged and passed out on the floor.

"Alex," she said, her voice cracking with relief. "Are you alright?"

"I'm good," he told her. "But we have a serious problem. Tell Jaze—"

"He knows what's going on. He'll meet you in the Wolf Den when you land," Brock replied.

The human's voice had a touch of distance to it Alex didn't recognize. "Is everything okay with the baby?" he asked.

"She's healthy," Brock answered. He paused, then said, "But Nikki's struggling to hang on."

The look on Cassie's face told Alex everything he needed to know. He let his head fall back against the helicopter wall and looked out the window. After the battle they had fought and the danger that loomed for werewolves and humans alike, he could barely comprehend the thought of losing

Nikki. She had been a mother for him when he arrived at the Academy. Her quiet confidence and the way she had loved him and Cassie when they were newly orphaned was such an example of selflessness that the thought of her gone from his life gave him physical pain.

"Let's wrap your leg."

Alex looked down at Jericho. The Alpha indicated the blood streaming down Alex's calf to the floor of the helicopter. Alex nodded numbly. The Alpha worked with fast but gentle fingers. Alex closed his eyes and let his mind wander.

A memory washed over him with vivid clarity.

"You have to eat something."

"I'm not hungry," Alex's young self replied.

Nikki crouched in front of him and held out a bowl of ice cream.

"Everybody loves ice cream," she coaxed.

Alex shook his head. His black hair fell in front of his eyes. "I don't like ice cream," he lied.

Nikki gave a little questioning sound that made Alex glance up.

"You know," she said, her voice kind. "It's impossible to stay lost inside yourself forever."

"Lost inside myself?" Alex repeated.

He didn't know why he answered her. He wanted to stay mad at the world. His parents had been murdered, he and Cassie had been shipped off to the Academy, and Jet, his rock, his idol, his big brother, had been killed. Starving himself was the only form of control he felt he had left. He had stubbornly not eaten for three days despite Cook Jerald coming up with the most tantalizing dishes she could create. Alex just couldn't find the ability to care anymore.

"Sometimes when tragedy happens, we lose ourselves deep inside," Nikki told him. A small, sad smile touched her

127

lips as if she knew exactly how he felt. "We feel numb, like we're just going through the motions of being alive." She brushed her hand along the cool stone of the steps he sat on. "Just feeling seems impossible because then we'd have to admit that we are still here while those we care about are gone."

Alex nodded. The brief admittance of how he felt made his eyes burn with tears.

"I know you don't want to be here," Nikki said. She set the bowl of ice cream down and knelt on the step below him. "I know you want to be with your mom and dad and Jet. I know you and Cassie just want to go home and pick up life where you left off."

The tears broke free. Alex ducked his head.

"I just want mom to hold me," he admitted in a voice that cracked with emotion.

"Oh, Alex," Nikki replied in a voice so gentle and understanding that he could hear his mother's words in the way she spoke. "Can I hold you for her?"

Alex nodded and the sobs encompassed him. She pulled him onto her lap and held him while he cried heartbroken tears, lost in a world that had taken everything from him, but that failed to take him, too. He felt so alone, so broken and betrayed. He didn't know how to face a world in which he and Cassie had survived and everyone else they knew had been killed. It didn't feel fair, any of it.

"What about Cassie?" Nikki asked quietly when Alex's sobs slowed.

"What about her?" he made himself ask. He wiped his tears on his sleeve.

"If you don't eat, you'll waste away, and then Cassie will have no one," Nikki said, her voice gentle.

Alex hadn't thought of that. Though his sister followed him like a shadow, she wasn't haunted by the nightmares that trailed through his dreams. At that moment, he knew Cassie was playing in the Great Hall with her new friend Terith. The girls had been close since she and her brother showed up.

But Alex couldn't let go and make friends with the other boys. He didn't want to accept anyone else into his life, because he could only imagine that doing so would push the memories of his parents and Jet further away. He didn't want to let them go.

"Cassie needs you," Nikki said gently. "We all need you. You're so strong, like your brother."

"But he wasn't strong enough."

At his lost words, Nikki brushed his hair back from his forehead the way his mother used to. "That's not the truth," she said softly.

"But he died," Alex replied. "He told me to never stop fighting, but he stopped." His throat ached at saying the words that had haunted his thoughts. He felt like he betrayed Jet by saying them, but he had to know.

"He never stopped fighting," Nikki told him. Her words were firm but still gentle when she explained, "Jet was so strong that he saved many, many families by fighting for what's right." She blinked and he realized that tears showed in her eyes as well. "Jet sacrificed himself to save Jaze and the rest of us. He fought so hard that they couldn't kill the werewolves the Extremists had captured. Did you know that?"

Alex shook his head.

"It's true," Nikki continued. "Your brother fought to his very last breath." Her tears trailed down her cheeks and she sniffed before she said, "He is the greatest hero I've ever known, and I know he's proud of you. Jet would want you to protect your sister because if he was here, he would do the same thing. Do you think you can do that for him?"

A little nod followed. The chance to make Jet proud filled

129

him with the first glimmer of hope he had known since arriving at the Academy.

"You're going to have to be strong to protect Cassie, you know that?" Nikki asked.

Alex nodded again. His stomach growled when he looked at the bowl. It was mostly melted, but the rocky road ice cream looked like the best thing in the world at that moment.

"If you could eat this ice cream, it would be a good start," Nikki urged. "Do you think you could do that?"

Alex nodded again. She handed him the bowl and he took a bite. His stomach twisted in hunger, so he took another one.

"Hello."

Alex and Nikki turned at the quiet voice. The small boy who had arrived with Terith the previous day looked down at them from the top step.

"What are you doing?" he asked.

Nikki smiled at him. "Eating ice cream. Would you like some? I know where Cook Jerald hides her secret stash."

Trent nodded. He looked at Alex. "I don't have anyone to eat with. C-can I come sit with you?"

Alex would be strong enough to protect Cassie; of that, he was sure. Looking at the little werewolf on the top step who had come to the Academy also as an orphan, Alex saw another person in need of protection. He made up his mind then and there to make sure the little werewolf always had someone to watch over him.

"You can come eat with me," Alex said. "The ice cream is good."

Nikki walked up the steps. Alex glanced behind him and met her smile.

"Jet would be very proud of you," she said.

He smiled back, the first true smile he had given since they had arrived.

"Who's Jet?" Trent asked.

Alex motioned to the wolf statue in the middle of the Academy's courtyard and said, "My big brother."

"Whoa, that's your brother?" the little boy said in awe. At Alex's nod, he said, "Man, that is so cool. I'm glad we're friends."

Alex smiled; perhaps Nikki was right. If he protected those around him, he could be like Jet. If Trent and Cassie needed him, he wondered how many others he could save to be like his brother.

Chapter Fourteen

Alex watched the sunrise from the steps where he and Nikki had first spoken so many years earlier. The door opened at the top of the steps and soft footfalls crossed the cement stairs.

"You did the right thing."

Alex looked back at the sound of Jaze's voice.

"How's Nikki?" he asked immediately.

Jaze motioned for him not to rise. "I need to sit for a bit."

The dean settled next to Alex with an exhausted sigh. The fact that Jaze didn't answer his question spoke multitudes.

"You saved Vance and got the humans out of there. You did the right thing," Jaze repeated. "We've sent out a nationwide notice about Drogan's Demons; the GPA is working on tracking them. They'll let us know as soon as they hear anything."

Alex recognized the dean's need to talk about things other than his wife who was drifting away despite everyone's attempts to save her.

Alex forced his weary mind to focus. "I let Drogan escape."

Jaze nodded. "But you saved both teams. That was the decision of a leader."

"It was the heat of the moment," Alex admitted. "I didn't know what else to do. Maybe I shouldn't have opened the trapdoor."

"I would have."

Alex was surprised by the dean's admission. "Even with the risk?"

Jaze nodded. "In order to allow werewolves to overcome the fear society holds over us, we need to get rid of the nation's most wanted criminal. If we can bring Drogan down, it'll take major steps toward resolving the prejudice against werewolves."

"So you would have risked the team?"

Jaze replied with a question. "Why was the team there?"

"To stop Drogan," Alex replied. "But I had a feeling when I saw the bomb…"

Jaze nodded. "Sometimes instinct can be the hardest battle we face. Instinct can save us, but it also makes us cautious." He waved a hand to indicate the Academy. "It was against my instincts to create a place like this with bricks and walls. Trust me, calling together all the werewolf youth to one school wasn't exactly the best act of preserving our race, if you know what I mean."

"It's almost been the end of us a few times," Alex replied. "But it saved us, too."

"It did?" Jaze asked. He watched Alex as if curious what

his answer would be.

Alex nodded. "If werewolves stayed in hiding, with our packs destroyed and living out our lives like desperate criminals, the race would be as good as gone anyway. What kind of a life is that? You and Nikki built something special here." His voice trailed away at the mention of her name.

Jaze closed his eyes. He squeezed them. "And now I'm losing her. Her body refuses to heal…" His voice cracked and he stopped talking.

Alex put an arm around the dean. He thought of how many times Jaze had comforted him the same way. When he lost his parents and Jet, and then losing Kalia, and almost Siale, he had always known Jaze was there if he needed someone to sit in silence with.

"I'm not me without her," Jaze said in a voice just above a whisper. He bowed his head, his elbows on his knees and his face hidden in his hands. "She's the reason my heart beats. I don't even know where I end and she begins anymore."

Alex didn't know what to say to fight against Jaze's agony. He swallowed and went with, "How is your little girl."

Jaze was quiet for a moment. He took a shuddering breath. "She's perfect. Your mother says she's eating like a champion."

"What will you name her?"

Jaze let out another breath. "Nikki chose the name Vicki Megan Carso, after our mothers. I wanted to change it around, but she said…" He paused as if the words were too painful to continue. After a moment, he said, "This school had always been a dream of my mother's, a place where werewolf children could be safe, fed, and educated. She said she wanted to thank my mom for bringing all of us together."

Alex gave a small smile. "I like the name Vicki."

"Me, too," Jaze replied with tears in his eyes.

Alex leaned against the dean. "No matter what happens,

we're family, Jaze. Don't forget that, and don't stop fighting."

Jaze looked at him. "That's what I'm supposed to say to you."

Alex nodded. "That's why I'm here to say it to you. Jet wouldn't want you to give in. Nikki's still here. We can hope, at least."

Jaze's gaze wandered to the statue lit by the golden morning sunshine. "Yes, we can," he agreed quietly.

About an hour later, the door opened behind them.

"You are a horrible assistant," Mr. O'Hare berated from the top step.

Before Alex could apologize for not checking in, Jaze stood so fast the human backed up and nearly tripped.

"Do I understand correctly that you brought one of my students knowingly into a dangerous situation with your colleagues?" he demanded.

Alex stared at the dean. He didn't know who had told Jaze what happened, but the anger that sparked in the dean's eyes made him glad it was directed at someone else.

"I, uh, perhaps," Mr. O'Hare stumbled over his words. "There was a situation, but I couldn't possibly have foreseen—"

"You endangered a student," Jaze replied with such vehemence even the stalwart Mr. O'Hare dropped his gaze. "Isn't that entirely against what you stand for? You're here to see that our level of education meets the standards set by the Board of Education, and yet you knowingly and willingly placed one of our children in danger. How dare you question what I do here if your intention is to look the other way when prejudice threatens the security of the very students you swear to champion?"

Alex knew Jaze's pent-up worry and frustration about Nikki's situation was fueling his attack on the Board representative. As much as he enjoyed seeing Mr. O'Hare get what he deserved, Alex didn't know how far Jaze would go.

The dean continued, "I don't know why I agreed to allow your sniveling, backstabbing ways into our school. Perhaps I hoped it would help our cause to allow these students the chance at a real life, but you've destroyed that, haven't you? The fact that your colleagues would readily attack one of our own who is still just a child shows how very far we are from that, doesn't it?"

The dean's hands clenched into fists and he took a step forward. Mr. O'Hare cowered against the door with his hands raised.

Alex set a hand on Jaze's arm. "Jaze, it's alright."

The dean spun to face him. "It's not alright, Alex! How are werewolves able to hope for a normal life when even the government officials who are supposed to be neutral are fighting against us?"

"They'll learn," Alex replied. "They'll have to." His gaze met Mr. O'Hare's. "I could have killed those men, but I didn't. They were the ones who lost even though they didn't have a bruise on them."

"But they don't learn," Jaze said. His body shook with the exhaustion of waiting every minute by Nikki's side in fear that she would breathe her last breath. The dean and his wife had accomplished so much, now he was on the verge of losing her. "Nobody learns because prejudice is blinding."

"We're fighting it," Alex replied. "Mr. O'Hare being here is a step toward overcoming prejudice." He looked at the Board member. "If we can just get humans to see that we all want the same goals, perhaps we can overcome this."

"But he set you up," Jaze said.

"It was unintentional, for the most part," Alex replied.

Jaze's eyes narrowed. "You believe that?"

Alex nodded. "I do, and I'm glad I was there. If I hadn't been, they may have gone after Mr. O'Hare. I'd rather it be me."

That took some of the fight from the dean's gaze. "You're reckless."

Alex shrugged. "But you're the one who assigned me to him."

Jaze gave a reluctant chuckle. "That's because I'm reckless, too."

"You need some sleep," Alex told the dean.

"I told Nikki I'd watch the sunrise for her," Jaze replied. "It's important to her." He sat back down, his tired gaze on the horizon.

Alex tipped his head at Mr. O'Hare to indicate that he should go back inside. The human opened the door and slipped into the school.

Alex sat down next to Jaze. Silence filled the space between them. Alex could feel the wall of sorrow that surrounded the dean.

"She asked me to remember her as she was," Jaze admitted quietly. "She asked me to watch the sunrise for her, and she hoped I would see her in it and remember the way we were." His voice broke when he said, "She said goodbye."

Alex stared at Jaze. "She did?" His eyes filled with tears. Jaze had known, and yet he let Alex have hope.

The door opened behind them. When Alex heard Meredith's steps, he knew.

"Jaze?"

Jaze nodded without looking back. His tears reflected the gold and rose hues of the sun spilling beyond the walls.

"I'm so sorry," Meredith said.

Jaze leaned his head on Alex's shoulder. Alex knew that the pain he had felt when he lost Kalia was multiplied a hundred times in the dean's heart. He ached for Jaze and sat beside him until the sun was high in the sky. Alex knew the professors kept the students from going outside so the dean

137

could have some peace.

Near noon, the door slid open again.

"Somebody wants her daddy," Siale said. "Cassie has little William."

Alex looked back to see his fiancé carrying Vicky wrapped in a pink and white blanket. The baby's face was red and eyes closed tight as she cried. Siale wordlessly settled the baby in her father's arms. Jaze stared down at the little face. The baby stared up at him and stopped crying.

"See," Siale said with a smile of satisfaction. "She's refused to calm down for anyone. She needs you." She blinked back tears and stepped around to Alex.

Without a word, Siale gave him a tight hug. Alex held her and felt a touch of relief from the sorrow of losing Nikki. He felt as though he could breathe again, and realized how much he had missed just being with Siale. Sharing their pain helped to ease it.

"How's your leg?" she asked quietly.

"Healing," Alex replied. "Jericho is a surprisingly efficient nurse."

She gave a small smile. "I'll tell him that."

"I miss you," he leaned close and whispered so Jaze wouldn't hear.

"I miss you, too," she told him. "But I'm glad you're here with Jaze."

Alex nodded. "Let me know when I can help."

She knew he meant with Nikki. The tears showed in her eyes when she gave him a smile of gratitude. "I will."

"She's strong."

They both looked down at Jaze. The baby was staring up at him and she held his pinky with her tiny hand.

"Just like her daddy," Siale said.

Jaze closed his eyes and put his forehead gently against the little girl's. "I'll take care of you," he whispered. "Your mom won't have any reason to worry. I'll make sure you're safe." A shuddering breath escaped him and a tear rolled down his cheek to land on the baby's. He wiped it away softly with his finger. "Your mom will watch over us, I promise."

Siale slipped her hand into Alex's. She looked like she wanted to cry, but she held it back. Alex squeezed her fingers, using her strength to keep him strong as well.

Vicki gave a little cry.

"Is she hungry?" Jaze asked, looking up at Siale.

She nodded. "Probably. Meredith said she ate about an hour ago, but she's got quite the appetite."

"That's my girl," Jaze replied. He pushed up to his feet.

Alex held open the door.

Jaze hesitated on the landing. He looked back at the courtyard, then up at the Academy as if entering took more strength than he chose to let show. Jaze's shoulders rose with the breath he took; he carried his infant daughter in his arms into the school.

Chapter Fifteen

"Where are you going?" Alex leaned against the door to Mr. O'Hare's office and watched the man pack his notebooks away in a box.

"I'm done here," the man replied without looking up.

Alex's chest tightened. "If you're leaving because of Jaze, you've got to know that he never really would've hurt you. He was just lost because—"

"I know," Mr. O'Hare replied, cutting him off without looking at him. "He lost his wife. He deserves to mourn. That's not why I'm leaving."

Alex took a step into the room. He made himself ask, "So you're done here?"

Mr. O'Hare nodded.

Alex pushed down his apprehension and asked, "What will you report? Are you going to shut down the Academy?"

Mr. O'Hare's movements slowed. He stared down at the book he had just placed in the box. His right hand brushed across one of the cardboard flaps. Alex could hear the minute friction of his fingers against the small fibers that made up the box.

"No."

The man's admission came out harsh as though he didn't want to admit it.

Alex knew Mr. O'Hare had been given plenty of reasons to shut the Academy down. It was obvious Alex was involved in dangerous missions with the professors outside of school, Mr. O'Hare had almost been attacked by a bear, the simplest of searching would reveal that the previous terms' curriculums contained classes that wouldn't fit into the Board of Education's guidelines, and he had almost been attacked by the dean.

Alex let out a slow breath. "Why not?"

Mr. O'Hare glanced at him but didn't appear to see him. The man blinked, then rubbed his eyes wearily beneath his glasses.

"Jaze was right."

Alex watched the human quietly but didn't press.

His patience was rewarded when the man said, "Your dean was right when he said I placed you in danger."

"It's not like—"

Mr. O'Hare cut off Alex's insistence that he could handle himself and continued, "I'm supposed to be an unbiased representative from the nation to determine whether or not this school meets the guidelines for educating the youth. Instead, I knowingly endangered a student."

When Alex tried to protest that Mr. O'Hare hadn't

known, the man met his gaze with a steely expression. "Why do you think I asked you along? I knowingly put you in danger. You're a kid."

"I'm the Demon," Alex replied.

Whatever Mr. O'Hare was about to stay was stopped and the man stared at Alex. "What?" he finally asked.

Alex crossed his arms. "You knew who I was when you arrived here. You hated me before I even had a chance to say hello. You knew what I was. Taking the Demon as a bodyguard isn't putting a student in danger; instead, you endangered your coworkers."

"You're a kid," Mr. O'Hare repeated, but with less conviction.

Alex shook his head. "I stopped being a kid the day my parents were murdered in front of me. I'm the Demon of Greyton, the devil, Drogan's half-brother. Whatever you want to call me, the fact remains the same. It wasn't my life on the line when we went to your office. Don't carry the guilt from the prejudice of your coworkers. You get credit for even daring to come to the Werewolf Academy. I can't imagine how scary that must have been."

Mr. O'Hare watched Alex with an unreadable expression. He finally said, "You really aren't a child, are you?"

Alex shook his head. "There's a reason I run missions with Jaze to save werewolves and stop Drogan."

Mr. O'Hare allowed a ghost of a smile to cross his lips. "You're not keeping any secrets."

Alex gave a shrug. "You chose to come here without fully understanding what you were getting yourself into. I respect bravery."

Mr. O'Hare shook his head and placed another book in the box. "All the same, I'm leaving. And no." He looked at Alex. "I won't be shutting down your school."

Alex felt as if a huge weight had been taken off his

shoulders. He held out a hand. "Thank you, Mr. O'Hare."

The man stopped him with a look. "Don't mistake my words as friendship, Mr. Davies. I still can't stand werewolves. Your dean is right. There are many huge hurdles for you yet to overcome if humans and werewolves are going to get along. I, for one, can't imagine sharing a bus with your kind, let alone approve of you in our schools as equal citizens."

Alex felt like he had been punched in the stomach. He watched the man carefully pack the last of his belongings, then sit at the desk again. Alex left him making notes in one of his infuriating little notebooks.

"Are you okay?"

Trent's voice jolted Alex out of the daze in which he wandered down the hall.

"Uh, yeah," Alex said, though he couldn't put much conviction into his words.

Trent's eyes narrowed suspiciously. "I don't believe you."

"That's because you know me too well," Alex replied.

"I was looking for you," Trent told him. "Come on."

Alex followed his friend without question. His mind was still on Mr. O'Hare when he realized they had arrived at Alex's quarters. Trent pushed open the door.

"Oh, good, you found him!" Terith said.

"About time," Von echoed. "We almost left without you."

"Left where?" Alex asked. He realized everyone was holding guns with canisters on the top. "Are those paintball guns?"

"They are," Siale said. She tossed the second one she had been holding to him. "You know you want to do this."

Alex didn't know what to say. It was the last thing he had been expecting to do considering all that had happened.

Siale knew him well enough to read how he was feeling

no matter how hard he tried to keep his face expressionless.

"Give us a minute?" she asked the others.

"Definitely," Tennison told her. "We'll meet you guys by the back wall. Come on."

Alex watched the pack that had adopted him trail out after Trent and Tennison.

"I'm still not quite sure why they're staying here," he said when Jordan closed the door behind her.

Siale gave him a fond smile. "That's why I love you."

"You love me?" Alex repeated as if surprised by the fact.

She laughed. "Of course I love you." She wrapped her arms around his neck and kissed him. "Why else do you think I'm marrying you?"

Alex stared at her. "We're engaged?" he asked with mock shock.

She smiled up at him. "I knew there was a reason I felt like the happiest girl in the world."

Alex ran his hands down her arms that were still wrapped around his neck. He couldn't believe his good fortunate that he had her. The thought of anything taking her away was too painful to even think about, though that was exactly what Jaze was going through. His smile faltered.

"I know," Siale said softly. Her own smile faded. "I know. I miss her, too."

"I don't think I can go out and pretend like nothing has happened," Alex said, his throat tight.

"That's not what we're going to do," Siale replied. "With losing Nikki and all the emotions in the Academy, the school feels like it's closing in on us. Everyone says they're about to explode. Jericho felt it was time to let off a little steam."

Alex nodded. "He's a good Alpha."

Siale put a hand on his cheek. "You are, too. Come do this with us and help your pack wind down a bit, alright?"

Alex couldn't deny her anything when she looked at him

like that. "Alright."

She took his hand and they walked out the door together. They found both packs waiting near the wall.

"Hey, Jericho," Alex said, shaking the tall Alpha's hand. "I appreciate this."

"I know Nikki was like a mother to you," Jericho told him. "We are all going to miss her."

"Me, too," Alex said. He fought down a wave of sadness. "Sometimes things don't make sense."

Jericho set a hand on his shoulder. "We're in this together. That's what it's all about." He tipped his head. "Come on. You need this more than any of us."

"I don't know if my head will be in it," Alex admitted.

Jericho shrugged with an easy smile. "It'll give me the chance to shoot you."

Alex smiled. "I'll bet you've been waiting for that for a long time."

The Alpha grinned in reply. "You have no idea."

Alex hefted his gun. "Let the chaos begin."

Jericho looked at the two packs. "Pack Jericho, you have orange paint, Pack Alex, yours is yellow. You know what a kill shot is." He speared them with a look. "And don't tell me that werewolves can heal. Two vital shots and you're dead. One headshot, and it's game over. You have ten minutes to find a place for your pack to defend." He pushed the gate open. "Ready? Go!"

The werewolf students took off through the trees with grins and laughter. Alex led his pack to the west. They wound along the river to the base of the cliff.

"Keep on your toes," Alex told them. "Jericho's fast and he's got Don as his Second. They also have eleven members against our eight. We could be in trouble."

Don was a quiet Termer who had turned into something of a trick-shot during weapons practice in Chet's class. The fact that Jericho had asked him to be his Second when Siale went with Pack Alex meant that Jericho knew exactly what the big werewolf's strengths were.

"Way to inspire the pack," Cassie said.

Alex grinned at his sister. "I said we could be in trouble. I didn't say we were going to lose." He winked. "I work best when the odds are against me, and we're going to do the same." He turned to Trent. "Take Siale, Jordan, Terith, and Von down the river so they won't smell you and circle back. As soon as you hear the commotion, attack."

"Got it," Trent said. He motioned to the others and they disappeared silently through the trees.

"Now there's only three of us," Cassie pointed out.

"Are you afraid?" Alex teased his sister.

She met his challenging gaze with a smile. "You wish."

"What does that mean?" Alex replied.

Cassie hesitated, then shrugged with a small laugh. "I have no idea, but it sounded good."

Tennison smiled at his fiancé. "If only we could terrify them with catch phrases."

Cassie's eyes lit up. "I would say things like, 'Better run away or I'll shoot you today!' or 'Yellow paint to the head, you're better off dead! Or 'Pack Alex rules and Pack Jericho drools!'"

Alex and Tennison exchanged a look.

"Should I tell her?" Alex asked.

Tennison motioned for him to go ahead.

"Cass, I don't want to break your heart, but those are the worst catch phrases I've ever heard," he told his sister. "In fact, I don't think you can honestly call them catch phrases."

She stuck her tongue out at him. "Just you wait. They'll be terrified, right Tennison?"

Tennison had been shaking his head, but as soon as she looked at him, he nodded quickly. "Uh, right. They'll be super scared."

She nodded. "That's right. Let's go hide."

"You're ridiculous," Alex called after her.

Her laugh came back to him through the trees. "I know!"

Alex crouched behind a bush and chuckled to himself. The little girl who had preferred the forest to crowds and followed her brother like a shadow was long gone. Instead, the young woman who joked and flirted with her fiancé reminded him of Meredith and the mother who had raised them. He saw quiet confidence, enthusiasm, and happiness in her eyes, and she looked complete with Tennison at her side as though she had truly found her other half.

A twig snapped to Alex's left. He almost shot, but after Professor Colleen's careful training, such a sound could only have been made on purpose to draw him out. He wouldn't give up his hiding place so easily. His fingers closed around the paintball gun that rested on his knee. The yellow balls in the canister rolled against each other with a hushed patter.

Alex's ears picked up the sounds of three individuals. He turned his head, tracking their progress through the trees. Whoever had snapped the twig had fallen silent; Alex kept his or her position locked in the back of his mind.

"They must be this way," a girl said quietly.

"Shh," another girl rebuked. "They'll hear us."

Alex smiled. Pack Jericho's attempt to send out targets for his team would fail. Thanks to hunting through warehouses and forests after Drogan's men, they knew better than to assume a target was as simple as it looked.

A paintball hummed through the air and a member of Pack Jericho yelled, "I've been shot! They're in the trees!"

Alex grinned at the thought of Cassie and Tennison shooting down from their hideouts. Footsteps ran through the trees as Pack Jericho locked in on their targets. The slight shushing of water against feet followed as his own pack closed in. The sound of shots being fired reached his ears. Students laughed and others crashed through the trees in an effort to escape.

"They're everywhere!" Don yelled. "Retreat!"

"They got me," another boy called out. "Run!"

The sounds of laughter and the splats of paintballs reaching home faded. Alex wondered what the headcount was, but he kept still.

"I know you're here, Alex," Jericho said quietly after a few minutes. "I can smell you."

"Your pack needs some work," Alex answered, following the Alpha's progress by the sound.

"They haven't had the same experience as yours," Jericho replied with the sound of a smile in his voice. "I can't say I'm sad about that."

"Me, either," Alex agreed. He heard Jericho pause near the tree closest to the lake. "It's good to get out of the school for a bit." Alex hesitated, then admitted, "I'm not as good at this Alpha stuff as you are."

He backed up at the sound of Jericho making his way around.

"You're good at being an Alpha," Jericho replied, drawing closer. "You're just not good at the school stuff."

"True," Alex acknowledged. "I've never been a great student."

"Too busy off saving the world," Jericho said. "Somebody's got to do it."

Alex grinned, knowing the Alpha was trying to distract him so he could get a good shot. Alex crouched lower, keeping the bush and several trees between them. "Why would you give up half your pack to me?"

"Who says I gave them up?" Jericho asked. "Maybe I was just hanging onto them for you."

Alex caught himself staring in the Alpha's direction. "Are

you saying you knew during the Choosing Ceremony that they weren't going to stay with you?"

"Perhaps," Jericho replied evasively. "Maybe I knew you should have been up there with me choosing them yourself."

"Why didn't you say anything?"

The sound of Jericho's voice swept to the right. "I didn't have to. You knew."

Alex let out a breath. He rummaged for a pinecone beneath the leaves and grass at his feet. "I was in denial," he admitted.

Jericho fell completely silent. Alex's senses prickled as he strained to pick up the Alpha's sound again. A breeze tickled Alex's nose, carrying Jericho's scent with it. Alex spun silently on his heels and pressed closer to the base of the cliff. The silence that flowed between them became complete.

The softest crackle of a leaf beneath the ball of a foot reached Alex's ears. He chucked his pinecone against the tree a few feet away. A brush of grass sounded when Jericho turned toward it. Alex took a chance and dove out from his hiding place. He fired three shots before hitting the ground. The first caught Jericho high on the forehead while the second and third splatted against his chest.

When Alex hit the ground, Don and Marky stepped out of their hiding places and shot him in the back and side.

"Dead!" Don exclaimed. "We killed you!"

Yellow paintballs sailed through the air and hit Don and Marky.

"And gone," Siale answered, jogging through the trees with Tennison and Cassie behind her. "Pack Jericho is finished."

Jericho looked down at Alex. "You did it again."

"Did what again?" Alex asked, feigning innocence.

Jericho held out a hand and pulled Alex to his feet. "You sacrificed yourself. You knew there were three of my pack

149

left. If you took out their Alpha, you would draw Don and Marky out."

"Then the rest of my pack could finish them off," Alex concluded. "Guilty."

Jericho shook his head. It was the first time Alex could remember seeing the Alpha truly disconcerted. "Let's take a walk."

Alex glanced at Siale. She tipped her head toward the school. "We'll meet you guys there. I think some of Pack Jericho's fallen members might be taking out revenge on Trent and Jordan."

"Let's rescue them!" Cassie shouted. She took off running and the others fell in behind her.

Chapter Sixteen

Jericho didn't speak until they were at the top of the small cliff that overlooked the lake. It was one of Alex's favorite places in the entire forest. A gentle breeze swept through the pines, causing them to stir like ocean waves. A surge of longing tightened Alex's chest at the thought of the ocean.

"I'm not sure if I'm missing something or if you are," Jericho said finally.

Alex glanced at the Alpha, but Jericho's brown eyes were on the darkening horizon.

"What do you mean?" Alex asked.

Jericho gave a slight shake of his head, his gaze still distant. Yellow colored the Alpha's brown hair where Alex's paintball had gotten him. "One of us has this leadership thing wrong, and I really have no idea which one of us it is."

Alex sat on the rocky ground and let his legs dangle over

the edge of the cliff. After a few minutes, he looked up at the Alpha. "Honestly? If one of us has it figured out, I put my dibs on you."

Jericho gave a small smile and took a seat beside his friend. "I'm starting to doubt that."

Troubled, Alex gave him a serious look. "What's bothering you? Is it the fact that I'm not afraid of bullets? I've felt enough of them that..." At the Alpha's look, his words died away.

"Alex, I don't get it." Jericho ran his fingers through his messed hair and looked at the yellow paint that streaked his hand. "I tried to do what you do. I knew you were in the bushes and if I made a sound, you would shoot me. I knew that your pack was ahead, and the only way to even get a little payback was to bring down their Alpha."

"Which you did," Alex pointed out.

Jericho nodded. "I did, but it went against everything."

Alex knew then what the Alpha was getting at. He ran his fingers across the rough edge of the rock he sat on and said, "Self-preservation doesn't seem to be one of my strong points."

"That's not it," Jericho replied. "You gave your pack a winning battle plan and you hid, knowing I would come after you; you wanted to survive, or else you would have waited in the open."

"Jer, it's paintball," Alex began, but the Alpha cut him off.

"You know as well as I do that wasn't a game. Paint might make up for blood, but when it comes down to it, stepping on that leaf was the hardest thing I've ever done. I knew it would bring you into the open for my pack to kill, but I also knew I would die doing it."

"Yet, you did it," Alex replied softly. He didn't look at the Alpha when he continued, "What makes us so different?"

Jericho picked up a stone and threw it. They both watched the rock plummet into the lake. Rings in the disturbed water grew from where the rock disappeared. They moved in larger and larger circles out to the shore.

"Did you hesitate?" Jericho asked when the rings subsided.

Alex wanted to give a flippant answer, but he could tell how much his response meant to the Alpha. He shook his head and said honestly, "No. I never hesitate."

"That's what makes us different." Jericho gave Alex a straight look. "When I hesitated, the hundreds and thousands of things I have to live for went through my mind. Even though it was a game, I pretended it was real, just for that moment, just to experience how it would really feel if that was going to be the end. And so I hesitated."

Alex threw another rock without a word.

"That's the key," Jericho said, breaking the silence that followed. "I think that's your key to defeating Drogan."

Alex stared at him, surprised by the Alpha's train of thought. "What do you mean?"

"You might not feel like an Alpha at the school, but throw you into battle or in a mission and you're all in. You don't show fear, you don't second-guess yourself, and every thought you have is on protecting those who look to you for safety. I think that's how it's going to happen."

Alex wasn't sure what Jericho was getting at. "So you're saying my willingness to get shot is how I'm going to end him?"

Jericho smiled. "I guess you could look at it like that. What I'm saying is that when you have the chance to end it, do what you do. Don't hesitate, don't second-guess yourself. He may be your half-brother, but he's destroyed so many things in this world he doesn't deserve to be a part of it any longer. Think you can do that?"

"If my Alpha commands it," Alex replied evasively.

Jericho chuckled and shook his head. "You've gone way past needing anyone to tell you what to do. You'll figure it out."

"Someone's got to save the world, right?" Alex said with only a hint of sarcasm.

"That's right," Jericho told him. "And somewhere along the line, you volunteered for the job."

A howl reverberated through the air and Alex's response died away. The pain and heartache in Jaze's voice tightened Alex's throat as the dean said goodbye to his one, his true love. The werewolves of Pack Jericho and Pack Alex appeared in twos and threes around the shore of the lake in wolf form. Different shades of gray stood out in the rapidly fading light.

Jericho gave Alex a sad look. "Our turn," he said quietly.

Both Alphas climbed low enough to phase in the privacy of the bushes. Alex reached the top of the cliff again first. Howls from the Academy combined with howls from the forest. The cries of heartache reverberated in Alex's chest until he couldn't contain it any longer.

Alex lifted his black muzzle to the dark sky. His song of sorrow rose to mix with the others in notes of loss, pain, longing, and anguish. Letting his cry spread through the forest eased some of the burden that tightened his shoulders and gripped his heart. He changed the notes, telling of the woman who had adopted them when he and Cassie were alone and gave them love when they felt like they had lost every bit of it in the world.

Alex closed his eyes and sang of a woman who led with kindness and showed true courage in the face of a world that tried to destroy them. He used the notes of the wild wolf to tell of the example Nikki and Jaze had been to him, and of his inability to ever repay them for their kindness. He ended his howl with the high notes of heartache and let it linger in the lower tones of gratitude for Nikki's selfless ways and the love she had always been so willing to give.

When Alex's howl faded away, those around him did as well. The echoes of their song caught within the trees and bounced off the mountain until only the ghost of it remained to whisper in the night breeze.

Alex went to his clothes and phased. He pulled them on and climbed back to the top of the cliff.

"It's hard to lose the people we care about," Jericho said quietly when he reached Alex's side once more.

Alex's hands clenched into fists. A waved of frustration swept through him. "If I could have fought someone to save her…"

Jericho gave him an understanding look. "You would have. But sometimes life has its own plan. Sometimes we can't change fate."

"But it feels so wrong. Nikki should be alive. She should be able to watch William and little Vicki grow up. Jaze needs her at his side. What will he do?" Alex blinked back the tears that made his eyes burn.

"He'll do what he always does," Jericho replied quietly. "He'll take care of his children, he'll watch over the school, and he'll live, because that's what we do."

Alex nodded. It was the only choice. Wolves didn't look back with regret, yet his human side longed for things that could never be.

"What are you doing?" Jericho asked.

Alex backed up until his shoes touched the descent of the cliff behind him.

"Living," Alex replied. He threw himself forward into a run and jumped off the cliff and into the empty air.

After seconds that felt like an eternity, Alex plummeted into the cool depths of the lake. A second impact resounded, telling that Jericho had followed him. For a brief moment, memories of fighting Drogan's mutants under the water clouded Alex's mind. He fought back a surge of panic. Something brushed his shoe. Alex bared his teeth and dove lower only to realize that he was face to face with a gnarled tree trunk.

Grinning to himself at his stupidity, Alex put his sneakers against the trunk and pushed off. He broke the surface and took a huge gulp of air.

"I thought you weren't coming up," Jericho said. The Alpha paddled in place with the inborn technique of the wolf.

Alex decided not to point out how ridiculous the doggy paddling werewolf looked. "I wanted to see what it felt like to be a fish."

Jericho sputtered and shook his head. "You are something else, Alex Davies."

They swam to shore and were met by the rest of Pack Alex and Pack Jericho.

"Ready to head back?" Siale asked quietly.

Alex nodded. He put an arm around her shoulders and held her close to him as they took the journey through the abnormally quiet forest. It felt as though even the trees still lingered, caught in the song of the wolves who had howled their torment to the moon.

Meredith met them at the Academy steps. She gave Cassie and Alex both a hug. "They're going to bury Nikki tomorrow in the town where she and Jaze met," she told them, her words soft. "Kaynan and Grace are keeping vigil."

Worry for the dean filled Alex. "Where's Jaze?"

Meredith's expression was sad when she replied, "I sent him to bed. He looked like he was ready to drop."

Alex held open the door for his pack mates and mother to walk through.

"Are you coming?" Siale asked when he paused on the

stairs to their quarters.

"I'll be up in a bit," Alex replied. "I just want to check on Jaze."

She gave him a soft kiss. "You care so much," she said. The little furrow that formed between her eyebrows whenever she was worried about him was there.

He brushed her arm with his hand. "I'll be up soon; I promise."

He jogged back down the stairs, then walked soundlessly along the hallway to the quarters Jaze and Nikki had shared. Nikki had insisted that the door never be locked in case Alex or Cassie needed them. Finding it still unlocked touched Alex. He pushed the door open and closed it softly behind him.

His sneakers sunk into the carpet when he walked down the hall to Jaze's room. He knew the photographs on the walls by heart and didn't need to look at them to feel Nikki's smile in the one where she crouched next to Cassie to look at the grasshopper the little girl had found, or the picture of Nikki laughing after she had pushed Jaze into the lake, followed by the next one where Jaze pulled Nikki in with him.

Alex lingered by his favorite one. It was a photograph of him shortly after he had arrived at the Academy with Cassie. He remembered the moment well. He had climbed onto the wall to see the trees he could smell on the other side. The seemingly endless expanse of forest had called to him, beckoning for him to jump down and just be a wolf, to run wild and free away from the pain of the world, to just be an animal and forget about the sorrow that dogged his every step.

Nikki had been the one to find him. The picture was of her sitting next to him, her arm around his shoulders and her own gaze on the trees beyond.

157

"It would be nice to just be a wolf, wouldn't it?" his young self had asked her.

"Yes," she had agreed with a smile. "It definitely would. But you know what?"

"What?"

"You would miss what makes being a werewolf special," she had replied.

Alex remembered his doubt when he had asked, "What makes being a werewolf special?"

"Well," Nikki had replied. "This, for one thing. Don't you think you would miss talking?"

Alex had shaken his head. "I could do without talking," he had replied with certainty.

The memory of her fond smile still lingered in his mind. "You remind me so much of your brother. Jet didn't talk much, either, but when he did speak, he said a whole lot with just a few words."

Alex had liked the thought that he was similar to his brother.

"What else would I miss?"

Nikki had thought about it for a moment. "Fingers. You wouldn't be able to make things or color. You'd have paws your whole life."

Young Alex had stretched out his hand and studied it. "It is pretty cool to make things," he had finally admitted. "Chet says he can teach me how to fight."

Nikki had nodded. "Fighting's pretty cool, especially if you can help those who are weaker."

"That's what Jet did," Alex had said with a smile. He had given a determined little nod. "That's what I'm going to do. I guess I better stay a werewolf, huh?"

"I think that's wise," Nikki had replied.

Alex set a hand on the picture. It made his heart ache to think that he wouldn't hear her voice ever again.

As if to contradict him, Alex heard Nikki's voice as clear as day say, "This is the happiest moment of my life."

Alex's heart slowed and he crossed the hall.

Chapter Seventeen

A light flickered in the living room. Alex paused in the doorway, uncertain about what he would find. The scene in front of him broke his heart.

Jaze slept on the couch with little baby Vicki curled next to him and protect by his arm from rolling off the side. She looked so comfortable and perfect sleeping in her father's embrace. Her cheeks were rosy and little wisps of curly blond hair showed beneath her tiny pink cap.

Alex's gaze strayed to the little boy sitting on the floor in front of the couch. Little William had his knees under his chin and his arms around his legs. His gaze was locked on the screen of the television Alex couldn't see from his vantage point.

Alex stepped into the room. He knew what he would

find, and how hard it would be to face. He let out a slow breath and turned to see Nikki on the television in her wedding dress. Her smile was huge as she walked with Jaze down the aisle.

"I miss her."

Alex's gaze shifted back to William. The three-year-old boy kept his gaze on the screen.

"I miss her, too," Alex said softly.

"When will she come back?"

Alex closed his eyes for a moment. He opened them and crouched in front of the little boy who was like a brother to him.

"What did your dad say?" Alex asked. His gaze flickered to Jaze, but neither the dean nor the little baby gave any sign that his quiet voice disturbed their slumber.

William dropped his gaze to the floor. "He said she had to go away, and we wouldn't see her again for a long time." The little boy frowned in concentration as if it was important to him that he got his father's words right. "He said she left to go see her mommy and daddy who were very far away."

Tears filled Alex's eyes. He sat on the ground. At his motion, the little boy climbed on his lap as if he just wanted to be held. Alex cuddled him close against his chest.

"She loves you very much, do you know that?" Alex asked. His voice cracked on the question.

William nodded, his cowlicked blond hair tickling Alex's chin. "She told me every day."

Alex smiled despite the tears that began to run down his cheeks. "That's good," he told the little boy. "Because it's true. Never forget that."

"Daddy said the same thing."

Alex nodded. A sob of loss filled his chest, but he kept it at bay. "You…you've made her very proud," he said. "Are you going to help your dad with baby Vicki?"

William nodded and he peered around Alex at his sister with a warm smile. "Daddy said Mommy gave her to us as a goodbye gift, and that it's my job to watch over her."

Alex smiled and wiped his tears on his sleeve. "He's right. Sisters are very important."

"Like Cassie?" William asked in his little voice.

Alex nodded. "Just like Cassie. Can you take care of Vicki the way I do Cass?"

"I will," William promised. "Because Mommy said if I did, I would always have a best friend." The little boy paused, then said, "But how long do I have to take care of her before I get a dog?"

Alex gave a soft laugh. "I think she meant that Vicki would be your best friend."

William looked a little disappointed. "So no dog?"

Alex shook his head. "But sisters are great."

"I suppose," William replied with a little sigh. "But she doesn't want me yet."

"Don't worry," Alex reassured him. "Soon, she'll be old enough to walk and play, and then you're going to have a great time together."

"Promise?" William asked doubtfully.

"I promise."

William gave a little nod and climbed down from Alex's lap. He sat on the floor and turned his attention back to the video. "Daddy said I can watch this whenever I want." He looked at Alex. "It's when they decided to be my mommy and daddy."

A wave of emotions filled Alex at the sight of Nikki and Jaze kissing. He felt like he either needed to smile or cry, and crying wouldn't help little William at all. He settled for saying, "I know they're very happy they decided to be your mommy and daddy."

William nodded. "Mommy told me that, too, before she

162

went away."

Alex attempted a happy smile, but it came out sad. "You know, my parents went away when I was only a bit older than you."

"Both of them?" William asked in surprise.

Alex nodded. "That's when I came to live here."

"With my mommy and daddy."

Alex smiled. "Your mommy and daddy took good care of me and Cassie."

"Will you be here to take care of me?"

Alex stared at the little boy. William's eyes were the same beautiful blue his mother's had been. Alex could almost see Nikki looking at him with a matching hopeful expression.

"Of course," Alex promised. "I'll always be here for you."

A yawn escaped the little boy.

"Are you getting tired?" Alex asked. A glance at the clock on the wall said it was far later than he had expected.

William nodded wordlessly.

"I'll tuck you in," Alex told him.

Alex turned the television off and walked with William to his bedroom. The little boy climbed on his bed and waited for Alex to pull up the covers. Alex kissed William on the forehead.

"Goodnight, Will. We'll hang out a lot more while your mom's gone, okay?"

"Okay," William replied with a tired smile. "I like that. It'll give me something to do while I wait for Vicki to be able to play."

"Good; it's a deal, then," Alex promised. He turned off the light.

The steady sound of William's sleeping breaths filled the air. Alex shook his head, amazed at how quickly the little boy had fallen asleep.

"Goodnight, William," he whispered.

Alex made his way back up the hallway. One more glance showed Jaze and Vicki still asleep on the couch. Alex wondered if he should help Jaze to bed, but thought maybe Jaze was avoiding sleeping without Nikki at his side. After checking to make sure Vicki was alright, Alex walked quietly back down the hall and shut the door.

The sight of Siale sitting on the carpet across the hall waiting for him filled him with an overwhelming need to hold her. She crossed to him silently and rested her head against his chest. He closed his eyes and, for the first time in what felt like way too long, he relished just having her in his arms.

Her sage and lavender scent filled him with each breath. He thought of how much it meant to him to have her scent around him every day. It was strengthening and filling. He thought about the first time he had smelled it in the hospital after they had been rescued from the body pit. He had fallen asleep in his bed and had a horrible nightmare about her dying in the pit. As soon as he awoke, he went to check on her, but her room was empty. Only the scent of sage and lavender remained, teasing him, beckoning to him. He knew at that moment that he would never be the same.

"I have an idea," he told Siale.

Ten minutes later, they were in the helicopter with Trent at the controls and Jordan in the seat next to him. Jordan's spikey red hair stood out all around the headset she wore.

"I'm not sure Jaze would approve of this mission," Trent said for the tenth time.

"Brock let us go," Jordan reminded him. "He must have thought it was a good idea."

"I won't get you in trouble," Alex told Trent. "You know how careful I am about following the rules."

Trent gave a snort of disbelief and Jordan laughed.

"Anything to help Jaze is a good idea," Siale said. "It'll be worth it; trust us."

Alex and Siale's fingers were intertwined as they sat side by side on the back seat.

"Thank you for coming with me," Alex told her.

She smiled up at him. "I want to be a part of this. It's important, and I get to be with you. I've missed you."

Alex lifted up his arm and she leaned against his side. He traced patterns on her arm and was amazed at how soft her skin felt beneath his touch. She did the same to his palm, lingering on the scars that traced his hand and reminded him of all it had taken to get to that point.

"This is it," Trent called a while later.

Alex looked out the window as the helicopter settled between long rows of short buildings. The gray light of dawn brushed the horizon, revealing more sheds in the distance.

"Will you guys stay with the helicopter in case anyone comes to check it out?" Alex asked Trent and Jordan. "I'd hate to get it confiscated or something."

"Four teenagers flying a helicopter early in the morning shouldn't cause too much controversy," Jordan said with a wink.

"I was going to get a hamburger," Trent replied wryly. "Think I can pull this thing up to a fast food window?"

Alex laughed. "If you're not here when we get back, we'll look for a burger joint with a helicopter wedged in the drive through."

He and Siale held hands while they walked between the buildings.

"Jaze used to tell me about this place." Alex looked around at the long stretches of pavement between the sheds. "He said they played football and hockey here. All the kids used to sneak out of their houses after curfew and hang out."

"Why was there a curfew?" Siale asked.

"Well," Alex replied with a grin. "There were rumors of werewolves in these parts. Who would have thought?"

165

Siale laughed. "Apparently, they were right!"

They stepped through the opening in the fence and followed the path across a long parking lot next to an abandoned shopping center. A lone streetlamp flickered in the middle of the parking lot. Alex brushed it with his fingertips when they passed by.

"It's strange to think about growing up in a time when nobody knew werewolves existed," Siale mused. "I mean, we are so free now, at least at the school. Could you imagine going to a school where everyone was human and you had to hide what you were?"

Alex's sneakers crunched on the dry grass that lined the alley between the fences where they walked.

"It might be fun," he replied. "But Jaze said when he first got here, the local pack didn't exactly like him."

Siale looked at him. "That was Chet's pack, right?"

Alex nodded. "And get this, Nikki used to be Chet's girlfriend!"

Siale stared at him. "No way! Did she know he was a werewolf?"

Alex shook his head with a grin. "Nope. She had no idea."

Siale smiled back. "That's amazing. I'll bet they have quite the story."

Alex nodded. "We'll have to ask Jaze to tell us all of it." He paused, then said a bit quieter, "Someday."

The hushed scent told him he was at the right place. "This is it," he told his fiancé." He looked at the back of the house Jaze had once shown him.

The Carso house and the house next door were still unoccupied. Signs had been posted on the doors and windows, but the lettering was faded and illegible. A punching bag hung in the back of the Carso house. It was tattered and worn from years of swinging in the tree. The leather on the outside was shredded and it looked as though a family of squirrels had taken up residence inside for the last several years.

Alex jumped the back fence and turned to help Siale, but found her already on the other side.

She smiled at him. "Werewolf, remember?"

"I was trying to be a gentleman," he pointed out.

She grinned. "We'll have to find a bigger fence, then."

Alex smiled and walked through the backyard. He paused by the punching bag, amazed the straps and chain still held. He ran his fingers along the worn leather and tattered cloth.

"It feels like we're walking through the ghost of memories," Siale said softly.

Alex looked up to find her gaze on the fence between the two houses. The wood was missing in places and broken in others. Alex hoped what he was looking for was there.

"That's why we're here," he said.

He made his way to her side and crouched. After a few minutes of careful searching, he grabbed two of the wooden slats.

"These are the ones I need," he said more to himself than to Siale.

Taking care not to ruin them, Alex used his werewolf strength to pry the boards from the fence. He checked the scent of the wood and broke the two boards in half, then leaned the upper parts back against the fence.

"It looks happy," Siale noted.

Alex glanced back. The fence almost looked like a half smile the way it leaned forward into the Carso yard. It warmed him to think of leaving the backyard that way, smiling at the memories of two people who had fallen in love and created a legacy that would remember them forever.

167

CHEREE ALSOP

Chapter Eighteen

"Jaze?" Alex tapped on the open door to Jaze's office. It was the first time the dean hadn't heard him and just welcomed him in.

Jaze looked up in surprise and gave Alex a small smile. "Sorry; my thoughts were elsewhere. Come in."

Alex and Siale entered with Cassie and Tennison close behind. Trent and Jordan lingered in the doorway.

"It's good to see all of you," Jaze said. "Can I help with something?"

"We made you a present," Alex told the dean.

Jaze watched him with a curious expression. "A present for me?"

Alex nodded. "We all worked together. It's, well, you'll see."

168

Cassie handed Jaze the gift.

He looked down at the wrapping for a moment as if he didn't know what to expect.

"Open it," Cassie urged. "You'll like it."

"Alright," the dean replied with a note of uncertainty.

He slid his finger beneath the paper Siale had wrapped it in and broke the tape. The blue and green paper fell away to reveal the frame.

"You guys," Jaze said softly. He stared at the picture. It was one Cassie had found of Nikki and Jaze standing in front of the partially built Academy. The frame of the main building was visible while only a few wooden posts showed where the dorms would soon be. Jaze stood behind Nikki with his arms around her waist; the smile on her face was so bright it lit the entire picture. "This is beautiful," Jaze said.

He moved the frame to look at the back and paused. Slowly, the dean lifted the frame to his nose. He sniffed it, then closed his eyes and inhaled.

"This was our fence," he said in a voice just above a whisper. Tears escaped from his shut eyelids and his voice broke when he said, "This is where we truly became friends."

Alex blinked back tears of his own. "Siale and I went there last night. I remembered the story you told me of when she was mad at you and you made her laugh."

Jaze nodded. He opened his eyes and wiped his tears with his shoulder. He appeared unwilling to let go of the frame. "She had a right to be mad." He smiled despite the sadness in his eyes. "I needed to apologize, so I did the manly thing and fake cried until she tried to comfort me."

Alex gave a soft chuckle at the thought of the dean pretending to cry.

"That worked?" Tennison asked. "I'm going to have to try that."

Jaze smiled. "It worked. She took pity on me, and when

she found out I was faking, she stuck her hand through the fence and tried to slap me." He paused, then said, "I caught her hand and kissed it. It was the first time I ever kissed her."

After a few minutes of silence, Cassie asked, "So she forgave you after that?"

Jaze nodded. "She had no idea I was a werewolf. I probably should have told her then, but her parents were Hunters before there was a truce, and they probably would have killed me."

"Good call," Trent said.

The dean chuckled. "I guess it was." He put the frame to his nose and sniffed it again. His voice was wistful when he said, "It's amazing how the smells linger after all these years. So many stories and so many memories." He smiled at all of them. "Thank you very much. I can't even tell you how much this means to me. This is the best gift anyone could have given."

One by one, the students hugged Jaze who had been like a father to each of them in his own way.

Siale was hugging him when Jaze's phone beeped. Brock's voice came over the intercom.

"Jaze, Drogan's Demons just attacked a city in New Mexico. The city's on lockdown. You need to come see this."

"We're on our way," Jaze replied. He set the frame carefully on his desk and motioned for Alex to open the panel.

The werewolves rushed down the tunnel. When they reached the Wolf Den, Brock had every screen tuned to different news stations.

"There're are other attacks in Utah and New York, and sightings of Demons in South Dakota," Brock said quickly. "Attacks happen, humans are killed, and the Demons disappear before the police can do anything. It's mass chaos!"

"No, it's not."

Everyone looked at Trent. The small werewolf studied the screen. "There's a pattern."

"I see it," Jordan said.

"What's the pattern?" Brock asked.

Trent pointed to the screens. "The attacks appear to be happening in succession, right? One after the other in random locations to throw the authorities off track?"

Brock nodded. "And your point is?" He looked so stressed out that the human didn't have anything to eat even remotely close by.

"My point is…" Trent grabbed the pointer from Brock's hand and followed the screens. "Look. One, two, three, or should I say nine, eight, seven."

"I don't see the pattern," Tennison said.

Brock's face washed white. "They're places his father hit."

"And in the same order," Jaze concluded. His jaw clenched. "Alex, get your team. We know where he's going to be."

Caden had the guns and other weapons already out when they ran down the stairs to the helicopter.

"The GPA will meet you there," Brock called over the sound of the chopper's blades as Mouse prepared to take off. "The Black Team is on their way, as well as SWAT and the CIA. This is being handled as a terrorist threat."

"It should be," Jaze answered. "Keep me informed."

"Be careful."

Alex spotted Trent and Jordan near the stairs. Jordan held his hand with both of hers as if hesitant to let him leave.

"I'll be with Alex, and he's always careful," Trent replied.

Jordan cracked a smile. "This isn't a good time for jokes."

"Sorry," Trent apologized with an answering smile. He stood on his tiptoes and kissed her. He broke away from his fiancé with obvious reluctance. "I'll see you soon," he promised.

171

Siale walked down the stairs with an extra headset in her hand. "We could use another set of eyes up here at what Brock calls the Battle Station and I call his refrigerator."

Jordan glanced at Brock. He shrugged with a sandwich in his hand that had appeared seemingly out of nowhere.

"What?" he asked with his mouth full. "I stress eat."

"Seriously," Siale said quietly. "We can really use you."

Jordan accepted the headset. "I'm happy to help."

Alex saw Trent mouth 'thank you' to Siale when Jordan's back was turned.

"The usual?"

Alex turned back to Caden who held out his Glock. "Yes, with two more clips."

"That crazy, huh?" Caden asked, shoving the extra clips into Alex's vest besides the others he always carried.

Alex didn't let his anxiety show when he replied, "We're heading back to D Block where I killed the General. It's going to be crazy." The GPA hasn't used it as a holding facility since Alex killed the man who was his father. The thought of going back there filled him with mixed emotions.

Alex wordlessly shrugged into the vest and followed the others to the helicopter.

Kaynan's dark red eyes met Jaze's. "It's a trap."

"That's why we're going," Jaze replied. "Things need to end one way or another. Drogan's not walking away from this one."

"You really think he'll be there?" Chet asked.

"I hope so," Jaze said.

Alex was surprised to hear the anger in the dean's words. Jaze met his gaze.

"I have some issues to address," the dean said.

"If by issues, you mean you want to destroy him and his Demons so the killing and fear ends once and for all, then I have issues, too," Alex replied.

Jaze cracked half a smile. "We have the same issues."

The instant they landed at D Block, it was clear everything was different than they had planned. Bodies of GPA agents, men in SWAT uniforms, and other government officials lay torn and mangled across the roof as if ravaged by dogs. Alex and the others jumped out of the helicopter. Mouse lifted it clear immediately under Jaze's orders so their escape wouldn't be cut off.

"I can't reach the Black Team," Brock told them in their earpieces. "And the GPA gives only static."

"We know why," Jaze replied, his voice tight. "Call back any who respond. Tell them not to go to D Block."

"I'll try," Brock said.

"Jaze?" Siale's voice came over the ear monitors. "Heat signatures show four Demons still left in the building along with Drogan. They're on the sixth floor." She paused, then said in a worried voice, "I think they're waiting for you."

The scent of blood was so thick it was the only thing Alex could smell. His pack grouped together in the middle of the carnage. Trent's eyes were wide as he stared around at the limbs and torsos. A need to protect his team and whatever humans remained surged through Alex. Drogan was inside the building, and the Extremist was responsible for all of the death and destruction that had taken place. Alex needed to make him pay. He began to succumb to the Demon inside him that demanded to be free.

Jaze grabbed his arm. "Alex, wait. I can't let you go rushing in there again like last time. I could just have easily have found you on the floor of that elevator instead of the General."

Alex pushed down the blue that colored his vision with difficulty. "Four Demons did this much damage," Alex said. "I'm the only one who stands a chance against them."

Jaze nodded. "Yes, but only if you keep your wits. Don't

173

rush into this blindly. That's what Drogan expects you to do." He voice filled with intensity. "We need to bomb this building."

Alex stared at him. It was the first time Jaze had ever recommended something so rash. With the werewolf's need to retaliate against Drogan, Alex knew it must be something else guiding the Alpha's decision.

Alex shook his head. "What if Drogan gets away?"

"Remember when we talked about instinct?" Jaze asked.

Alex nodded. "Instinct can be the hardest battle we face."

"Exactly," Jaze replied with his gaze on the door that led from the roof. "I want to fight Drogan as much as you do, but instinct warns me that I shouldn't go through that door. I have too much to live for, and you do, too."

Alex's hands clenched into fists. "But what if there are humans down there."

Jaze shook his head. "Not left alive." He looked around at the bodies. "Trust me. We blow it."

Alex hesitated, but Jaze had never steered him wrong. He finally nodded.

"Mouse," Jaze said, "We need the explosives."

The small werewolf landed the helicopter on the roof just long enough for Trent to grab the bag.

"Jericho and I will stay with Trent to make sure nothing goes wrong," Alex said.

Jaze nodded. "We'll set the explosives around the base and come back to pick you up. Be careful."

"We will," Alex replied.

His senses thrummed when the helicopter took off. The fact that four Demons waited in the building below along with his half-brother made the Demon pulse at the edge of his self-control. He followed Trent to the east corner and watched the small werewolf begin to set the explosives.

"Take your time," Mouse said over their earpieces. "If we

174

plan this right, we'll bring the building down on top of them. Nothing could survive."

"I hope so," Trent muttered.

He finished placing the bundle, rechecked one thing, and then Alex followed him to the next corner.

A sound sent a shudder down Alex's spine. Not wanting to distract Trent, Alex touched Jericho's arm, then tipped his head at the door. Jericho nodded. Alex left Trent and quietly crossed to the closed metal door.

"The Demons are moving," Siale said quietly.

"Got it," Alex replied.

Trent had finished with the second charge and started the third when the sounds Alex had heard intensified. He let the Demon take over. His limbs elongated, his claws grew, and his shoulders tore through his shirt when he shoved his claws into the frame on either side of the door.

Chapter Nineteen

The Demons hit the door with the force of a battering ram. Huge chunks of cement from around the door cracked and fell. Alex scrambled to hold it. The Demons shoved again and his clawed feet slid backwards across the roof.

Jericho shoved his shoulder next to Alex's.

"Almost done!" Trent said.

"Please hurry," Alex replied, his voice gruff and scratchy.

Even with Jericho at his side, they were no match for four Demons. The entire frame was ripped free of the wall and the two werewolves slid an inch at a time backwards. Alex's heartbeat thundered in his ears above the growls and clawing from behind the door. Four Demons against his one. The odds were stacked high against him.

The sound of the helicopter increased.

"Done!" Trent called.

There was no time. A glance behind Jericho showed that the helicopter was too far away. Trent stood at the edge of the roof watching in horror as the Demons forced their way through. All three werewolves would be killed like the scattered remains of the teams around them.

"Get Trent out of here."

Alex stared at Jericho. "If I let go of this door, you're dead!"

Jericho met Alex's gaze. There wasn't fear in the Alpha's eyes, only determination. "Get Trent to safety. That is an order from your Alpha."

No matter what had changed in Alex's life, Jericho had been his leader through most of his time at the Academy. Alex's instincts demanded that he listen. Trent was once in Jericho's pack, and the werewolf was now under Alex's. Both Alphas' nature demanded that they protect their own.

Alex shoved the door as hard as he could to give Jericho a chance, then took off for Trent. He reached the small werewolf in three strides. Trent gave a small yelp when Alex grabbed him roughly beneath the arms. The helicopter was about ten feet away with its doors wide open. Alex didn't slow down. He threw the small werewolf away from him as hard as he could.

Trent flew through the open door of the helicopter with surprising accuracy. Hands grabbed him to slow his landing. Alex spun on his heels.

Time slowed. The Demons were all over Jericho. Blood showed on claws and muzzles. The Alpha's cries of pain sliced into Alex with brutal force. He couldn't see anything but Jericho's hand reaching out through the four demonic creatures. A shadow stood in the doorway with a pleased smile.

177

One word rang through the air. "Kill."

The snarls of the Demons grew in answer and Jericho cried out in pain.

The bomb closest to Alex let out a soft beep and the second followed. The building was being detonated. It was the only chance they had to ensure that Drogan was in the building with four of his Demons. Alex stood in the middle of a death trap.

Alex did the last thing he knew anyone expected. He charged into the midst of the four Demons, grabbed Jericho from their clutches without slowing, and launched himself off the building.

"Alex!" he heard Siale cry into Jericho's earpiece.

"No!" Trent shouted from the helicopter.

The building exploded.

Alex rolled to the right just before they hit the trees, shielding Jericho with his body. He slammed into one branch, then another. Two more branches and they landed on the ground so hard Alex felt like every rib in his body broke. He gasped for air as explosions ricocheted around them. Huge pieces of the building flew past, smashing through tree trunks and carving huge gouges through the earth.

Alex forced his battered body to turn so he could shelter Jericho from the debris.

Jericho moaned. The sound cut through the crash of the falling building and straight to Alex's soul. The Demon faded from Alex, leaving him filled with pain from the fall as he stared down at his friend.

"Jer?" he forced out.

The Alpha moved his hand. Alex's heart twisted. The werewolf's stomach had been torn completely open. The blood and mess pooled around them.

Alex's gaze clouded with tears. "Stay with me, Jericho."

The werewolf opened his eyes. His gaze was hazy and it

took him a minute to lock onto Alex. When he did, his lips moved in a small smile before they twisted into a grimace of pain.

Alex didn't know what to do. He wanted to take away the werewolf's pain. He wanted Jericho to stand up and laugh it off. He needed the Alpha to lead as he always had, to show Alex by example how an Alpha was supposed to act.

But it was impossible. Blood colored the werewolf's teeth and trickled from the side of his mouth. Alex wiped it away.

"Jericho, don't go," he said, his voice breaking.

Jericho closed his eyes. He moved a bloody hand away from his stomach. It took Alex a second to realize the Alpha was trying to reach in his pocket.

"You need something in there?" Alex asked.

Jericho tried to speak, but gave up and instead nodded.

Alex reached into the Alpha's pocket. His heart slowed when he found the small velvet ring box. He pulled it out and opened it slowly.

"Give…" Jericho said weakly. "Tell…Cherish…"

Alex nodded. He could barely see the ring through his tears. "I'll tell her; I promise."

Jericho gave one last smile, then closed his eyes.

"Jericho?"

The werewolf's labored breathing stopped.

Alex shook his head. "No, Jer. Don't go."

Alex tried to draw in a breath, but it felt like his ribs were knives cutting into his lungs. Every breath gave the sensation that he was suffocating. He tried to suck in another gasp, but the pain was excruciating. Dark spots filled his vision. He clutched the ring box to his chest and fell into the grass next to the Alpha.

Thoughts of Siale filled his mind. He couldn't let go. He fought to keep his mind alert and not give into the haze. The seconds felt like hours in the grass beneath the falling building.

"Alex?"

The voices sounded as though they called from a far distance. Alex tried to open his eyes, but his eyelids wouldn't respond. He felt like he was drowning.

He didn't know how much time had passed before people surrounded him and Jericho. He could hear frantic voices, but nothing penetrated the tar that coated his mind. He gasped, a horrible gurgling sound.

The tattered remains of his shirt were torn away. Someone put a hand on his chest. Words that sounded like, 'I'm sorry, Alex', reached his ears a second before something stabbed into his chest with such sharp pain Alex gasped. Some of the tightness released from his lungs and he drew in a ragged breath.

"Get him back to the Academy before we lose him," Jaze's strong voice commanded.

Hands grabbed Alex and lifted. He smothered a cry at the agony, but tears leaked from the corners of his eyes. Despite the haze, all Alex could think about was Jericho lying all alone on the forest floor.

"J-Jericho," he forced out.

A reassuring hand gripped his arm.

"We've got him," Jaze said, his voice gentle. "He's coming home, too."

Alex felt himself be set on the floor of the helicopter. He tried to move and another stabbing pain shot through his chest. His back arched as he fought to draw in breath.

"The other lung!" Kaynan said.

A force slammed into his chest. He drew a sharp breath and the drowning sensation lessened. Despite the voices repeating his name, Alex couldn't keep awake. His muscles relaxed and he gave into the embrace of darkness.

***

The beeping that filled Alex's ears when he awoke was disorienting. Images raced through his mind and he couldn't figure out when or where he was. He thought he and Siale had just been freed from the body pit, then memories of awakening in the cage with Dr. Kamala watching him sent shudders down his spine that turned into shivers from cold. But werewolves weren't supposed to get cold. Alex realized he was kneeling in the snow with a body in his arms. Each tear that fell from his eyes turned to icicles before they hit the ground and shattered into a million pieces.

The memories changed. Alex was kneeling on the forest floor and another body lay in front of him. He clutched something in his hand so hard it cut into his skin. Alex opened his hand and looked down at the ring. Jericho had meant to propose to Cherish. The Alpha was in love with a human who loved him back just as much. It was beautiful. It was lost.

Alex opened his eyes. The room was dark. The steady beeping near his head let him know that he was hooked up to monitors. He took a slow breath to keep his heartbeat measured so as not to alarm his mom. He needed a minute to think things through.

Jericho was gone. Drogan's Demons had killed another of his friends, another werewolf who could never be replaced and who had been torn out of the life he deserved to live.

Alex rubbed his eyes. His head ached. He couldn't remember when it had ever hurt so badly. He tried to sit up, but movement made pain flood through his lungs with such knife-edged agony he could barely breathe.

Alex pulled the hospital gown down far enough to see his chest. The light of the moon that spilled through the window revealed bruises splayed all down his torso. He could tell with the simple movement that worse bruising covered his back. He wondered how many ribs he had broken. Perhaps jumping off a building and crashing through trees before landing on his back on the forest floor had been a bad idea. He hadn't been able to save Jericho.

Alex ignored the pain and pushed up slowly. Sitting made the stabbing pain worse. Alex gave up sitting and slid his feet to the tiled floor of the medical wing of the Academy he knew very well. It was both a relief and a humbling experience to stand there because even though it took some pressure off the breathing, standing made him realize how very weak he was.

He ran his hand along the bed.

"Alex?"

Instead of jumping and spinning in the defensive moves Chet had trained into his muscle memory, Alex took a shallow breath and turned. The sight of Siale crossing to him made his knees weak. Alex caught her in a hug so fast she gasped in surprise and he gasped in pain.

Siale stepped back.

"Are you okay?" she asked worriedly.

Alex nodded breathlessly. "I should have thought that through."

"Can I help you sit down?"

He shook his head. "Sitting hurts."

"You should be lying down in bed. Your mother isn't going to be very happy with you," Siale told him. The little furrow formed between her eyebrows. "Really, Alex. You're going to fall over."

"Give me a moment," he asked softly.

At her nod, Alex closed his eyes. He focused on the moonlight that fell across his left side. The touch of the moon was cool and reassuring like a blanket woven from the night. Alex pictured the moonlight flowing into his skin,

182

healing and repairing wherever it went. When his image of the moonlight reached his chest, he willed his lungs to fill completely. There was pain, but Alex felt better able to handle it. His headache lessened with the surge of oxygen. Alex pulled in another breath, then another. He opened his eyes to find Siale watching him.

"Is that better?" he asked.

"Yes," she replied with a hint of surprise. "It is."

Alex turned back to the bed. He lifted the blanket and searched along the white sheet.

"What are you looking for?" Siale asked him.

"The ring. I think I dropped it," Alex replied. He fought back a feeling of panic when he realized the ring wasn't there.

He was ready to tear apart the entire room to look when Siale said, "I've got Jericho's ring."

Alex let out a breath of relief and hid a wince. He leaned against the wall in an effort to regain some of the precious strength he had expended. Siale held the small gold circle on her palm. The diamond winked like a star caught in the first light on the horizon, simple, beautiful, and exactly what Alex pictured Cherish wearing.

He reached for it. "I'm taking it to her."

Siale stiffened and closed her hand. "No, you're not. There's no way you can go anywhere in this shape."

A surge of frustration filled Alex. "Yes, I am. Jericho asked me to." He pulled the IV from his wrist and detached the monitors.

"Then wait until you're feeling better."

Alex shook his head. "I can't. I need to let Cherish know what happened."

"We can call her," Siale urged. She set a hand on his arm. "Alex, you shouldn't go anywhere like this. Meredith said you had a double pneumothorax. Both of your lungs collapsed because you broke so many ribs in your fall and they

183

punctured your lungs. You're healing, but it could happen again if you don't give yourself time to rest."

Alex shook his head. He could see Jericho's pleading gaze when he asked Alex to take the ring to Cherish.

"I'm going," Alex said. He took two steps and his legs gave out.

Siale caught his arm before he hit the ground. The jolt was so sharp Alex almost growled.

"Let me go," he demanded.

He yanked his arm from her grasp with more force than was necessary. With sheer strength of will, Alex walked through the door. He slammed his hand on the panel across the hall and the door slid aside. Alex stepped into the darkness.

Chapter Twenty

It took much longer than it should have for Alex to reach the secondary vehicle storage room Trent used as his private workshop. He felt horrible for the way he had spoken to Siale, but the drive to fulfill his promise to Jericho kept one foot in front of the other. By the time the door slid open, Alex was gasping for breath. He was grateful that he at least wore pajama pants and a tee-shirt instead of a hospital gown, though he shied away from thinking about who had changed him out of his tattered clothes from the rooftop.

Alex took two steps into the room, then had to steady himself against a table.

"Are you really planning to ride a motorcycle in your condition?"

Alex's head jerked up and he stared at Siale.

"How did you get here?" he forced out. He put a hand to his side to stop the throbbing of his ribs.

She gave him an empathetic look. "I've been here for almost ten minutes. I thought you might have changed your mind. Besides, you forgot the ring." She opened her hand to show him the ring she still held.

Her words stole a bit of Alex's bravado. He leaned against the table and crossed his arms gingerly in front of his chest.

"I promised him." His words were quiet but the emotions they stirred in him made him clench his hands into fists.

Siale crossed to him and, without speaking, put her arms around him. He bowed his head against her. He didn't cry. It was enough to know that she felt his pain and she shared it; in the end, she understood.

"I'll drive," Siale said after several minutes had passed.

Alex cracked a smile. "You'll drive what?"

Siale pointed at the tarp Trent had put over Alex's motorcycle. "I'll drive your bike."

Alex stared at her. "Uh, you're kidding, right?"

Siale gave a little laugh Alex would have found endearing except for the fact that she was completely serious. "Give me a chance," she said.

She walked to the motorcycle, leaving Alex to watch her pull off the tarp and run a hand across the paint.

"It's pretty." At Alex's exasperated look, she smiled. "Come on, Alex. I'm teasing. It's a very manly bike. It's a bit bigger than the one Trent taught me on, but I think I can handle it." Her smile faded and seriousness took over her tone. "You want to give Cherish the ring, and you can't ride in your condition. Trent gave me a few lessons. Trust me, okay?" She picked up the spare helmet and strapped it on.

Alex crossed to the bike. He eyed Siale. "You asked Trent to give you a few lessons?"

186

Siale met Alex's gaze. "I know how important your motorcycle is to you. If you ever wanted me to, I had to make sure I could go with you."

All of the fight left Alex. He watched Siale as he spoke. "I know there are things I've done that have left you out. I guess I didn't realize how much that bothered you."

She gave him a small smile. "I know you have things you need to do." She hesitated, then said, "I guess I just hope that eventually I can be a part of them all."

Alex realized there was no choice if he was going to keep from hurting her. He nodded. "Let's go."

Siale grinned and attempted to buckle her helmet. Alex watched her failed attempts for a few seconds before he caught her hands in his.

"Let me help you."

She watched him wordlessly as he pushed the strap through the ring, looped it back, and pulled it to ensure it was snug before he buttoned the strap down.

The look in her eyes showed how grateful she was that he agreed to let her come along. It ate at him that it meant so much to her.

"How's that?" he asked quietly.

"Perfect," she replied.

Before he could repeat his apology for leaving her out, she rose up on her tiptoes and kissed him on the nose.

"Let's go," she then said with an air of command.

Siale swung her leg over the motorcycle and pulled the bike straight. It took her a second to get the kickstand up, but when she did, she gave him a confident nod.

Alex fought back a smile and climbed gingerly onto the back.

"This is a first for me," he said.

She glanced at him over the shoulder.

"Being the passenger," he explained. "I've never ridden

187

on the back."

"Then you better hold on," she answered.

She handed him his helmet from where it hung on the handle. He buckled it on with surprising difficulty. Pride kept him from admitting that lifting his arms to the straps was painful enough to make him wonder if he had punctured at least one lung again. By the time he was settled, he was struggling to breathe.

Siale let out a small breath as she reached for the starter. Alex realized she was nervous. He leaned closer to her.

"That's it. Hold in the clutch." A smile spread across his face at the rumble of the engine. He wondered how he had gone so long without riding. "Okay," he continued. "Rev the gas. Easy on the clutch. It's a bit touchy, but once you get used to it, this will be the best motorcycle you've ever ridden."

Siale drove carefully across the floor. Alex hit the button Trent had placed within easy reach and the garage door slid up. They rode into the courtyard.

"Wha-who is driving Alex's bike?" Trent's voice demanded over the headsets.

Alex chuckled, then winced at the pain. "It's me, Trent."

"Alex?" Trent replied, his tone shocked. "How, I mean, when, I mean, I didn't think you'd be out of bed yet."

"He shouldn't be," Siale replied. "But he's stubborn."

Trent let out a relieved sigh and said, "Siale, I'm glad you're with him. Who knows what he's up to?"

"I'm right here," Alex reminded them.

"It's okay, Trent. Thank you for being such a good friend," Siale said. "Would you mind opening the gate?"

"For you, no problem," Trent answered.

"Would it have been a problem for me?" Alex asked.

"Yes," Trent and Siale replied at the same time.

Alex shook his head, but he couldn't fight back a small

188

smile at the actions of the people who cared about him.

"We're going to Cherish's," Siale told Trent. "I don't know when we'll be back."

"Thanks for letting me know. At least *somebody* keeps me posted on what's happening," Trent replied pointedly.

"I let you know," Alex protested.

"Before or after you're gone?" Trent queried.

"Uh, after," Alex replied. "There's no reason to tell you before. What if I change my mind?"

"Has that ever happened?"

"No," Alex admitted.

The gate opened and Siale drove the motorcycle through.

"Thanks, Trent," she said.

"You're welcome, Siale. Be careful, both of you."

"We will," she promised.

Alex could feel Siale's tension as she drove the motorcycle down the small road.

"Don't fight it," he said. "Loosen your grip and listen. The engine will tell you what it needs."

Siale's shoulders relaxed and the roar of the engine fell into a comfortable growl. Alex leaned into the turns. With each movement, he had to bite back making any sound at the pain. He knew he should have waited another day or so for his body to heal, but he had never been one to second-guess a decision.

"Relax."

Siale's voice was soft within the sound of the engine and the hum of the road beneath the tires.

"What?" Alex asked.

He could hear the smile in his fiancé's voice when she replied, "I can hear how much you're hurting when you breathe. Relax. Lean against me. I'm stronger than you think I am."

Alex fought back a wry grin. He thought he had been

doing so well at pretending to be fine.

The road leveled out after the forest. The moonlight, now unfiltered by the trees, settled on Alex's shoulders like a cloak. The moonlight was strong; the full moon was only a few days away. Alex felt the light seep into his skin, encouraging his body to heal. Alex let his breath out slowly and gave in to Siale's words.

He slipped his arms around her waist. Siale's hand came off the brake and rested on his for a moment. Alex leaned his head on her shoulder, his helmet touching hers. With another outlet of breath, Alex willed his muscles to relax. He hadn't realized just how much pain he had been causing himself by sitting up so straight. The release of tension seeped out of him and was replaced by the warmth and exhaustion of healing. Alex closed his eyes.

After blissful hours of darkness, Alex found himself on the building of D Block. The Demons were forcing their way through the door. Alex ran toward Jericho, but his legs stuck to the roof like glue. It pulled at his feet, slowing him while the Demons tore his friend and Alpha apart. Alex fought with every ounce of his strength, but he couldn't get free. Jericho was being flayed in front of his eyes.

"Jericho!"

Alex jerked awake. Siale's hand on his arm kept him from falling off the motorcycle. Night had changed to day while Alex slept. The warmth of the sun bathed him as they rode.

"It's alright," she reassured him. "You're with me. We're on our way to Cherish's."

"I failed him."

Siale shook her head. "I saw the entire thing from the helicopter camera. You didn't fail him. You did everything you could to save him. If it wasn't for you, Trent would be dead, too." She paused, then said, "Alex, you jumped off a building to save Jericho. You did everything you possibly could have to help him come home alive."

Alex asked the question that plagued him. "How do we tell Cherish?"

Siale's hand tightened on his. "We do it together."

The silence that surrounded them was comfortable and warm. Alex had jumped off a building. He could have died as easily as Jericho except for the Demon that ran through his veins. He didn't know what it was or where it came from, but now there were still at least eight of them loose and terrorizing the land.

Trent's voice came over the headsets.

"Siale, you still awake?"

"Yes," Siale answered, her tone warm. "Thanks for checking."

"I am, too," Alex said. "Just in case you wanted to know."

Trent chuckled. "I didn't want to ask in case you were getting some much-needed sleep. Your mom asked about you, by the way. I think she's a little tired of finding your hospital bed empty. I told her you were with Siale, so she's not too worried. But try to get some more sleep if you can. I built you a smooth-riding motorcycle and then taught your fiancé how to drive it for a reason."

"Thanks," Alex replied.

Trent's tone became serious. "Now for why I called. The GPA has been sifting through the rubble that was once D Block; they found pieces of four Demons." He paused, then said, "As well as Drogan's hand."

Alex's stomach tightened. "Are they sure it's his?"

"We just received DNA confirmation," Trent replied. "They're saying he's dead. You did it, Alex."

Alex shook his head. "You and Mouse did it," he said numbly. "And I'm glad. Good job."

"Same to you." Alex could hear the sadness in the little

werewolf's voice when Trent concluded, "Please tell Cherish I'm sorry about Jericho. Kaynan and Grace are with Mrs. Hunt making preparations. The funeral will be in two days."

"I'll let her know," Alex answered his friend. "Thanks for everything, Trent."

"Have a safe trip, you two."

"We will," Siale said.

After a few minutes of silence, Siale was the one who broke it. "I don't believe the GPA."

Alex stared at the back of her helmet in surprise. "You think they're lying?"

She shook her head. "I think they found his hand, but I don't think he's dead."

Relief filled Alex. It was the same way he had felt when Trent told him the news. "I know; I agree. So what do we do?"

"There's a homicidal werewolf-killing Extremist whose goal is to wipe you and anyone you love from this earth. We need to stop him."

"You sound like you have a plan," Alex hedged.

"We draw him out." She sounded surer of herself by the second.

"Alright, I'll bite. How?"

"Our wedding."

Alex couldn't have been more shocked. "Let me get this straight. You want to use our wedding to draw Drogan out into the open so we can take him down?"

"We'll throw a fake wedding," she replied. She slowed the motorcycle around a turn. "It has to look real. That's the only way he'll fall for it. We can't tell anyone except your team."

"Our team," Alex said, still trying to get his mind around what she was suggesting.

"Our team," she replied with the sound of a smile in her voice. She tipped her head back. "Let's focus on Cherish;

we'll plan our fake wedding on the way home."

Chapter Twenty-one

Alex knocked on the door.

"I usually climb up the fire escape," he said in an effort to push down the sadness that filled his chest.

Siale slipped her hand into his. They listened to footsteps cross to the door.

"Alex?" Cherish said when she pulled it open. Her hair was mussed and she looked as though they had woken her up. She glanced to his right and her eyes widened. "Siale?" Her voice cracked. She shook her head. "No. This can't be right. You aren't supposed to be here."

Siale set a hand on Cherish's arm. "I'm so sorry."

Tears spilled down Cherish's cheeks. "It can't be. I talked to Jericho yesterday. He said he was leaving on a mission to stop the Demons."

Alex nodded. "The Demons overpowered us." He blinked back tears of his own. "Jericho saved mine and Trent's lives."

Cherish began to sob. Siale wrapped her in a hug. Alex cried with them, his eyes shut tight and his hand squeezing them in an attempt to slow the tears that refused to obey.

"I'm so sorry, Cherish," he said. "I tried to save him. I really did."

Cherish took a shuddering breath and looked around as though she had just realized they were still standing in the hallway.

"Please come in," she said, wiping her tears. New tears took their place. She led the way to the small living room and motioned for them to sit on the couch. "You must be exhausted. Let me get you some water."

She was gone far longer than filling cups would normally take. Alex and Siale sat on the couch and held hands.

Siale took the ring from her pocket. "I feel like you should give this to her," she said, her eyes bright with tears.

Alex took it without a word and then held her close. Her shaking shoulders brought sobs to his chest, but he forced them down. The girls needed him to be strong. He would be there for them the way Jericho had always been there for him.

When Cherish came back, her eyes were red and puffy and she carried a picture frame instead of cups.

"I forgot the water," she apologized.

"We're fine," Siale replied. "You don't need to get us anything. We're so sorry we had to come here under these circumstances."

Alex opened his hand. The ring glittered on his palm. "The last thing Jericho said was to give you this," his voice caught, but he forced himself to say, "And to tell you how much he loved you."

Cherish picked up the ring with shaking fingers. She gave a watery smile. "It's beautiful."

Siale nodded and smiled through her tears. "It's gorgeous."

Cherish slipped it on her finger, and though fresh tears trailed down her cheeks, the smile stayed. "He was the one who broke me down. I said I'd never marry. But I would have said yes to him."

"I think he knew that," Alex told her. "He knew how much you loved him."

She gave him a grateful smile. "And I know how much he loved me. He said it whenever we spoke on the phone. It was the first thing he always said when we got together, and the last thing he said before he left." She blinked quickly. "It was the last thing he said to me when he hung up the phone before your mission."

Alex bowed his head. "Cherish, if I could have done anything to save him…"

"I know," she said. "That's why I brought this." She held out the picture frame.

Alex took it. When he saw who was in the photo, his breath caught.

"Is that Jet?" Siale asked.

Alex nodded.

Cherish leaned closer. "That's Jericho in the middle. I think he said he was nine when the picture was taken." She pointed to the woman on Jericho's left. Alex recognized Mrs. Hunt. "That's his mother, and those two little boys," she gave a fond smile, "Those are Jericho's twin brothers, Zach and Zeb. They're three years old in that picture."

"They look like little angels with their blond hair and blue eyes," Siale said. "They're so adorable."

"In real life, they're much more mischievous than they look," Cherish said.

Alex stared at the picture. "I didn't know Jericho had brothers." His gaze kept straying to Jet standing behind the twins. His brother didn't smile, he had seldom ever smiled, but he had the satisfied look on his face that said he had just finished a job that ended well. Alex knew the expression by heart.

"They're not werewolves, they're human," Cherish explained. "They're eleven now, and they never phased. Zach and Zeb go to public school."

"They look so happy," Siale noted with a smile.

Cherish nodded. "They were just reunited. Extremists killed Jericho's father and captured Jericho's mom and brothers when he was out with his friends. He thought he would never see them again. He said Jet saved their lives." She set a hand on Alex's knee, bringing his gaze up to hers. "That's why I brought this out. Jericho told me it was one of his most prized possessions. He gave it to me in case anything happened to him."

That caught Alex's attention. "What do you mean?"

Cherish looked at the picture. "He said if there was ever a chance to repay Jet for saving his mom and brothers, he would take it." She met Alex's gaze again, her green eyes filled with emotion. "He said he would gladly give his life for yours if the opportunity ever called for it. He asked me to understand if it happened."

Alex shook his head, refusing to comprehend her words. "He knew this might happen?" he asked incredulously. He stared at the picture. "He was willing to give his life away just to save mine?"

"No, Alex," Cherish replied.

Alex stared at her, wanting his heart not to ache the way it did at her words, hoping for something that would make him feel less responsible for his friend's death.

"It wasn't *just* to save your life. It was to save you because saving you meant repaying your brother. Jet gave Jericho his family back, and do you know what Jericho did?" Cherish paused, then said, "He saved the life of the werewolf who has almost single-handedly given his werewolf mother and his younger brothers the chance at a normal life. Jericho loved you like a brother."

Alex let his head hang. "He was a brother to me, too."

The warmth in Cherish's voice cut through his sorrow when she said, "Then remember him as a brother who was happy to have been your Alpha. He felt like he learned as much from you as you did from him."

Alex took in a shuddering breath. "That's why he choose me as his Second."

"When?" Siale asked.

Alex realized neither girl had been there. "In Jericho's first term at the Academy, he choose me as his Second. It was the first time a Termer Alpha had ever chosen a Lifer to be his Second." He shook his head with amazement. "That's why he gave me a chance. He was repaying Jet."

The thought brought a smile to Alex's face. The fast bond he and Jericho had created was in part because of Jet. It was another way his big brother had looked out for him long after his death.

"Jericho was amazing," Alex concluded.

"Yes, he was," Cherish said. Her voice broke.

Alex could see the tears she had yet to cry etched in the sorrow of her eyes. He gave her a hug. Cherish started to cry again. Siale hugged her as well and the three cried together in sorrow and in joy at the memories of the werewolf who had meant so much to all of them.

"I need to talk to my mom," Cherish said. She sniffed and wiped her cheeks with her sleeve.

"We'll walk with you there," Alex replied.

He and Siale walked beside Cherish through the streets of

Greyton. Evening had fallen. Cars drove by and pedestrians filled the streets on their way home from work. Alex looked for gang symbols, but they had been washed from the sides of buildings and street signs. Children played on the steps they passed and mothers chatted as they watched their children. The appearance of a city held siege by the gangs that filled it were gone.

"Jericho always helped me appreciate the little things," Cherish said after they had walked several blocks. She gave a sad smile and nodded to a little vine that clung to the side of a building and grew toward the sunlight. "He always pointed this plant out. He said it was beautiful the way it persevered in the middle of concrete and bricks."

"It is beautiful," Siale agreed. She touched a leaf from the vine.

"Jericho always talked about how pretty the sky was, and how much he loved being a werewolf because of how the animal senses worked with his human ones." She blinked quickly. "He used to try to describe it to me so I would understand. He didn't want me to feel left out."

Alex noticed that she fidgeted with the ring on her finger. He caught her hand and looked at it. "The ring looks beautiful on you."

"It's a perfect fit," Cherish said.

"Jericho would have been so happy to see it on you," Siale told her. She gave Cherish another hug.

They walked together in front of Alex. Siale threw him a grateful smile that Alex returned.

Alex and Siale waited near the door of Frenchie's Food. The sound of Mrs. Summer's surprised gasp and both women crying made Alex's heart ache. He glanced at Siale. The answering tears trailing silently down her cheeks was almost too much. Alex lifted his arm; she ducked under it and buried her face against his chest. Alex felt Siale's tears soak his shirt.

He closed his eyes and held her, each of them supporting the other and sharing their strength along with the heartache.

Alex opened his eyes when footsteps drew near. He wiped the tears that had escaped and met Mrs. Summers' teary gaze.

"Thank you so much for coming," Cherish's mother said. She gave them both a hug. "It's so much better than finding out such things over the phone."

Cherish nodded behind her. "You two have been such great friends. Thank you very much for all you did for Jericho."

"He did so much more for me," Alex replied. "I'll always be grateful to have had him in my life."

"Us, too," Mrs. Summers said. She tipped her head toward the dining room. "Why don't you two come have a bite to eat? You must be hungry."

Alex shook his head. "I'm not sure either of us could eat right now."

Siale nodded in agreement. "We should probably be on our way back to the Academy."

"Thank you for coming by," Mrs. Summers said. She gave them each another motherly hug.

Alex and Siale walked slowly down the street. The lamplights had come on, lighting golden pools within the gray hush of nightfall. Siale's hand felt warm in Alex's. He felt her ring against his fingers. With losing Jericho and seeing how hard it was on Cherish, so many emotions battled in Alex's thoughts. There had been many times he had almost not come home to Siale and his family. He couldn't imagine causing Siale such pain. The thought almost made him regret proposing to her, except for the fact that he couldn't imagine living a life without her at his side.

Chapter Twenty-two

"Alex, look!"

Torn out of his thoughts, Alex looked to where Siale pointed. In the window of the restaurant across the street, Alex made out the forms of Brock and a blonde woman at a table. Alex smiled when he realized it was Jennifer Stauffer, the woman Brock had helped track down and reunite with Mrs. Summers. They had been best friends when they were children, then Jennifer disappeared. After their reunion, Brock and Jennifer had hit it off. Whenever Brock was found missing from the Wolf Den, it was inevitable where he would be.

"They're so cute," Siale said.

The warm smile that spread across her face made Alex smile, too. He made up his mind and held out his hand.

201

"Come with me."

"Where are we going?" Siale asked when they walked past the street where the motorcycle was parked.

"You'll see," he replied.

Alex led Siale through the entrance of M's, the finest restaurant Greyton City had to offer.

"Alex, what are we doing here?" Siale asked in a whisper before the steward saw them.

"Siale, you agreed to be my wife and I haven't even taken you on a proper date. You deserve better." He ran his thumb over the ring she wore. "I'm going to take a page from Jericho's book and start appreciating the little things as well as the big. You are such an amazing person, and you should be treated like a queen instead of a fiancé wondering if her future husband is ever going to come home."

Siale's soft gray eyes shone bright in the elegant lighting. "You don't need to do this," she protested.

Alex smiled at her. "Yes, I do."

"Will you require a table for two this evening?" a man in a black shirt and gray vest asked politely.

"Yes, thank you," Alex replied.

He realized after the steward had seated them that he was actually nervous. Couples sat at stylish glass tables spaced just far enough apart to give those around them privacy. The sounds of silverware on glass plates and the chink of wine glasses overtook the quiet conversations.

Alex had never been in a place so fancy. He felt suddenly grateful for the money Trent had always insisted he carry in case of an emergency. He figured realizing how very much he had taken Siale for granted and needing to show her he loved her would be considered just such an occasion.

Siale's fingers twisted in the cloth napkin. He noticed she had barely eaten a bite of the fancy little dinner roll that sat in the middle of her plate next to a flower-shaped dab of butter.

He almost laughed out loud at the thought that she was nervous, too. It relieved him to think that he wasn't the only one who didn't feel like they fit into the fine atmosphere.

"This is a bit much, isn't it?" he asked. "We don't exactly fit the type that requires an extra small fork for shrimp." He held up the amusingly tiny object in question.

Siale's dimples showed when she gave an answering smile of relief. "Not at all."

Alex winked at her. "Then let's enjoy it. We'll pretend to be all fancy and talk with proper enunciation." He sat up straighter and held his shrimp fork between his thumb and finger. "Do you suppose this is better held like so, or between my thumb and middle finger? Is there a better name for the middle finger? It seems a bit crude. I don't suppose the shrimp mind either way, seeing as how they've already been cooked. Although, I'm not quite sure how I feel about eating cold fish."

"I don't think shrimp is a fish," Siale replied, playing along. Her eyes danced at the game and she held up her little fork as well. "I recall hearing once that shrimp are considered a member of the shellfish family, although," she eyed the shrimp on her fork. "This one is definitely a bit shrimpy even for a shrimp."

Alex chuckled. "I'll bet he got made fun of in school."

Siale laughed out loud. She immediately covered her mouth and looked around.

Alex grinned at her. "Don't worry. It's okay to laugh."

"Alex, people are staring."

Alex glanced to his right. Several of the finely dressed couples around them had indeed stopped their own conversations and were looking in his and Siale's direction.

"Maybe we shouldn't have made fun of the shrimp?" he guessed. An uncomfortable shiver ran up his spine at the attention.

203

"Do we need to leave?" Siale whispered.

Alex shook his head, but he wasn't certain. He attempted to turn his attention back to the shrimp, but with everyone watching them, it was impossible to even pretend to be interested in the food.

Siale's gaze locked over his shoulder.

"Alex," she warned.

Alex's muscles tensed and he reached for his wine glass so he could smash it in case he needed a weapon. He glanced back. The cook, who was bald and wore a black chef's hat at a rakish angle along with a black apron bearing the restaurant's italic red M, walked beside a man in a tailored black suit and a black tie with a matching golden M tie tack. Neither men appeared armed. Alex didn't grab the glass, but he rose and placed himself between his fiancé and the potential threat.

The man in the black suit stopped a few feet away and surprised Alex with a warm smile.

"Mr. Davies, I am honored that you would bless my establishment with your presence." The man bowed. He looked past Alex at Siale and bowed again. "And the soon-to-be Mrs. Davies, the honor is mine. You are even lovelier than you were on television."

Alex was still in awe of the fact that the man had bowed at them. He didn't know people even did that anymore. Unsure of whether it was appropriate to bow back and feeling entirely underdressed in his pajama pants and tee-shirt, Alex went with his gut and held out a hand.

"The pleasure is ours."

The man in the black suit shook his hand with another warm smile. "I am Keith Earl Bucherer, the owner of this restaurant, and this is our head cook, Kenyon Manson."

The cook shook Alex's hand as well. "I must admit, I never thought I would cook for werewolves."

Silence fell across the entire room. Alex didn't know how to respond. He wasn't sure if the man was taking a jab and his words were a polite warning for them to leave, or if he was joking.

Cook Manson smiled. "I've heard that with a werewolf's acute sense of smell comes the ability to enjoy every nuance of the spices and herbs used to accentuate a plate. I would be honored to know what you think of the Peking duck Mr. Bucherer has asked me to prepare for you this evening."

"Uh, I'll be glad to let you know," Alex replied.

The cook smiled again and excused himself.

Mr. Bucherer motioned for Alex and Siale to take their seats again; he even assisted Siale by maneuvering her chair to a comfortable position beneath the table.

"Your meal is on the house," Mr. Bucherer continued. "As well as every meal you choose to partake of at M's, which I hope will be many." He smiled. "Just think of this as your fine dining experience away from home." He turned away to follow the cook back through the restaurant.

Alex was touched by the man's kindness, but he had to know why. The other guests at the restaurant had gone back to their own hushed conversations. Alex took the opportunity to ask, "Mr. Bucherer?"

The owner turned back. "Yes, Mr. Davies."

Alex glanced at Siale. She looked as concerned as he did about the situation. Alex went with the straightforward question. "Why are you being so kind?"

Mr. Bucherer smiled and gestured to the chair on Alex's left. "May I?"

"Of course," Alex replied.

Mr. Bucherer sat down. He was silent for a minute, his gaze distant. When he spoke, the surety had left his expression and instead, to Alex, he looked lost.

"I've gone over time and again the things I would say if I

205

ever had the chance to speak to the Demon face to face."

Alex and Siale gave him the silence he needed. Siale's hand slipped into Alex's under the table.

When Mr. Bucherer spoke again, the man's forehead was furrowed and gaze stark. "Yet putting thoughts into words brings the memories to life again. I didn't expect that." He turned to face Alex. "Mr. Davies, my wife had been kidnapped by the Fivers. By her account, she was being held hostage with three other women in the back of a delivery truck when the Demon appeared and helped them escape." Tears filled his eyes. "I never thought I would see her again. The police had been searching, but the women kept getting moved and they couldn't locate them. Days went by. I couldn't eat, I couldn't sleep. I kept wondering what she was going through."

His eyes filled with tears and he bowed his head. When he took a shaky breath and looked back at Alex, the expression in them was so stark and bare that empathy surged in Alex's chest.

"Then I saw her on the news. She was being helped into an officer's car. The reporter said the women had been rescued by the Demon. In the far left corner of the screen, a huge wolf limped into an alley." The man's eyes followed a drop of condensation down the side of Alex's water glass. "I paused the image. I couldn't imagine why something so ferocious would save my Melody."

"I'm not..." Alex began.

Mr. Bucherer cut him off with a shake of his head and a smile that chased away the agony that had filled his expression. "Of course you're not, Alex. That's what I came to realize. When I picked up Melody at the hospital, she told me how brave you had been. Neither of us could believe you weren't even old enough to be out of high school, yet you risked your life to save strangers." He met Alex's gaze. "You gave me back my wife, you gave us back our city, and you changed the prejudiced views of someone who felt he was on a different level than werewolves." He gave a self-deprecating smile. "I appreciate that you changed my mind."

Alex smiled back. "I'm glad I could help, and I'm glad Melody's alright. Please let her know."

"I will," Mr. Bucherer said, rising to his feet. "And now I'll stop interrupting your evening. Please enjoying the Peking duck. It's a specialty of ours."

"We will," Siale told him. "Thank you."

Alex waited until the man was out of earshot before he said, "That went far differently than I expected."

"Me, too!" Siale said breathlessly. "I'm so happy for him."

Alex nodded. "I'm happy for them both."

Siale set a hand on Alex's. "You gave them their life back. That's so wonderful."

Alex set his hand on hers. "See how romantic I am? I got you a duck for dinner, and I didn't even have to catch it."

Siale laughed. "I'm glad. I get tired of feathers."

"Me, too," Alex agreed. "They taste horrible and the stick in the back of my throat. Do you think Cook Manson cooks his duck with them on or off?"

"Off, I hope," Siale said with a giggle. "I couldn't imagine them on."

"What if Peking means with feathers?" Alex asked.

They were both relieved when the dishes arrived without feathers and cooked to perfection.

"Maybe we should ask Cook Manson to host our fake wedding luncheon," Siale suggested.

Alex smiled at her joke, but the comment turned his thoughts to their earlier conversation. "Are you sure you want to stage our wedding just to draw Drogan out?" Alex asked.

"I'm absolutely sure," Siale replied. "It's the best chance we have to catch him and end his reign of terror once and for all. If we have to fake a wedding to do it, then so be it."

"What about your dad?"

Siale let out a small breath.

"I think we should keep it a secret from our parents, as hard as that will be," she answered. "We need everyone to act as though it's a real wedding."

"And if Drogan doesn't show up?"

He heard the smile in her voice when she replied, "Then we'll get married."

The thought of catching Drogan if his half-brother was indeed alive tempted him almost beyond reason, yet Alex wanted to make sure he was being rational. Asking his fiancé to fake her wedding felt far beyond what he knew he should expect from her, but Siale was adamant. Her determination to catch Drogan matched his own.

"Let's do it," Alex finally agreed.

There was a hint of teasing in Siale's voice when she said, "We better start talking about details."

"What details?"

"Wedding colors, cake flavors, flower arrangements."

Alex groaned and let his head fall to the table.

Siale laughed and gave his shoulder an affectionate squeeze. "I'm just kidding. I know how much guys don't like that stuff. I'm sure your mom and Cassie will be happy to help."

The thought of deceiving his mother and sister ate at Alex, but he knew how important it was to make the ruse look as real as possible. A building had fallen on Drogan, but until they found his body, Alex wasn't going to accept a hand as a sign that he was dead. The mayor of Greyton City had already offered to host the wedding. If the best case scenario happened, they would be married. If the worst came to pass, Drogan would attack and they would finally bring the nation's number one criminal and terrorist to justice.

Chapter Twenty-three

Alex leaned against the back of the couch, grateful he had healed enough on their ride to Cherish's to at least pretend to be relaxed.

"Let me get this straight," Professor Chet said. "There are at least eight Demons left out there after the destruction of Block D. They've been killing and pillaging faster than any force can stop them, and you and Siale decide to take a little ride to Greyton? Did this seem like a good idea to you?"

Alex met his mother's worried gaze, then Cassie's. The professors standing around Jaze's couch all had matching expressions of frustration and anger. Siale sat up as though she wanted to speak, but Alex knew it was his fault. He wouldn't let her take the brunt of their fury. It wasn't the first time he had managed to ruffle the feathers of everyone at the Academy.

"I'm sorry." He said the words with full honesty and met the gazes of every werewolf in Jaze's living room. "I shouldn't have left, and I shouldn't have taken Siale with me, but I made a promise." He looked at his mom. "I know everyone here feels Jericho's loss as strongly as I do, so you understand when I say I made him a promise. I couldn't let Cherish find out what had happened without telling her in person. I had to give her the ring."

"The ring?" Cassie's hand rose to her mouth. "He was going to propose?"

Alex nodded. Siale's hand tightened in his. He used it for strength. "He loved her, and she would have said yes." The admission made his eyes burn with tears he wouldn't let fall. "Cherish loved him as much as he loved her, which you all know was a great deal. Jericho was my Alpha and he died saving mine and Trent's lives." He looked back at his friend who stood near the door with Jordan at his side. "It was the least I could do."

Trent nodded; the little werewolf's face and nose were red with the signs that he had been crying.

"Why did you call us all here?" Kaynan asked quietly.

Alex looked at Siale. His fiancé nodded encouragingly. Alex took a steeling breath. "We want to get married as soon as possible."

Meredith's mouth fell open in surprise. "I thought you wanted to wait for the summer!"

Alex shook his head. "Losing Jericho taught me…" He hesitated and looked at Siale. Her warm smile answered his unspoken question. "Taught us," he corrected, "To seize the moment. With the Demons out there, we don't know what's going to happen. I love Siale and she loves me. You all know how reckless I am." Cassie nodded and a few of the other

211

professors followed. Alex lifted his shoulders in a small shrug. "I guarantee with Siale at my side that I'll be less reckless."

"That would be good," Siale said.

Laughter followed her words and lightened the tension in the room.

Alex gave his mom his most winning smile. "What do you say, Mom? Want to plan a wedding?"

Cassie let out a little squeak of excitement and grabbed Tennison's arm. "Let's do it! Let's get married right away!"

Tennison nodded with excitement in his own eyes. "Alright. When are you thinking, Alex?"

"Next week."

Everyone stared at him.

"Next week?" Professor Colleen said. "Are you serious?"

"There's so much to get done," Grace echoed. "I don't know if we could do it in time."

"I don't know about that," Kaynan replied from her side. He gave Alex a searching look. "You want to get married in a week? Let's make it happen."

"Okay," Meredith agreed. "Let's plan a wedding."

"How exciting!" Gem hopped from foot to foot as if she was filled with so much happiness she couldn't stay in one place. "Dray, we can work on the flowers!"

"And I can help with the catering," Colleen offered.

"Am I going to have to cook?" Rafe asked, his golden gaze wary.

Colleen laughed, her violet eyes sparkling. "Only if you want to."

Rafe shook his head. "I think I'll stay away from the kitchen."

"I'll help!" Brock offered.

Professor Mouse shook his head. "You'd eat everything before we got it to the tables."

"I didn't say I'd be any good at it," Brock countered.

"Maybe I could be a taste tester. You know; make sure all the food is good before it goes out to people? You don't want to serve low-quality food to your guests."

Jaze raised his left hand. His right cradled little Vicki to his chest. She was asleep and gave out a little contented sigh at the sound of her father's voice. "School's about to start for the day. I suggest making plans after lessons have been taught. Meredith, can I leave the preparations up to you?"

He appeared relieved when she nodded. "Of course. I'll take care of all the wedding plans."

"With lots of help," Gem shot in.

Meredith smiled. "With lots of help. You have your little ones to manage. Just don't forget to ask if you need us."

"I appreciate it," Jaze replied. He smiled down at the sleeping baby. "I think I have things handled for now."

The bell rang. Alex and Cassie rose to follow the professors out.

"Alex, stay for just a minute," Jaze said.

Siale kissed him on the cheek. "Catch you later."

"See you at lunch," Alex told her.

He waited until Professor Mouse pulled the door shut, then turned around. The expression on Jaze's face made a knot tighten in his stomach.

"You want to get married next week?" the dean asked, his eyes searching Alex's face.

Alex dropped his gaze and ran his fingers across the green and white afghan across the back of the couch Nikki had knitted when she was pregnant with Vicki. The wool yarn caught against the calluses of his hand.

"Why wait?" he asked, hoping he sounded nonchalant. "I love Siale. I don't see a reason to put it off any longer. Greyton City is on board and the mayor has already given us—"

"You're setting a trap for Drogan."

213

Alex paused and glanced up at Jaze. "I'm what?"

Jaze's eyes narrowed. "Don't pretend like I'm stupid, Alex. I know exactly what you're doing. You don't think Drogan's dead, so you're using the wedding to draw him out."

Alex watched him just as closely. "Do you think Drogan's dead?"

Jaze was quiet for a moment. He looked slowly around the room, then at his favorite overstuffed chair. The dean finally took a seat. Vicki stirred and nuzzled underneath Jaze's chin before she stilled; her breathing fell back into a restful rhythm.

"No, I don't," the dean finally admitted.

Grateful for Jaze's honesty, Alex sat back on the couch. "Me, either. If the Demons are still attacking cities, I think their Alpha must be the one commanding them to do so."

"You want to cut off the head of the snake."

Alex nodded. "It's the only way to stop them."

Jaze's voice was quiet when he asked, "And get revenge for Jericho?"

Alex nodded. "He deserves vengeance."

Jaze's voice held him when the dean said, "Yes, he does. Just be careful that when you do seek your revenge, you keep the living in mind."

Alex asked quietly, "Instead of the dead?"

There was steel and determination in his voice when the dean answered, "Along with the dead. We'll never forget those who gave their lives so we can survive. We live in their memory, instead of dying for it."

Alex thought about the dean's words. "I think I under—"

"Alex!"

William flew through the door and tackled Alex. Alex laughed and fell off the couch. William sat on top of him with the proud smile of a three-year-old.

"I got you!"

"You sure did!" Alex replied with a chuckle. "You got me good."

William climbed off and offered Alex his small hand. "Need help?"

Alex grinned and took the hand. He pulled William down and tickled the little boy.

"Not fair!" William giggled. "That's not fair!"

Alex sat back on the couch and patted the seat next to him. William took it happily. The little blond haired boy smiled up at Alex, his blue eyes so like Nikki's Alex couldn't help thinking of her.

"Your mom would be proud of how big you're getting," he told William.

"She'd say I'm going to be bigger than Daddy," William replied. "She always told me that."

"I think it's true," Jaze said. He smiled at his son from across the room. "Your mom was always right."

William nodded. "She was in my dreams last night."

Jaze smiled at his son with a shadow of longing in his gaze. "What did she say?"

"She told me to listen to the statue."

Alex stared down at him in surprise. "What statue?"

"The one in the yard," William replied. "The wolf one."

Heat ran across Alex's skin. He could feel Jaze's rapt attention when he asked the little boy, "Does the statue talk to you?"

"Sometimes," William answered.

Alex kept his tone light when he asked, "What does the statue say?"

William's blue eyes reflected the warmth of the lamp next to Alex when he replied, "Jet said the Demons are coming."

Alex and Jaze looked at each other. Alex could tell the same chill had gone down the dean's spine.

"We need to evacuate the Academy," Alex said.

"I agree," Jaze replied. "But let's do so quietly. If Drogan hears, he'll pull his Demons back and attack before the students are clear. The sooner we can get this wedding underway, the better."

"Will they come back?" Alex asked.

"You mean the students?" At Alex's nod, Jaze gave a small smile. "For many of them, this is home, but it's our duty to ensure that it's safe. Right now, we can't promise that."

Vicki stirred and began to cry.

"She's hungry," Jaze told Alex. "Spread the word to the professors. I'll catch up to you."

Alex stood. William followed Jaze to the backroom, leaving Alex to wonder what had just happened. He found Siale waiting for him when he left Jaze's quarters.

Siale paused before giving him a hug. "You look like you've seen a ghost," she said.

"Something like that," Alex replied. At Siale's questioning look, he explained, "We're evacuating the Academy."

Siale's eyes widened. "Why?"

Alex said what he knew Jaze would want him to tell the professors. "With the wedding coming up and the Demons loose, we don't want the Academy to be a target. It'll be safest to have all of the students gone until Drogan is accounted for."

Siale nodded. "Okay. I'll talk to my dad about taking the Lifers. I think he'd be happy to have them at the warehouse until things are under control."

Alex felt guilty for not telling her the complete truth. He took her hand and led her down the steps to the courtyard. They walked in silence to the big wolf statue in the middle of the grass. Comfort filled Alex when he set his palm against the cool metal. Siale waited near him without question. He appreciated the way she gave him the time he needed to gather his thoughts.

"William says Jet's statue talks to him in his dreams," he finally told her.

He didn't know if he wanted it to be possible or not. Jaze was completely willing to make a decision that affected the entire Academy based on the three-year-old's words. Alex wasn't sure what to believe.

"He said Jet told him that the Demons were coming to the Academy. Do you think that's possible?" he asked, careful to keep his tone level.

Siale studied the wolf statue for a few minutes. When she spoke, her eyes were on the seven emblazoned on the wolf's shoulder. "Maybe it's instinct."

"What do you mean?"

Siale set a hand on the seven. "Maybe what William feels is instinct, and he doesn't know how else to describe it."

"That's possible," Alex acknowledged. "He said his mom told him to listen to Jet. That's why we're evacuating the Academy."

Siale set a hand on his arm. "It's bothering you, isn't it?"

Alex nodded. His words were quiet when he said, "I've talked to Jet's statue ever since I got here." He paused, then continued, "It helps me clear my thoughts, but I've never gotten an answer like that."

"Haven't you?"

He met Siale's gray gaze in surprise. "What do you mean?"

She gave a small, warm smile and said, "Isn't it Jet that tells you to keep fighting? Isn't he the one that pushes you to try every way possible to defeat Drogan?" She looked at the statue. "Isn't it your brother you follow to protect those who are weaker and need your help? At first, it seemed to me like you lived in his shadow. But now I know that the same blood

217

flows in your veins. Jet's been a part of you since you were born."

Alex felt the truth of her words as soon as she said them. He shook his head and smiled at her. "You always surprise me by how well you really know me."

She smiled back at him. "That's love. The more I know you, the deeper I respect you, and that respect is tied with how very much I love you."

He kissed her in front of the statue. The sun shone down on their shoulders while the scent of turning leaves and frost in the shadows hinted at the fall that would soon embrace the Academy and the forest. Alex walked with Siale hand in hand back to the Academy. They had a lot to do before the wedding, and the first step was going to be the hardest. He wasn't sure how the professors would take the news that the Academy was to be evacuated, but he trusted his dean and the little boy who looked at him with the eyes of the woman who had once been the only mother in his life.

Chapter Twenty-four

"It's so empty," Cassie said as they wandered through the Academy.

"It feels like ghosts roam the halls," Tennison replied.

Alex trailed behind the pair. The last of the students had left earlier that day so that they could get home long before the full moon rose. The tremors that crawled beneath Alex's skin intensified the closer it came to nightfall. Only those students who would be attending the wedding remained, and they had sat as long as they could stand it in the library until Trent suggested walking the halls in an effort to stave off the need to phase.

"Maybe they do," Terith replied. She looked down the halls they passed as if searching for ghosts.

She and her brother seemed a bit lost without Von and Jordan at their sides. Even though Alex had asked Jaze's permission for both werewolves to attend the wedding, the dean had denied his request. Worry that Drogan and his Demons would surface meant every security measure had to be taken. The fewer werewolves both the team and the GPA had to protect, the better.

"You believe in ghosts?" Siale asked her.

Terith nodded. "Definitely. Don't you? It's like memories walk through the halls. Look." She gestured into Chet's empty training room. The evening light spilled through the windows to light the empty mats and wrestling ring. "You can almost see Boris and Torin fighting it out. Their Seconds would be cheating, trying to give their Alpha the upper hand. Chet always had to yell at them for interfering with rank duels."

Alex leaned against the open doorway. "It amazes me that neither ever won. They could fight the entire class period, and Chet would always have to call it off when the bell rang because they were so equally matched."

"You beat them both."

Alex looked at Trent. "Not in here."

"It doesn't matter," Trent replied. He nodded at the empty ring. "Here, in the courtyard, in the forest, it's all the same. You're the top dog."

Alex was about to protest when Siale said, "He's right. They always wondered who was strongest, but it was you."

Alex remembered the feeling of defeating each Alpha. He hadn't needed the Demon to come out on top. Something had filled him with strength. He knew that same thing was responsible for his now black fur when he phased, and the way the other students looked at him when he walked into a room.

"Jericho knew."

The name Cassie spoke settled over everyone. Alex's sister nodded in certainty. "He knew what you were. That's why he chose you at his first Choosing Ceremony. He believed you were more than even you knew."

Alex and Siale exchanged a glance. Alex gave her a small smile. Their conversation with Cherish had let Alex know exactly why Jericho had chosen him. Alex had kept the same thought at the forefront of his mind during the funeral the day before. Jericho's decision to honor Jet's sacrifice in saving his family had impacted Alex's entire life. When he howled with the others, it was in remembrance of the Alpha who had become not only his mentor, but his friend.

"I learned as much from him as he did from me," Alex replied, his voice soft.

Silence settled over them. Alex's thoughts were swept away to the first time he had met the tall, skinny Alpha in the courtyard. So much had changed from the time Jericho had called his name in front of the entire Academy. It was the first time a Termer had ever called a Lifer to be a part of his or her pack, let alone be the Second. Alex would never forget the honor Jericho had bestowed on him that day.

Siale slipped her hand into his. "I can't believe we're getting married tomorrow. I'm nervous." She read the concerned look on his face and hurried to say, "Not about marrying you, but about doing it in front of so many people."

Alex knew she was worried about Drogan and the Demons more than anything else. Keeping up pretenses with their families had been tough on them both. He was ready to have it over with no matter what was going to happen. He forced a smile and pulled her close. "Me, too," he admitted. "I can't believe how much Greyton's putting into this."

"You have a ballroom and everything," Terith reminded him. "I can't believe the Mayor is the one officiating!"

Trent shook his head. "Talk about making a statement.

221

I've got to give the man credit for taking a stand."

Tennison smiled. "Greyton's already known for having Alex as their protector. They want to be known as the first werewolf-friendly city on the map."

Cassie leaned against her fiancé. "It's all a dream come true, but it feels so fast. I can't believe it's tomorrow! I don't think I'm going to sleep tonight even after the full moon."

"Let's phase," Trent suggested. "I can't stand it anymore. Jordan's not here. I've lost my sense of stability and any reason for control. Let's go be wolves."

"I couldn't have said it better," Terith replied, throwing her brother a relieved smile. "I feel like I've lost my arm or my heart without Von at the Academy. Being a wolf is easier. We don't have to think about it."

Everyone looked at Alex. He realized they expected him to make the final decision. With the others gone, he truly was the Alpha.

Alex nodded. "Let's go."

His friends rushed up the stairway to phase. Alex walked up more slowly.

"You're in your mind a lot these days."

Alex smiled at Siale. She waited at the top of the stairs with a quizzical expression and her head tipped slightly to one side. Her gray eyes watched him with the knowing look of someone who guessed Alex's thoughts but waited for him to state them.

"I think I'm starting to realize what it means to be an Alpha," Alex admitted when he reached her.

"Professor Kaynan would be proud of you," Siale replied, slipping her arm through his. "Remember his philosophy class? 'The best Alpha thinks of him or herself last, puts the pack first, and remembers that the pack is only as strong as its weakest member.'"

Alex cracked a smile. "I remember when Torin replied,

'But if the pack is there to serve the Alpha, what good is it if the Alpha places himself last?"'

Siale grinned. "Kaynan wasn't thrilled."

Alex chuckled. "Leave it to Torin to find the self-serving side of being an Alpha."

Siale pushed open the door to Alex's quarters. It still amused him to see that the others had chosen his used-to-be lone wolf rooms as their own without so much as asking him. He smiled at the sight of Trent running around in wolf form with Tennison's shirt in his mouth. Cassie's fiancé was trying to corner the wolf between the couch and the fireplace without luck while Cassie just watched and laughed.

"You seriously need Jordan here," she said with a shake of her head.

Trent barked in agreement. Tennison dove at that moment and managed to yank the shirt from the werewolf's teeth. He held it up with a dismayed expression.

"It's all slobbery. That's gross, Trent. Just wait until I phase and chew up your favorite shoe," Tennison threatened.

Cassie laughed. "Are you a shoe-chewer, Tenn? Are there other bad habits I'm going to have to break you of after we're married?"

"Just put lemon oil on everything," Siale replied. "Chewers hate the taste of lemon oil."

Alex and Cassie both grimaced at the thought.

It was Siale's turn to laugh. "You two really look like brother and sister when you do that."

"Alex also screams like a girl," Tennison replied. "You might have to train him on that."

Alex threw off his shirt and phased. Before Tennison could escape, Alex snatched the werewolf's shirt from his grasp and darted out the door.

"Alex, get back here with that!" Tennison yelled.

Trent fell in close behind. Both werewolves huffed in

laughter as they flew down the stairs and out the door Siale had thankfully thought to prop open.

A few seconds later, the rest of the werewolves chased the pair through the forest. Alex dodged a tree trunk and threw the tee-shirt to Trent just before Tennison tried to snag it in his jaws.

Trent ducked beneath a bush and darted left around a stand of aspens. Tennison slowed to get around Alex, then used his long legs to lope between both wolves. Alex barely caught the tee-shirt before Tennison got to it. He circled right and followed a game trail down to the stream. To Tennison's dismay, Alex proceeded to jump into the ankle-deep water. He then gave showy splashes designed to soak any wolf who got within reach of the shirt.

By now the tee-shirt was a sopping wet mess with mud on one sleeve. Alex didn't know why Tennison bothered to get it back. Taking pity on the werewolf, Alex lowered his head to the water to wash the shirt.

Tennison yipped with frustration. His ears were back and he pawed at the edge of the river like a puppy who didn't want to get wet. Alex gave a wolfish grin and lowered his muzzle into the stream.

Something bowled him over so hard Alex lost his grip on the tee-shirt. Soaked from head to toe, he staggered back to his paws. Surprise filled him at the sight of Kaynan standing in wolf form on the far side of the river with Grace, his mate, at his side. The crimson-coated Alpha had the tee-shirt in his jaws. Glee showed in his red eyes.

Alex glanced over his shoulder. His pack looked completely surprised by the professors' appearance. Kaynan gave a bark of challenge and both he and Grace disappeared through the trees.

Alex waved his tail and looked back at his pack mates. He wasn't about to let the challenge go lightly. It was his pack against Kaynan and Grace. They could handle two werewolves.

Alex gave a bark of command and leaped up the far bank in the moonlight. The sounds of splashing heralded his pack following close behind. They took up a protective fan formation. Shadows trailed them on either side. Alex made out the forms of Dray and Gem on his right with Colleen and Rafe on his left.

Alex caught sight of Kaynan ahead of them. He felt as much as saw Siale close in on his right. She sped up when he did, her ears back and mouth open in a wolfish grin at the challenge. Alex's paws drummed along the ground. Kaynan's cedar and clove scent along with the lingering strange chemical smell that colored both him and his sister Colleen filled Alex's nose.

Alex pushed harder. His pack loped behind him on nearly silent paws. Alex felt a surge of pride at the way they ran in formation, leaping over logs and between the trees as though they were of one mind and thought. Alex felt like an Alpha, a true leader. Even the professors couldn't match his pack.

He was ready to give the order for his pack mates to split to the right and left the way they used to drill when suddenly Kaynan and Grace, Rafe and Colleen, and all of the others were gone. Alex ran past the last place he had seen the first two, spun on his heels, and circled back. Their scent disappeared completely.

Baffled, Alex watched Siale and Cassie search the same way. Tennison sniffed around the trees while Trent and Terith jogged back to see if they had somehow missed the werewolves in the bushes.

Alex couldn't believe it. He snorted in disbelief, spinning in a complete circle to see if somehow the professors were playing a trick on him.

A pine branch hit him in the head. Alex looked up. His

mouth dropped open at the sight of Kaynan and the others up in the evergreens in wolf form looking down at him. Alex thought of the time he had jumped up in a tree to beat everyone back to the Academy. Wolves and trees didn't mix well; the balance was off and it just felt completely wrong. He had to give the professors credit for making it work quickly enough to throw his pack off the trail.

Kaynan gave a huff of laughter and let the now soggy and shredded tee-shirt fall through the branches to land at Alex's feet. Alex snorted. Tennison trotted up and snatched it from the forest floor. To Alex's surprise, the werewolf then proceeded to worry and shred the shirt himself while the others looked on.

Kaynan and Grace jumped down with Colleen and Rafe close behind. Everyone watched Tennison finish destroying his own shirt. Trent grabbed one of the shreds and raced around the trees. Rafe picked up another. The quiet professor with the golden eyes shook it. When he let go, the ruined shirt hit Alex in the face. Rafe barked a laugh.

Alex grinned and took off after him. The others fell in close behind. During the night of the full moon, they were just wolves, animals united by comradery, loyalty, and the kindred nature that came from growing up among the trees. The other wolves from Rafe's pack joined them in their flight through the shadows.

Wolves brushed past Alex's shoulder, leading them deeper into the forest. Alex and Siale followed. Cassie and Tennison and Trent and Terith ghosted close behind. Besides Tennison, they had been the first students at the Academy. When little more than gangly-legged pups, the professors had run with them the same way, leading them through the forest and teaching them to love the meadows and glens, valleys and peaks.

Alex ran with the reminder that though life was fragile

and could twist in ways that left holes gaping in his heart, there was also stability among the ancient trees and peace within the forest depths to counterbalance the pain. The way of the wolf was one of quiet acceptance. His journey as a werewolf was filled with highs that made him feel like he was flying and lows he had survived through sheer determination. Being a wolf helped him place both of those in perspective.

The world continued whether he fought Drogan or not. Trees grew and the sun rose, the rain still fell and the crickets chirped regardless of what he did. The thought made him feel small and filled him with hope at the same time. It took some of the weight off his shoulders and chased away the fear of what would happen if he failed. The way of the wolf helped to remind him that the best he could do was to live for his pack. They were his world, his strength, and they would be at his side every step of the way.

Chapter Twenty-five

Drogan pressed the gun harder against Siale's head. She winced. A slight breeze toyed with the hem of her wedding dress, wrapping the white fabric around both her and Alex's half-brother. Alex tried to reach her, but his feet felt like they were trapped in tar. He yelled her name, but it came out as a whisper. A single tear trailed slowly down Siale's face. It reached her delicate jawline and fell with agonizing slowness to the floor. Alex followed the tear, straining, reaching, and unable to do anything but watch the iridescent drop reflect his own hopelessness.

When the tear hit the ground, it shattered with the sound of a bullet exploding from a gun.

"No!" Alex yelled.

He sat up so quickly the room spun. Reality clashed with the nightmare. He couldn't clear Drogan's scent from his nose. Shadows moved out of the corner of his eye, out of place amid the dawn that spilled through the window after their midnight run. Alex turned his head and froze.

Drogan stood in the middle of his room. His half-brother held Siale by the throat. There was a gag in her mouth. Drogan's right arm ended in a jagged blade attached to the stump where his hand had been. Siale's eyes widened when he pressed the blade to her neck.

"Let her go!" Alex yelled.

"Quiet," Drogan growled. "Your professors will hear you." He paused, then said, "Or will they?"

"What do you mean?" Fear sent ice through Alex's veins. He willed the Demon to take over. Blue tinted his vision.

"Do it and she dies," Drogan said in a voice that left no doubt he would follow through with his threat. "You evacuated the Academy. Smart." His eyes narrowed. "Smarter would have been to disappear. You knew I wouldn't give up, Alex, yet you stick around. Why can't you just die?"

Alex stood slowly with his hands up to show that he held no weapons. A glance behind him revealed two Demons hulking near the hallway where the rest of his pack slept. The werewolves had been exhausted after the full moon run; Alex doubted any of them had awoken yet. If the Demons went on a rampage, everyone would die. "Then kill me, Drogan. Kill me and let Siale go. You don't have to hurt anyone else."

Drogan's mouth twisted in a smile that scared Alex more than any glare.

"If only it was that easy," the Extremist said. He motioned with his bladed hand. "Let's move."

To Alex's dismay, Drogan pushed the hidden panel with his shoulder and slid it to the side to reveal the tunnel. Alex had no choice but to walk in front of Drogan and one of his

229

Demons down the walkway. The fact that the other Demon stayed in his quarters wasn't lost on him.

"I'm the one you want," Alex said. "You don't need to hurt anyone else."

Drogan's silence followed him down. His brother's demeanor terrified him. Usually, Drogan was prone to talking about how much he hated Alex and wanted to kill him. The silent, impassive Extremist was another story.

Drogan paused near the entrance to the Wolf Den. The door was shut. Drogan didn't bother to push the panel.

"Let us in," he growled.

The door slid open.

Alex's chest tightened at the sight of all of the professors standing below Brock's station with four of Drogan's Demons guarding them. Tears escaped down Meredith's cheeks when he met his mother's gaze. The professors looked the worse for the wear, bruised and bleeding. Chet sat on the floor with blood on his shirt while Grace applied pressure to a wound on Kaynan's back. Dray tried to smile at Alex, but the combat professor's lips twisted into a grimace when Gem tightened the bandage on his arm.

Alex paused at the sight of Jaze chained to a chair in the middle of Brock's command center. There was a poorly-tied bandage around the dean's forehead and dried blood showed at the corner of his mouth. Little William sat on the floor at his father's feet with baby Vicki sleeping in his lap. The usually calm and hungry Brock sat at his computers, his face pale and gaze worried.

"How did this happen?" Alex asked quietly.

Drogan glanced back at him. "Unlucky for you, werewolves are slaves to the full moon. After gaining access to the Academy, all we had to do was wait it out until everyone returned exhausted and fell asleep. A few put up a fight, but my Demons convinced them it wasn't a good idea.

You're lucky I didn't just kill them all in their beds."

Alex felt the gaze of every person and Demon in the room on him as he followed Drogan and Siale to the stairs.

"Why didn't you?" Alex forced himself to ask.

Drogan didn't answer.

Alex tried another question. "How did you get inside the walls?"

Drogan looked up the stairs. Alex followed his gaze to Brock.

Alex shook his head. "There's no way. Brock would never betray Jaze."

Brock hung his head, unable to meet Alex's gaze.

Drogan merely replied, "It helps to have the right leverage."

Brock turned away from Alex and touched his fingers to the screen on his right. Alex's heart fell at the sight of Jennifer Stauffer, the girl Brock had taken to dinner in Greyton City, bound and gagged. A man in a mask stood behind her chair with a knife to her throat. Tears and a bruise on the woman's cheek were enough to set Alex's teeth on edge.

"You're going to pay, Drogan," Alex growled.

Drogan's mismatched eyes met Alex's. "That's where you're wrong," he replied. "I'm going to enjoy every second of this."

Alex had reached the end of his frayed patience. "Every second of what?" he demanded, his voice rising. "What can you possibly want? Money? Fear? Power? There's nothing you can gain by taking over an Academy the world already knows about!"

Drogan shoved Siale to a sitting position on the stairs. When she tried to move, the tip of his bladed hand was enough to still her attempt.

"After all this time, I thought we understood each other,"

231

Drogan said, his voice casual while his eyes held Alex like shards of green and blue ice. "I don't want money, power, or fear."

With four Demons guarding the professors, another in his pack quarters, two more at the door, and another unaccounted for, Alex couldn't think of a way to gain the upper hand. The scent that flowed from his brother revealed the insanity in the Extremist's actions. Alex had no doubt whatever Drogan's goals were, his brother intended to carry them out completely.

Alex's voice was quiet when he asked the question, "Then what do you want?"

Drogan grabbed Siale's arm and pressed his blade to it. She winced. Alex took a step forward, but the Demon closest to his mother put his claws around her neck. Alex froze.

Drogan drew his blade down Siale's arm. The skin parted in a line of red. Drogan watched the blood pool. "The only thing I want is for you to suffer, Alex," he said, his voice calm. "I don't care about anything else other than making sure that my *brother* takes his last remaining breaths with the utmost pain possible." His voice darkened. "The world can rot for all I care. You took everything from me; now I get to make you suffer until you take your last breath at the point of this blade."

"Then do it!" Alex commanded. He held out his arms, willing Drogan to carve them instead of his love's. He couldn't take the sight of her in pain steps away from him and him unable to do anything about it. It was the worst form of torture he could think of. "Take your vengeance out on me. I'm here, right now, standing in front of you." His voice tightened with hopeless frustration when he concluded, "Take me instead. Please."

Drogan paused, his blade still in Siale's arm. Tears trickled down her cheeks and her lips trembled with the effort it took to stay silent. Alex wanted to hold her so badly his arms ached, but he didn't dare take a step forward for fear that his mother would pay for his actions as well as his fiancé.

"I will kill you," Drogan said. Before Alex could feel any hope that his friends and family would be safe, the Extremist continued, "But first, I will knock you from the platform of glory you have built for yourself. The world worships you. I will make them fear and loathe you. Your professors care about you; I will make them regret the day they ever let you set one foot in this Academy." He met Alex's gaze. "Your fiancé loves you? I will slice her to pieces in your name until she curses the day you pulled her from my pit."

Siale's head jerked up.

Drogan looked down at her with a cruel smile that darkened his gaze. "Oh, you thought I didn't remember you?"

Siale ducked her head.

Drogan pulled the blade from her arm and used it to raise her face back up so that she would look at him. Red blood coated her chin.

"I remember everything," Drogan said, his voice soft and taunting. "I remember how your skin was like satin beneath my fingertips. I remember how you begged me to stop."

Alex's hands tightened into fists.

Siale tried to glance away, but Drogan grabbed her hair with his good hand, forcing her to look at him again.

"I remember how much stronger you were than your mother," Drogan continued. "I loved watching your pain, the way you tried to stay silent." He tipped his head closer to her and whispered loudly, "But in the end, you couldn't."

Siale slammed her forehead against his face.

Drogan cupped his nose as bright red blood flowed through his fingers. He laughed and dropped his hand. Red stained his lips and mouth when he said, "I should have remembered that, too." He shook his head and glanced at Alex. "You have your hands full with this one, just like I did."

Alex took another step. Meredith cried out in pain. Guilt flooded Alex when he saw the deep claw marks along her shoulder from the Demon. Alex's hands clenched and unclenched. He couldn't win. If he tried to protect Siale, his mother got hurt. If he stood by and did nothing, everyone was in danger; Drogan had him hedged in on every side. It was a lose-lose situation no matter how he looked at it.

The only thing he could think of was to distract the Extremist from his attention to Siale.

"What are you going to do, kill me in front of the nation?" he asked.

Drogan turned away from Alex's fiancé and faced him again. "We're going to have a wedding."

Alex watched him closely. "What do you mean?"

Drogan gave a chilling smile. "The world loves you." He looked down at Siale. "You two are the werewolf sweethearts who have captured the nation's attention. Everyone wants to see true love between their *Demon*," he twisted the word, "And the love of his life." His smile deepened. "They'll get their precious wedding and so much more when you decapitate the mayor of Greyton City in front of your beloved humans, and then give the order for my Demons to slaughter the rest of them like livestock."

"Drogan, you're a sick, twisted monster," Chet growled.

"You can't make Alex do that," Meredith protested.

Ice was coursing through Alex's veins. "I won't do it."

"You'll do it," Drogan replied. He tipped his head toward Jaze. "I have the leverage, and as we've seen with Brook, leverage truly is power."

"It's Brock," Brock muttered without taking his eyes off the screen showing Jennifer.

Alex thought quickly. "If I'm going to have a wedding, I'll

need my family there and witnesses from the Academy. It'll look strange otherwise."

Drogan nodded. "Of course. You'll have your beloved professors, your mom, and your fiancé." He ran his tongue across his lips when he looked at her. Siale shivered and stared at the floor. Drogan grinned as if he enjoyed her discomfort and continued, "Thanks to your careful planning, you'll also have your sister and her fiancé there as well. However," he looked up at Jaze. "If the prestigious Dean of the Werewolf Academy is absent after his wife's not too distant death, I don't think anyone will think twice. He is in mourning, and it isn't too farfetched to believe a wedding is just too much to handle after such a loss."

Alex locked gazes with Jaze. The dean didn't look surprised at Drogan's words, but worry showed beneath the Alpha's calm demeanor.

"He needs to be there," Alex protested. "He's family and his presence will be just as important as the mayor's."

Drogan shook his head. "Werewolves are pack creatures, Alex." His lips tightened for the briefest moment. "I've gotten over that fact, thanks to you destroying anyone I even remotely considered part of my pack. Now, with infusions of human blood—"

"Infusions?" Alex repeated.

Drogan sighed as if Alex's attempt to stall him in order to create a plan were mere annoyances. "Yes, Alex. Human blood has been highly effective in turning away the undesired effects of being a werewolf, like the control of the full moon. It was the perfect time to hit the Academy with pretty much everyone out of commission after the predictable run. The human blood has also thankfully wiped out any sympathies I might have toward the fact that we share the same bloodline, or at least half. Your other half is a little lacking." He looked at Meredith meaningfully.

Alex bristled. "Using humans for blood is disgusting. It's something your father would have done."

"Our father," Drogan reminded him, "Which gets me back to the discussion of packs. Werewolves will do anything to save their pack, and I know you well enough to understand that Jaze has been your Alpha from the day I sliced your adopted parents' throats. If you don't kill the mayor with all the world watching, I will slice his stomach with the same blade and watch him die in front of his children, then I'll let you hear them scream when I do the same to them." His gaze sharpened with his threat. "You will kill the mayor, sic my Demons on the crowd, and watch the acceptance you have been trying to build for werewolves fall down in blood and ashes at your feet. If you don't, Jaze and his kids will die."

Chapter Twenty-six

Alex fought back the urge to tug at the neck of his tuxedo. The cameras broadcasting the wedding to the nation were no doubt recording his every move. He glanced at Siale. She gave her father a weak smile. Red grinned proudly back at her while he fiddled with his cufflink for what had to be the twentieth time.

Alex couldn't see how beautiful Siale looked in the wedding dress Jericho's mother had tailored for her. He wasn't able to enjoy standing next to Cassie and Tennison as they all prepared to say their vows. Worst of all, he couldn't look the mayor in the eyes while the man read from the book he held and smiled at the young couples in front of him with the innocence of someone who didn't know he was about to die.

"Stay calm, Alex," Drogan said into his earpiece.

Alex's jaw tightened. Having Drogan in his head every step of the way made it worse because he knew the man's bladed hand was inches away from Jaze. The fact that Drogan had placed the same blade he had used to kill Alex and Cassie's parents on the stump of his arm was twisted enough to let them all know just how far the Extremist would go.

The professors sat on the chairs below pretending to enjoy the wedding while waiting for the inevitable to take place. Only Brock, Drogan, Jaze and the children remained at the Academy. Trent and Terith sat side by side, both siblings looking as though they were about to be sick. Alex wished it was Trent's voice in his ear reminding him to be calm. It was all Alex could do to keep his composure. His whole world was about to implode no matter what he did.

"My dad gave Jaze the same conundrum," Drogan said, his voice irritatingly calm. "Jaze had the gall to let his own mother die to save the nation's views of werewolves. Naming a school after her doesn't exactly make things better, does it, Jaze?"

Alex couldn't hear the dean's muffled reply, but Drogan laughed. "You can try to justify it, but you killed her. That's what will happen to you if you fail, Alex. You'll kill Jaze as surely as if you sliced his stomach yourself. His blood will be on your hands. Your mentor, your dean, your Alpha, will be dead because of you, and so will the kids. Don't slip up, or you can add three bodies to the others hanging over your head."

Alex could see the hulking forms of the Demons hiding in the alley just beyond the courthouse. With William held at knifepoint, Jaze had been forced to tell the Black Team and the GPA to stand down. He denounced the wedding as not a threat, and told them their time would be better spent tracking down the Demons by following the false leads Drogan gave him. Alex felt the absence of the teams he trusted. He hadn't realized how much he appreciated having them at his back until they were gone.

"Your attention is wandering, Alex," Drogan said. "I can just imagine how it will feel to slice the stomach of your newest little cousin. She's awake now; should I see if she likes my new hand?"

"Touch her and die," Alex growled under his breath.

The mayor paused. "Did you say something?" he asked politely.

"Easy, Alex," Drogan warned in his ear. "Be smart. I want you to kill him right after you say 'I do', not before. Step lightly or Jaze dies before you draw your next breath."

Alex forced a smile that felt more like a snarl on his lips. "Sorry, mayor. Something got caught in my throat."

"Of course," the mayor replied with a warm smile. "I'll continue." He lifted his book and continued reading passages about love and life that rushed past the hum in Alex's ears.

He looked down the row of professors below him. They were his only hope, yet they were as tied as he. Drogan had made it perfectly clear that if a werewolf tipped off the mayor or police force in any way, Jaze and the children were dead. Drogan would also signal his Demons to attack the crowd and annihilate them regardless of what anyone did, so they would doubly lose.

The expression of loss on all of their faces hit Alex hard with the realization that it was their Alpha on the line even more so than Alex's. Jaze had been there for him in so many ways, yet they had grown up with the dean, survived incredible hardships with him, and followed him without question. The fact that they were now unable to stop their Alpha's death if Alex slipped up showed in the frozen expressions and intense attention to the proceedings. Alex

239

knew it wasn't fair to expect them to step in. With Jaze's life on the line, his pack would do all they could to save him.

Alex's gaze stopped on his mother. Meredith's hands were knotted together in her lap and she looked pale in her beautiful light blue dress. She had cried on and off since Drogan made it to the Academy; now, there was a determined look on her face, her eyebrows pulled together and her jaw clenched as her gaze roamed restlessly across the beautifully decorated stage in the manicured grounds of the courthouse. Alex wished he could read her mind. He needed desperately for someone to tell him what to do. Every decision he made would mean someone's death, and many people stood to suffer if Drogan's plans were carried out.

"Tell your sister to stop crying," Drogan said. "A few tears are expected at a wedding, but if she keeps it up, she's going to shed suspicion on the whole occasion."

Alex glanced at Cassie who stood across from him next to Siale. Though his sister's face showed no expression other than a forced smile, tears trickled down her cheeks.

"Cass, you've got to be strong," he whispered while attempting to keep a smile on his face.

"I know," she replied with a matching fake smile. "I just can't help it." She looked at him and more tears echoed her words. Alex's heart went out to her. She looked so beautiful and grown up in her tailored white dress; no bride should cry with such despair in the same minutes she was supposed to marry the man she loved. Siale's hand gripped Cassie's; their fingers were white with matching terror. Alex could hear their thundering heartbeats and stilted breaths.

Tennison's hand moved as if he wanted to hold his fiancé, but he couldn't and still keep up appearances for the wedding.

"What do we do?" he whispered from Alex's side.

Alex shook his head. Fear warred with outrage in his

thoughts. Was he about to let his sister and fiancé watch the audience be ripped apart by bloodthirsty Demons? Was he going to start the bloodshed by decapitating the mayor as Drogan commanded? Would he let Jaze, William, and baby Vicki die because he refused to do what his half-brother demanded of him?

Alex bent down with his elbows on his knees and buried his face in his hands.

"Um, Alex, are you okay?" Mayor Hendricks asked, pausing in the middle of his sermon on dedication to one's spouse.

"What are you doing, Alex?" Drogan asked, his tone touched with warning. "You're acting out a little early."

Alex let out a little groan.

"Are you feeling sick?" the mayor asked. He raised his voice. "It is normal to feel a little anxious on the day of your wedding, but it'll pass."

Several members of the audience chuckled in response.

"Get it together, Alex," Drogan snapped. "You're supposed to wait until after the I Do's, not before."

A hand touched Alex's back. He knew the worried expression he would see on Tennison's face. The student loved his sister. He saw it in the way Tennison treated her each day, how he cupped Cassie's cheek in his hand, the way he stole kisses in the cafeteria when he thought no one was looking, and now in the tense, determined, yet fearful scent that wafted in the air. Tennison wanted to protect Cassie, but he didn't know how.

Alex had vowed to keep Siale safe. He had promised her she wouldn't have to know fear again like what she had experienced in the body pit, yet here they were, fear entangled with her sage and lavender scent. He didn't want to meet her gaze, because he knew he would see the same fear in her soft gray eyes. She didn't deserve this; none of them did.

241

Jericho's voice came in his head. It was calm and self-assured in the way that he always spoke. Alex used to wonder how Alphas had all of the answers. After becoming one, he realized they didn't, they just had a way of projecting confidence about their decisions. He had always admired Jericho's way of reasoning; remembering the Alpha's assurance of his own words made them echo even stronger.

"I think that's your key to defeating Drogan."

Alex had stared at his friend, wondering how a death wish could ever impact his half-brother. "What do you mean?"

"You might not feel like an Alpha at the school, but throw you into battle or in a mission and you're all in. You don't show fear, you don't second-guess yourself, and every thought you have is on protecting those who look to you for safety. I think that's how it's going to happen."

Alex had watched him closely, wondering if the Alpha was making a joke. "So you're saying my wanting to get shot is how I'm going to end him?"

Jericho had smiled his easy smile. "I guess you could look at it like that. What I'm saying is that when you have the chance to end it, do what you do. Don't hesitate, don't second-guess yourself. He may be your half-brother, but he's destroyed so many things in this world he doesn't deserve to be a part of it any longer. Think you can do that?"

"If my Alpha commands it," Alex had replied evasively.

Jericho gave his usual chuckle and shook his head. The Alpha knew Alex too well. "You've gone way past needing anyone to tell you what to do. You'll figure it out."

"Someone's got to save the world, right?" Alex had replied with only a hint of sarcasm.

"That's right," Jericho told him. "And somewhere along the line, you volunteered for the job."

The truth to the Alpha's words rang through him.

Drogan's voice growled over his earpiece, "You look like

an idiot. Stand up and do what you need to do." When Alex stayed down, Drogan's voice deepened. "Don't ruin this like Jaze did when he let his mother die. You can save him and your little cousins. Kill the mayor, now."

Alex let out his breath slowly and straightened back up. He met the professors' gazes followed by his mother's. Everyone looked strained beyond what a wedding should require. It was time to end things.

Siale gave him a pained smile. "Are you alright?" she asked.

Alex straightened his shoulders. "It's going to be okay."

Siale nodded with a light of hope in her eyes. The fact that she believed in him spurred Alex on.

Alex looked back at the mayor. "I'm sorry. I had to settle my stomach a bit. I guess I'm a little nervous."

Mayor Hendricks exchanged a knowing glance with Chief Harrington who stood near the edge of the crowd watching over the proceedings. "Don't worry, son. Our own chief had to say his vows twice; Jack was so shaky no one could understand them the first time!"

"At least I didn't forget the ring for my wedding," Chief Harrington replied with the good-natured grin of friends who ribbed each other often.

Mayor Hendricks smiled at Alex. "Back to the important questions. Do you, Siale Andrews, take Alex Davies to be your lawfully wedded husband?"

"I do," Siale said.

They were already at the vows. Alex's hands began to shake. He balled them into fists, then realized the camera would pick up his nervousness. He willed his fingers to relax. Mayor Hendricks turned to him.

"Do you, Alex Davies, take Siale Andrews to be your lawfully wedded wife?" Mayor Hendricks asked.

Alex knew what he had to do. As Drogan had reminded

243

him, Jaze had been in the same situation. Alex didn't need to ask what his mother or brother would do. He had already had the greatest example of sacrificing to save what they had worked so hard to accomplish. He only hoped the others would forgive him.

"Do it."

The shock of hearing Jaze's voice in his earpiece spurred Alex to action. He spoke loud enough that his voice would carry across the lawn that had been packed to standing room only. "Mayor Hendricks, your life is in danger. Drogan is holding my dean hostage, and he is going to kill Jaze and his children if I don't kill you on national television. He wants to destroy the way the world has accepted werewolves, and he is going to give the order for his Demons to attack the audience. You need to act, now!"

Mayor Hendricks stared at him. A yell rang out in Alex's ear so loud he yanked the earpiece out. Whether it had been Jaze's or Drogan's, he had no way of knowing. Screams of terror sounded through the crowd. The humans bunched back from the alley where the Demons had waited. Blood-thirsty growls answered. Drogan had given the kill command.

Alex grabbed Siale's hand. "Get the humans out of here. Drogan won't stop until they're dead."

"Tennison, Cherish, with me," Siale called.

"Chief Harrington, call your men!" Alex shouted as he jumped off the stage and ran for the Demons.

Alex willed his own Demon to surface. Blue colored his vision. His tuxedo that Jericho's mother had so lovingly crafted split in two. His muscles lengthened and claws curved his hands. The crowd ran past him. Alex placed himself between them and the advancing Demons.

Chapter Twenty-seven

The eight Demons rushed at Alex. They would kill him; of that he was sure, but if he stalled them long enough, some of the humans would get away. He would uphold all he and Jaze had fought for, and he would use his Demon to destroy as many of his brother's as he could.

The sounds of their snarls as they advanced sent a chill down Alex's spine. If the false wedding had done anything for him, it was the realization that he wasn't ready to die. Siale was worth living for and fighting for. Alex gritted his teeth and drove his claws into the sidewalk. If he had to die so that she could live, so be it.

Someone fell in beside him. Alex glanced over and shock filled him. It was Dray, but as he had never seen the

245

professor. The werewolf's blue eyes were the same, but he was huge and bulky, a Demon with gray fur and sharp claws.

"We face them together," Dray said, his voice gruff.

"They'll kill us," Alex replied.

Dray glanced over his shoulder. Alex followed the professor's gaze to Gem. The tiny werewolf Alex had never seen frown a day in her life helped as many humans flee the courthouse lawn as she could.

Dray turned back to the Demons. "It's worth it."

The beasts hit them with the force of eight bulldozers.

Alex was shoved to the ground by four of Drogan's Demons. Claws tore into his arms and legs. Fangs sunk deep into his shoulder. They matched him strength for strength. Each time he got ahold of one, another would tear him free with unforgiving claws that marked his body in crimson ribbons.

Alex willed the panic to keep away. Muscle memory took over. He attacked with the skills honed into his body by years of training under Chet and Dray's tutelage. He gave as much as he got, and was rewarded by yelps and cries of pain.

Two Demons caught Alex by the arms and another sunk its claws into his legs. Alex struggled to break free, but they pinned him to the ground. A Demon with Drogan's mismatched eyes clamped onto Alex's neck. Alex rolled from side to side, but couldn't turn over with the Demons holding him down.

He struggled to breathe as the Demon's fangs ground together. He could feel his blood pouring down his chest. Black filled his vision along with the intense pain. He was going to die. The realization hit Alex like a bucket of icy water. Siale's face filled his vision. The Demons would go after her and the others. He wouldn't be able to save them.

Dray threw off one of the Demons he fought and it slammed into the one pinning Alex's right arm down. Alex clenched his claws into a fist and drove a haymaker into the face of the Demon who tried to rip out his throat.

The Demon yelped and let go. It snarled down at Alex and opened its mouth to bite him again. Alex shoved his hand into the Demon's mouth. Startled, the Demon jerked back. Alex held onto its tongue and was yanked to his feet. He used his momentum to bowl the Demon over. Still keeping ahold of the Demon's tongue, he drove the creature to the ground. He shoved his other hand into the Demon's mouth with the first.

Alex roared with the force of his rage and balled both hands into fists. The Demon's teeth cut into his arms. He ignored the pain and forced his hands apart. The Demon let out a throaty yelp of panic. It clawed at his stomach with its feet. The other Demons tried to pull Alex back, but he wouldn't let go. Alex gave one more roar of rage and jerked his hands open. The Demon's jaw dislocated. He raised his hands high into the air, bringing the Demon with them, and slammed his fists to the ground. The impact of his fists between the Demon's skull and the cement made a sound like dropping a melon onto the road. The Demon quit struggling.

Alex spun around, certain the other Demons were about to tear him apart. Instead, they backed up uncertainly.

"What are they doing?" Dray asked. His breath wheezed through his chest and blood coated his skin.

Alex couldn't tell what was from the Demons and what was the professor's. Dray held his mangled right arm to his chest. Both bones protruded through the skin.

"They almost had me," Dray continued. "Then they dropped me at the same time." He glanced at the lifeless form at Alex's feet. "You killed one of them!"

Alex nodded, his attention on the other Demons. "It was luck."

The creatures had backed up to the alley. They looked in

different directions, their eyes no longer filled with anger and hatred, but with panic.

Realization hit Alex. "Their Alpha. Something happened at the Academy."

Alex spun, searching the lawn. He found Trent near the mayor. The werewolves had blockaded as many of the humans as they could inside the courthouse. When the Demons made it through Alex and Dray, the others were prepared to fight for the lives of the humans they protected.

Pain flooded through Alex when his Demon left his wounded body. He stumbled on the lawn.

"Trent!" he yelled, his voice raspy through his mangled throat.

Relief filled his friend's gaze when he spotted Alex, but the expression changed to shock. Alex wanted to run, but his legs weren't willing. He sunk to his knees on the grass.

"Alex!" Trent called at the same time that Siale screamed his name.

Both werewolves ran to him.

"Alex, we have to get you to a hospital," Siale insisted. She touched his shoulder and her hand came away bloody.

"Seriously, Alex, you need help," Trent replied. The werewolf's gaze flickered past Alex to the alley. "What happened to the Demons?"

Alex didn't need to look back to know they were gone. "Drogan…" He struggled for breath. "The Academy…something happened."

Trent's eyes widened. "Their Alpha gave the order to attack and they stopped. Jaze did something."

"We've got…" Alex couldn't form the words.

Siale dropped to her knees in front of him. "We've got to get back to the Academy, but you can't go anywhere like this." She raised her hand to his throat as if she wanted to stop the blood, but her fingers shook. "This is too bad, Alex.

I don't know what to do." She raised her voice. "Meredith!"

The fear that filled the name gripped Alex's heart. "You…shouldn't…" He swallowed painfully and tasted blood. He closed his eyes and said, "Be afraid."

"I'm afraid of losing you," Siale replied.

A familiar hand touched Alex's shoulder. Something was pressed to his throat.

"Hold this," his mother said, her voice tight with command.

He wished he could open his eyes to see her in action, but just kneeling on the ground with his head bowed took all of his strength. He hoped Trent was getting the helicopter, but he couldn't give the command to make it happen. He could only hope the small werewolf knew what needed to be done.

"Lyra, bring me more bandages," Meredith said. "Siale, put pressure here. Alex, we're going to lay you down."

More hands than Alex thought would be available helped lower him to the ground. He willed his eyes to open for a brief moment. Faces blocked out the setting sun. Strangers that had come for the wedding, humans and werewolves alike, looked down at him with worried expressions. He caught sight of the mayor and Principal Dalton. Officer Dune looked on from further back; Alex recognized his young daughter at his side.

Alex's eyes shut of their own accord.

"Stay with me, Alex," his mother said. "Don't you fall asleep. You've got to fight."

"I…" Alex gave a small, pained smile, "Don't want to…stop fighting."

It was the first words he had said to Jaze when he reached the Academy. The thought of the dean forced him to open his eyes again.

"We've got to…" He drew in a ragged breath. "Get to the Academy."

Meredith shook her head. "We can't move you. You've lost so much blood. If I can't stop it, you're going to bleed out before Dr. Benjamin can get here."

She put another bandage around his throat. Siale held pressure on the wound. Lyra returned with a bag.

"Have Trent radio for Dr. Benjamin again," Meredith said. "How's Dray?"

"He has fractures to his arm and femur. He might have a collapsed lung," Lyra replied. "Gem is helping me."

Meredith nodded. "Let me know if he needs an emergency decompression."

His mother's voice faded as Alex's eyes closed again. He wished he could tell her how proud he was of the person she had become. Memories of the beaten, starved woman Jaze had saved merged with the strong, confident woman his mother was. He couldn't believe how much she had changed. Life at the Academy had been exactly what she needed. The thought that it had also been what he needed made him anxious. He needed to make sure Jaze was alright. He had to get to a helicopter. They needed to leave, now.

Alex pushed himself up at the same time that the beating of helicopter blades touched his ears.

"Alex, don't move!" Meredith commanded.

"I've got to get to Jaze," Alex replied. Strength filled him at the sight of Trent lowering the helicopter to the lawn of the courthouse.

"Alex, I don't think you should do this," Siale told him.

Alex wanted to stand. He put every bit of willpower into wanting his legs to hold, but his body refused to move any higher than his sitting position leaning against Siale for support.

"I can't stay here," he said. Frustration at his weakness touched his voice. "Jaze…Jaze might need me."

Hands reached down.

"We've got you, Alex," Mayor Hendricks said.

"You've done so much for us," Officer Dune told him as he helped pick Alex up.

"Now it's our turn," another man from the crowd said.

The feeling of dozens of hands carrying him across the lawn left Alex speechless. He looked into the grateful, smiling faces of the Greyton citizens he had just fought to save from the Demons.

He caught Mrs. Summer's gaze.

"You're family," she said, her eyes shining with tears.

Other humans nodded.

Someone stumbled and Alex winced at the pain that coursed through what felt like every inch of his body. Other hands reached in to steady him.

A young girl slipped her hand into Alex's. "You're our Demon."

She held his hand as he was set gently on the floor of the helicopter. Her big green eyes held his gaze. "Come back, okay?" she asked, her voice small but hopeful.

Alex nodded tightly. "I will. Thank you."

Meredith and Siale climbed in next to Alex. Kaynan, Chet, Rafe, and Vance followed.

"Do we know what happened at the Academy?" Vance asked, his deep voice gruff with concern.

"No idea," Trent replied from the front seat as he lifted the helicopter into the air. "Communications are down. I'll get us there as quickly as possible."

Alex heard a cloth rip. He opened his eyes to see Siale press a piece of her wedding dress to his shoulder. She ripped another cloth free and wrapped the wound from one of the Demon's fangs the best she could.

"You'd be a good..." His words slurred and Alex couldn't get himself to finish the sentence. A deep rushing sound filled his ears. Darkness took over his gaze before his eyes closed.

"Alex?" Siale said. Alarm touched her voice. "Alex, stay with us!"

"Come on, Alex," Vance's voice beat against him like the banging of a bass drum.

"What's going on?" Trent asked from the front seat.

"He's lost so much blood," Alex heard Meredith reply.

A zipper opened, the sound strange and muffled to his ears. Something stabbed his arm. He gave in to the insistent embrace of nothing.

Chapter Twenty-eight

Voices broke through the darkness in Alex's mind. He felt like he was swimming across freezing cold water as the uniting chant pulsed through his thoughts.

"My brother, a body of flesh and blood no longer your soul holds. Run without the confines of bone and sinew, howl without the constriction of lungs or breath, and live within the embrace of the moon and her welcoming light. Your life is one with wolvenkind, and your heart will beat with ours forevermore. You will not be forgotten."

Alex recognized the voices. Jet's quiet words were entwined with Jericho's confident voice and Kalia's softer tones. His adopted mother and father chanted with the others, their caring and love audible within the phrasing.

253

Nikki spoke with the smile he always remembered, and even Pip's squeaky voice could be heard in the background.

Another voice said the chant. It was deep and gruff, filled with anger the way it had been in life. The General, his hatred of Alex thick even in death, repeated the words with those Alex had loved and lost. The words were a threat, a reminder. Alex had won that battle, but there were so many others left to fight. He would never stop fighting.

Alex's eyes flew open.

"Never forgotten, always one," Jet's voice whispered in the back of his mind.

Alex gasped for breath. Moonlight spilled into the helicopter. They had positioned him near the open door so he could get the full effect of its healing touch. Kaynan sat between him and the door to keep him from falling out. Siale and Meredith knelt on his other side.

"Alex?" Siale said.

He tipped his head to look at her. The relieved smile that spread across her face filled him with warmth.

"I thought I was dead," he told her. His voice was croaky and dry. Talking hurt.

She touched his cheek. "So did we. You weren't breathing well." She blinked quickly to keep back the tears that made her gray eyes shine in the moonlight. "Your heart kept slowing down." Her words stopped as though her throat had tightened too much to speak. She merely smiled down at him, her lips pressed close together in a smile that looked as though it held back a sob.

"You lost too much blood," his mother said. She smiled when he looked up at her. "We did a transfusion, but I thought it would be too late."

Alex followed her gaze to the tube in his arm. He traced it back to the port at her own elbow.

"Mom," he protested.

She gently set a hand on his chest to keep him from rising. "That's what moms are for."

Alex didn't like the fact that she could hold him down so easily. If they found Drogan at the Academy, he would have to be able to fight. He struggled to rise again.

A hand covered Meredith's, pressing down stronger. "Stay there, Alex. You scared us all," Vance told him. "Get the rest you can. We're almost at the Academy."

Alex let out a slow breath and nodded. He didn't want to show how much the huge werewolf's hand hurt.

"How far are we?" he asked, his voice quiet among the steady thumps of the chopper's blades.

"Almost there," Trent replied. He looked back at Alex from the front seat. "Good thing I'm the only pilot we have. I would have been the one to give you blood."

Alex huffed a small chuckle that sent pain through his chest. "Are we even a match?"

Trent shrugged. "Who knows? That's one way to find out."

"He'd be dead," Siale reminded the small werewolf with the tone of someone repeating the same argument.

"Or alive," Trent replied. "I'm going with alive."

Alex smiled at Meredith. "Thank goodness you're here."

His mother brushed his hair away from his forehead with gentle fingers. "I don't always get the opportunity to be your mother. I'm just glad I can be there when you really need me."

"I always need you," Alex told her. He thought of how he had felt listening to her give orders when he was fading. "I'm proud of you."

That brought a smile to his mother's face. "Why?" she asked, her expression puzzled.

Alex sucked in a breath through his damaged throat and let it out slowly. "Because you remind me that…you don't

255

have to have muscles to be strong." He swallowed, then concluded, "You have to have heart."

Tears showed in her eyes and she leaned down to kiss his cheek.

"Oh my goodness."

Trent's gasp brought everyone's attention to the front of the helicopter.

"No!" Kaynan exclaimed.

Alex struggled to rise. "What is it?" he asked.

He didn't need a response. Trent angled the helicopter to the left and the werewolf's shock was explained.

The Academy lay in ruins. The Great Hall had collapsed inward, the students' quarters lay in a broken mess where the classrooms had been, and half of the wall had fallen in. Dust clouded the dark air, blocking out the moonlight with debris.

"What happened?" Meredith asked in dismay.

"Jaze must have had no other option," Kaynan replied. Sorrow filled the red-eyed professor's voice.

"He did that?" Siale asked. Her hand gripped Alex's hard.

The wounds from the Demon's teeth didn't hurt nearly as bad as his heart at the sight of the fallen Academy.

Vance nodded. "The Academy was designed with this in mind if something like Drogan's Demons attacked and there was no way to destroy them." He didn't take his eyes off the wreckage when he concluded, "I just never imagined it would come to that. I don't know how Jaze could have gotten out."

"What about the children?"

Meredith's question hung in the air as Trent landed in the courtyard. Parts of the yard had collapsed inward into the Wolf Den, leaving gaping holes where students had once played and learned to embrace their heritage.

"Stay here," Vance told Alex as soon as the struts hit the ground. "We'll let you know what we find."

Meredith held Alex's other hand while she and Siale

stared after the others. Thoughts of little William and baby Vicki swarmed Alex's mind.

"You can't stay here," he said.

"We're staying," Meredith replied firmly, but her gaze strayed to the fallen school.

"They need everyone to help find Jaze and the kids. William and Vicki need you," Alex urged.

Siale shook her head. "We can't leave you, Alex," she protested.

"You've got to look for them for me," Alex pleaded. "I'd be out there, but I can't. It kills me to think of them hurt and alone. They're probably so scared." He let go of Siale's hand and cupped her cheek. "You've got to find them for me. They've got to be alright."

"Okay," Siale breathed. She kissed him quickly on the cheek. "I won't give up until they're back here, alright?"

"Thank you," he replied with relief.

As soon as Siale was gone, Alex turned to his mother. "Every person counts in a search like this."

"I know," Meredith said.

"They're our family," Alex reminded her. He could see William sitting on his lap again as they spoke about losing his mother. Little Vicki had been snuggled in her father's arms while they both slept. Alex wouldn't forgive himself if they were crying for him and he didn't do what he could to make sure they were saved. "Mom, you've got to go find them."

"I know I do," Meredith replied. Alex could hear the worry in her voice. She hesitated a moment, then looked at him. "You'll stay here?"

"I'm not going anywhere," Alex reassured her. He tried to sit up, but the pain made him lay back down. "See?" he said wryly, frustrated by his weakness.

Meredith gently pulled the I.V. line from his arm and pressed a bandage to the exit hole. "You promise you'll stay here?"

"I promise," he repeated. "Please go find them."

Alex listened to her footsteps cross the lawn. He could hear the others combing through the wreckage. The sound of bricks collapsing and the heavy scent of dust in the air let him know how recently the explosion had happened. He could only pray they would find Jaze and the children.

Alex closed his eyes and willed his body to soak in the moonlight. His torn neck and lacerated body ached as it healed. The sensation was warm but hurt at the same time. He could feel the damp helicopter floor below his bare back. The stickiness reminded him that the moisture was from his blood. He shifted his body in an attempt to find a more comfortable position.

A groan reached his ears. Alex froze.

"Kaynan?" he called. "Chet?"

There was no response. Alex pushed up gingerly. He felt the healing parts of his body pull in protest. Fresh blood dripped down his chest.

Alex moved slowly to the edge of the chopper. He put his feet on the ground and held onto the helicopter as he pushed up. His knees held by sheer strength of will.

The groan sounded again. Alex gritted his teeth and took a step forward, then another. He reached the edge of a hole. His eyes adjusted slower than usual to the murky darkness that had once been the Wolf Den. A slight glimmer caught the moonlight.

Alex squinted. His heart slowed at the sight of the silver seven that matched the one on his shoulder. His eyes traced the black shadow he knew by heart. Jet's statue had fallen through the Wolf Den's ceiling. Dirt and debris from the collapse had fallen with it.

The groan sounded again and a form moved beneath the statue. Adrenaline ran through Alex's veins when he realized who he looked at.

"Drogan," Alex growled.

He jumped into the hole. The voice in the back of his mind mentioned that the move might have been a bit foolhardy given his current condition. Alex bit back a gasp when he hit the ground and his knees gave out.

A pained chuckle sounded that set Alex's teeth on edge. "My Demons must have made an impact."

Alex fought back the urge to yell. He preserved his strength and said quietly to hide his pain, "You sicced them on the crowd."

"You…didn't uphold your promise," Drogan replied.

"You mean my word to kill an unarmed human?" Alex demanded. He rose back to his feet and barely felt the pain as he made his way to his half-brother's side. "The word you knew I would never keep?"

"You are Jaze's blood," Drogan replied dryly.

"You are, too," Alex reminded him.

Alex paused when he got close enough to really see Drogan. Jet's statue had landed fully on the Extremist. Drogan's ribcage was crushed beneath the black wolf's head. Blood ran across the floor in a dark puddle.

"You're dead, Drogan."

They were words Alex had wanted to say ever since the Extremist killed their parents. Alex had trained every possible moment at the Academy to seek his revenge. So many lives had been lost and others lived in terror that Drogan would seek them out. The Extremist had haunted Alex's every step, killed his friends, and threatened the peace and security he and Cassie had fought so hard to achieve. Now, that moment had come.

Alex's strength waned. His knees let go and he sank back to the ground.

Drogan gave a weak smile; blood coated his teeth. "You

look about dead yourself."

Alex glared at him. "Don't get your hopes up. I'm pretty hard to kill."

"You're telling me," Drogan muttered. The Extremist coughed. The cough turned into a hack that colored his lips with blood. He closed his eyes.

Despite his façade, Alex could feel his wounds taking their toll. As much as he wanted to end Drogan's life, his condition made him inclined to just sit back and watch.

"Kill me." Drogan's eyes opened and he gave Alex a pleading look, the first Alex ever remembered seeing. The Extremist winced with an expression of severe pain. "Alex, please."

Alex warred with the empathy he definitely got from his mother rather than the General. He could end Drogan's suffering and give the Extremist peace. He was looking at his brother, his own flesh and blood. The only thing Drogan wanted from him was to die, the exact thing Alex wanted from Drogan himself. He was tempted to do it when the memory of burying Jericho surfaced in Alex's mind. Cherish wore a ring without her love at her side. A pack stood without an Alpha. A mother lived without her son and the brothers Jet had worked so hard to bring back together.

Alex shook his head. "Suffer," he said, his voice level.

Drogan closed his eyes again. His breath rattled in his chest. Alex didn't know how the Extremist was still alive. The same moonlight that had illuminated the seven on the statue's shoulder was centered on Drogan's chest. He wondered if it healed the werewolf just enough to keep his heart beating.

"She's some girl." Drogan's eyes were closed. He spoke without opening them. "I enjoyed causing her pain. She used to be so fresh and new, before I got to her."

Alex tried not to listen. He told himself that perhaps Drogan was talking about somebody else. Maybe the

Extremist was remembering a girlfriend; that would be bad enough. Perhaps he was disoriented from the loss of blood. Maybe he didn't know what he was saying.

Drogan's eyes opened and his mismatched gaze locked on Alex. "I made Siale suffer every way I could think of."

Alex rose to his feet.

"When I ran out of ideas," Drogan continued, "I asked my men. They always came up with something."

Alex grabbed a huge chunk of cement from the floor on his way to the statue.

"When she stopped screaming, I knew I was really getting somewhere," Drogan said, his eyes closing again. "I used to—"

His words ended when the block of cement crushed his head.

Alex rested his forehead against the statue, his strength rushing out of him.

"It's done, Jet," he whispered.

"Alex!" Siale yelled.

Chapter Twenty-nine

Alex ran through ruins of the Academy toward Siale's voice. The fear in her tone spurred him faster. He forgot about pain, Drogan's death, and the Academy itself. All that mattered to him was reaching his love and making sure she was alright. Fear that the Demons had reached the school pulsed through him. Now that their Alpha was dead, there was no telling what they would do.

"Alex!"

He rounded the corner of the fallen Wolf Den. His steps faltered at the sight in front of him.

Kaynan and Chet stood on one side of a huge cement support beam. Vance and Rafe stood on the other. Both sets of werewolves were trying to lift the beam off of Jaze. Siale knelt by Jaze's side and held his hand with tears streaking down her face. The pain of the dean's expression ate through Alex. Brock, his face covered in dried blood and one arm held tightly to his side, tried to do what he could to ease Jaze's pain.

Alex ran forward and forced the Demon to take over. Though his injured body tried to protest, Alex forced it to obey. Blue filled his vision and the Demon surged through his limbs.

"Alex, wait!" Kaynan protested.

Alex ignored him and grabbed the end of the cement beam. Using all that remained of his strength, he lifted the pillar. Alex's knees shook. He gritted his teeth and lifted higher. It took every last ounce of strength from the Demon to hold the beam high enough to clear the dean's crushed body.

Kaynan reached under and pulled Jaze free.

"Clear," Chet shouted.

Alex let the beam go. It fell to the floor with a resounding crash and broke into pieces.

Gray swirled through Alex's vision when the blue left. His legs buckled and he fell forward.

"Easy," Rafe said. The golden-eyed werewolf lowered him to a sitting position on the ground. Siale put a hand on his arm, her soft gray eyes filled with tears.

"Alex."

The sound of the dean's voice was enough to bring Alex back to his knees. With the help of Rafe and Siale, he crawled to Jaze's side.

Jaze held up a hand. His fingers shook with the effort. Alex took it in his own shaking hand and wrapped his other one around it.

"Alex," Jaze whispered again. His dark brown eyes were filled with pain and his breath wheezed each time he sucked in a gasp.

"I'm here," Alex reassured him.

Jaze looked at him, but his gaze was distant as though he didn't see the younger werewolf kneeling in front of him. "Take care...of...William and Vicki," the dean said. His words grew quieter with each syllable.

"Jaze, are they alive?" Siale asked anxiously.

"We can't find them," Kaynan said, agony bright in his crimson eyes.

Jaze lifted his free hand and pointed with a trembling finger. Siale jumped to her feet and raced with Kaynan to the corner where Brock's cousin Caden used to prepare the weapons. The huge gun safe had been embedded in the wall. Dents showed in the black metal, but the door was otherwise unharmed.

"What's the combination?" Kaynan called.

Jaze closed his eyes. A tear slipped down his cheeks. "Six, one, one."

Kaynan spun the dial.

"The day Nikki and I got married," Jaze continued. His words were more of a sigh that spilled from his lips. A drop of blood followed.

A baby's cry broke through the air.

"Oh, thank goodness," Alex heard Kaynan say from the safe.

"Aunt Siale," little William sobbed.

"I've got you," she replied.

Jaze said something Alex couldn't hear. He leaned down. The dean raised his free hand to the empty air and whispered, "Nikki, I've missed you so much."

Alex's tears fell on the hand he clasped. "Don't go," he pleaded.

A slight smile touched the corners of Jaze's mouth. "You're even more beautiful...than I remember."

His labored breathing sounded harsh to Alex's ears.

"I-I don't know what to do without you," he told the dean.

Jaze's gaze focused on his face. A knowing look Alex recognized touched the dean's pained expression. "You'll…know," he said. He winced and shifted as though trying to find a more comfortable position. He gave up and a weak smile touched his lips. "You've…always known."

Alex shook his head. "You've always helped me." His tears dripped down his nose to the dean's hand.

Jaze's focus shifted past Alex's shoulder. His smile grew bigger. "Jet…" He took a wheezing breath and said. "Jet, you came back."

A sob tore from Alex's chest. He didn't want Jaze to leave. He couldn't imagine a world without the dean in it. Jaze had always been there for him, guiding him even without seeming to. Now, Jaze's loved ones had come back for him. Those the dean had left behind during their fight to free the werewolves, the humans and werewolves Jaze had been forced to say goodbye to, had come back to welcome him with open arms. Alex couldn't keep him from that no matter how lost he felt at letting Jaze go.

Jaze sucked in another breath. "Mom," he said. Tears spilled down his cheeks. "Alex, they're all here."

Siale's hand touched Alex's shoulder. He glanced up to see Vicki resting quietly in Siale's arms. The baby's eyes reflected her father's broken form. Kaynan reached them with William at his side. The little boy broke free and knelt next to Alex. Alex pulled him close.

"Is Daddy going to be okay?" William asked.

Alex looked down into the boy's blue eyes. He had never lied to William. He knew there was no reason to start.

"No," he said, his voice gentle. "But I'll take care of you." He met Siale's gaze. "We'll take care of you."

She nodded with tears on her cheeks.

Alex set a hand on Jaze's shoulder. "Go to them," he told the dean. "Your children will be safe with us."

"Love them…" Jaze's whisper barely moved the dust in the air. "Love them all…like I love you."

Alex nodded. His throat was so tight he couldn't say anything else. He knelt down and pressed his lips to the dean's forehead.

"I love you, too, Jaze," he whispered.

A sigh left Jaze's lips, flowing out with his last breath.

Alex sat back and William climbed on his lap. The little boy held his father's sleeve. Alex listened to Jaze's slow heartbeat. Jaze's hand, the one he had held out to Nikki, Jet, and the others, dropped back to his chest. His heart gave one more beat, then stilled.

"Daddy," William cried. He pressed his head against Alex's chest.

Alex gently loosened his hand from Jaze's and wrapped the boy up in a tight hug.

"I've got you, William," he promised. "And I'll never let go."

Chapter Thirty

The nation mourned Jaze Carso's death and honored him with flags at half-mast and a funeral ceremony broadcasted across the country. Words of gratitude for his bravery in ridding the nation of its number one enemy were spoken from leaders and civilians alike. Werewolves were granted citizenship in his name, and Extremists were confronted with extreme force.

Despite the beauty of the proceedings and the solemnity with which Jaze was granted a final resting place next to Nikki in the city in which they had met, Alex's favorite part, the one he would always remember, came after the sun set.

"Our brother, a body of flesh and blood no longer your soul holds." The words of hundreds upon hundreds of werewolves rang out through the forest.

267

"Run without the confines of bone and sinew, howl without the constriction of lungs or breath, and live within the embrace of the moon and her welcoming light." The trees stilled as though in reverence to the wolf who had run beneath their forest canopy.

Silence spread. The honor and love was so profound Alex could feel it with every breath. Little William held his right hand and Siale held his left with baby Vicki asleep in her arms. The forest spread out below them, a vast, dark carpet that hid the world Alex had grown up in. The ruins of the Academy could be seen as a mound of black in the night beyond the crumbled walls. It was a tribute to Jaze, a place Alex would always consider home.

He tipped his face to the moonlight and said, "Your life is one with wolvenkind." The voices below him joined in and concluded, "And your heart will beat with ours forevermore. You will not be forgotten."

When the last word had finished its echo across the land, Alex cupped his hands around his mouth. The howl of remembrance he sang to the sky was joined by the hundreds of voices, werewolves giving tribute to the leader who had given everything to make sure they were safe. Jaze had united them and brought together the nation by destroying the enemy who had threatened to tear them to pieces.

Drogan's violence and the extent he was willing to go to in order to bring human and werewolf-kind to their knees had united both races. Jaze had given up everything, including his life, to stop Drogan. That selfless act spurred a movement of patriotism that joined werewolves and humans in, if not friendship, at least the beginnings of acceptance.

Alex howled his gratitude to the father-figure who had taught him the value of love, loyalty, and pack. He told of his appreciation for Jaze's trust in including him on the missions, and of the dean's understanding when things didn't always go as planned. Alex howled his thankfulness for the Academy Jaze had built that had become a home to so many, and he promised Jaze that he would do his best to follow in the dean's footsteps.

They waited at the top of the rise until long after the howls had died away and werewolves left the forest. The rising sun reflected on the lake Alex had jumped into first as a dare, then as a means of escaping his enemies. The lake was now his final memory of Jaze Carso, the werewolf who had changed a nation.

"Never forgotten; always one," he concluded quietly. A feeling of peace rose in his heart at the thought of Jaze with his loved ones again.

When Alex and Siale walked back down the hill, their friends fell in around them. Cassie and Tennison held hands in front of the pair, and the professors met them in the forest. Together, the students and teachers of the Academy walked one last time beneath the trees to the school that meant something different to each of them, yet in their hearts, everyone had considered it a home.

***

Alex was awoken by Trent later that morning; his friend had caught him still in bed at the hotel in Greyton the city had thoughtfully provided for the werewolves while they were figuring out where to relocate.

"What is it?" he asked sleepily.

"It's a phone call," Trent told him. "You're going to want to take it."

Alex accepted the cell phone with the wolf paw Mouse emblazoned on the back of everything he could.

"This is Alex," he said.

"Alex, this is Agent Sullivan of the Global Protection Agency."

Alex sat up. "Yes, sir?"

"Mr. Davies-Carso, I was a friend of Jaze's and I would like to express my condolences for your loss. The country has lost a fine man."

Alex pushed his messy hair back from his forehead. "Thank you."

"Now to business," Agent Sullivan said. "According to our research, your father, Jared Carso, also known as the General, amassed a great deal of money in several private accounts. Policy normally dictates that this money be absorbed as an asset; however, in gratitude for your diligence and the sacrifices you have made to bring these terrorist threats to rest, the money has been transferred into an account for your use and the use of your posterity."

Alex stared at Trent. The small werewolf nodded excitedly.

"Uh, thank you," Alex said, still not quite sure he understood the man correctly.

"The account information and access will be sent to you within the next two days. We will call you back at this number with the details," Agent Sullivan said.

Alex was about to say goodbye when Trent interrupted him.

"How much is it?" Trent asked excitedly.

"Um, if you don't mind me asking, how much are we talking about?" Alex repeated.

A smile could be heard in the agent's otherwise professional tone when he replied, "There are a few more accounts we are attempting to locate, but at this time, we are talking hundreds of millions of dollars. Good day, Alex."

The agent hung up, leaving Alex to stare at the cell phone in disbelief. An enormous weight had just lifted off his shoulders, but he barely dared believe what he had heard.

Trent jumped up at down. "Hundreds of millions! We could put every student through college!" He laughed. "We could build a werewolf theme park with that much money!"

Alex grinned at his friend's enthusiasm.

"We'll know what to do with it," he replied with a smile.

***

"I do," Alex said.

"Do you, Siale Leanna Andrews, take Alex Davies-Carso as your lawfully wedded husband?" Kaynan asked.

Siale gave Alex her special smile, the one that made him warm all over and sent tingles down his spine. It was only by reminding himself that they were in the middle of their real wedding that he was able to keep from kissing her right then and there.

"I do," she said.

"And do you, Cassie Ann Davies-Carso, take Tennison Matthew Hughes as your lawfully wedded husband?"

Alex had never seen his sister as happy as at the moment when she echoed, 'I do.'

"And do you, Tennison Matthew Hughes, take Cassie Ann Davies-Carso as your lawfully wedded wife?"

The tall, pale-eyed werewolf smiled a sure smile at Alex's twin sister. "I do," he answered.

"I now pronounce each of you husband and wife," Kaynan concluded. "Alex, Tennison, you may kiss your brides."

Alex pulled Siale to him. Feeling the softness of her lips against his with the realization that she would be at his side forever made him the happiest he had ever been in his life.

"I love you so much," she whispered.

"I love you," he replied, staring down into the soft gray gaze he would get to see for the rest of his life.

A baby cried.

"He wants you," Grace said. She held the little boy with dark red eyes up to his father.

"Now, Jaze, don't make such a fuss," Kaynan chided; he then tickled the little boy until he giggled.

Meredith smiled at them happily from her seat on the

front row. Little Vicki and William were contentedly playing with the blocks she had brought. William took the block Vicki was trying to eat and stacked it on top of his tower.

"Uncle Alex, look!" the boy exclaimed.

"That's wonderful!" Alex told him.

Vicki knocked the tower over. For a moment, William looked like he wanted to cry; then the same determination Alex recognized from William's father came over him. He quietly picked up the blocks again.

"Now Vicki, please wait until I tell you next time," he told her patiently.

Alex and Cassie passed Brock and Jennifer sampling the cheese and cracker appetizers Alex had picked out specifically for them.

"Did you hear about the explosion in the French cheese factory?" Jennifer asked her boyfriend.

Brock grinned. "I'll bet all that was left was de Brie!"

They both laughed.

"I don't get that," Siale said.

Alex smiled at his wife. "Me, neither. We should leave it that way."

She laughed her musical laugh and he kissed her on the nose.

Trent and Jordan caught up to them.

"Look how cute!" Jordan exclaimed.

Alex followed her gaze to where Gem and Dray played with their little girl. Jordan and Siale hurried over to talk to the couple. Colleen stood nearby with Rafe behind her. He had his arms wrapped around her sides with his hands resting on her large belly.

"Any day now," Colleen told Gem.

"Our kids will have so much fun together," Gem replied happily.

"Thank you again, Alex," Lyra said, smiling up at him

273

with Mouse at her side. "I can't believe it."

"Please believe it," he told them. "You've done so much, all of you. It's the best way I could think of to thank you all." He winked at Mouse. "And the best way to ensure that you all stick around."

Mouse grinned. "I don't know if you needed to go as far as a private werewolf neighborhood, but I'll take picket fences over Extremists any day. At least with the privacy, the kids will have somewhere safe to be on full moons."

"We don't have to worry anymore," Lyra said. "We're safe, remember?"

Mouse grinned at his wife. "Old habits die hard, sweetheart. It can't hurt to be safe."

Trent and Alex wandered the grounds where the ceremony had been. The structure felt new and old at the same time. Bricks from the Academy had been carried a long distance to help with the foundation.

Alex paused at his favorite overlook. The ocean rushed in and out below, sending spray up over the rocks in an arch that captured the daylight in a rainbow. He couldn't wait to go surfing later that afternoon. Jerry, Brooks, and the others were already preparing for the barbecue on the beach. Alex had no doubt it would also involve a game of football.

Alex took a deep breath of the sea air. "So much for the Werewolf Academy," he said with a slight feeling of loss.

Trent shook his head. "Who needs an Academy?" He waved an arm to indicate the building behind them.

Alex turned around to see the great black wolf statue that stood in the courtyard of the beautiful building. Sunlight caught on the silver seven on the wolf's shoulder.

Trent smiled. "We don't need a Werewolf Academy. We have a Werewolf University!"

CHOSEN

About the Author

Cheree Alsop is an award-winning, best-selling author who has published over 50 books. She is the mother of a beautiful, talented daughter and amazing twin sons who fill every day with joy and laughter. She is married to her best friend, Michael, the light of her life and her soulmate who shares her dreams and inspires her by reading the first drafts and giving much appreciated critiques. Cheree works as a fulltime author and mother, which is more play than work! She enjoys reading, traveling to tropical beaches, riding motorcycles, playing the bass for the band Alien Landslide, spending time with her wonderful children, and going on family adventures. Cheree and Michael live in Utah where they rock out, enjoy the outdoors, plan great quests, and never stop dreaming.

Never stop dreaming!